THE LATE-NIGHT VISIT

James Ffolliott towered before the girl named Silence, his waistcoat half unbuttoned, his cheeks flushed from brandy, his arrogant mouth tightened as if with secret pain. With one hand on the edge of the great oak table he steadied himself; with the other, he motioned for Silence to approach.

"You understand," he said, "you're not to be a servant here. You're to be my stepdaughter's friend and dearest companion. Anything you need, anything you want, ask for it, and it will be yours."

Silence's dark brown eyes met his icy blue ones. He stared at her face as if spellbound . . . his powerful arms seemed about to reach toward her. . . .

"Get out of this room now!" he said savagely. "Get out of my sight! And quickly, do you hear? Quickly!"

SILENCE IS GOLDEN

❧ Elsie Lee ❧

A DELL BOOK

Published by
Dell Publishing Co., Inc.
750 Third Avenue
New York, New York 10017
Copyright © 1971 by Elsie Lee
All rights reserved. No part of this book may
be reproduced in any form or by any means without the
prior written permission of the Publisher,
excepting brief quotes used in connection with reviews
written specifically for inclusion in a magazine or newspaper.
Dell ® TM 681510, Dell Publishing Co., Inc.
Printed in the United States of America
First printing—January 1971

CHAPTER ONE

We were always encouraged to read the works of Mr. Dickens, particularly *Oliver Twist* and *Nicholas Nickelby*. Miss Carey greatly approved Jane Eyre, as well. She was fond of pointing out to us that Belliston Parva orphanage was in no way similar to the institutions in which other little children languished.

"No one of you has ever been hungry at meal's end," she stated impressively. "Simple fare, perhaps, but this is best suited for young stomachs in any case, and there is always enough. Ah, poor little Oliver and Jane should have been at Belliston Parva! Such kindness, such pleasant companionship—a tree for Christmas, frolics for holidays, *cake* for Sunday tea—I declare it is beyond anything great!"

In justice, she was right. We were never punished physically; there were no whippings or boxed ears. Occasionally we were deprived of Sunday tea cake, or (for serious depravity) sent to Coventry for a day—which meant being placed alone and apart from everyone in classrooms or dining hall. You were not allowed to speak to anyone, and no one could speak to you. I found this dismal the one time I was naughty enough to incur Coventry, but Tommy Six stoutly maintained he enjoyed it. "Good as a vacation—nobody nattering at you!"

There was space for twenty boys and thirty girls, as well as a nursery for ten foundlings until permanent arrangements could be made. We all learned the three R's and worked in the gardens, with plenty of domestic skills for the girls and useful trades for the boys. As we grew up we were hired out to help in the big houses and estates of the locality, but we never had to work in the mills; and after a drunken farmer brutally assaulted the girl his wife had taken for kitchen help, we were only rented by the day.

Yes, as orphanages go, we were lucky at Belliston Parva. Some thought was given to our capacities, and our natural talents were encouraged. We worked hard, but never beyond our strength, and in the end we faced the world with healthy bodies and clear, if humble, minds. Dimly, I knew it was because of Miss Carey, who allowed us to laugh and play games for a while after meals. Behind her bovine exterior was a very shrewd mind that said the trustees would preen themselves on a model institution with an outstanding record of success after discharge. Our boys became butlers and head keepers to dukes and earls; our girls became housekeepers or head nannies in castle nurseries. It was all most gratifying to the trustees, and produced extra funds fairly easily.

So we were kindly treated—but it was still an orphanage, and when I was sixteen I should have been glad to leave in the usual way. Unfortunately, no one wanted me—or so Miss Carey said. I do not think she tried very hard, because I was so useful with the nursery class and the best personal maid she ever had. In time I was more of an assistant, saving her steps about the rambling old house, for she was no longer young and was inclined to be overweight. I had a certain authority, although I avoided the appearance of giving orders. The staff considered that I "knew my place," and cooperated good-humoredly.

On the whole I was happy, proud to be trusted with bits of responsibility or the recipient of confidential gossip on the trustees. All the same I felt . . . peculiar. What, in fact, *was* "my place"?

I could see that the requests for orphans ready to leave Belliston Parva did not fit me. I was an excellent needlewoman, but without apprentice money for a first-class dressmaker. I delighted in cookery, and gradually took over preparation of Miss Carey's dinners—to the satisfaction of both kitchen and headmistress, for I need not say her menus were different from the dining hall! I could wash and iron, clean floors and wash delicate china, put a fine patina on old mahogany and polish silver or brass to a sparkle, mend and darn, and tend a lady's wardrobe impeccably. I could knit, crochet, and embroider skillfully. I could plant a garden, get more out of my plot than anyone else, preserve fruits and berries, arrange flowers tastefully, manage the teapot when Miss

Carey wished to concentrate on a trustees' meeting, or hand the cups gracefully when she preferred to pour.

The trouble was that I was already fitted to be a housekeeper, head nannie, nursery governess, or personal maid to a marchioness when I was only seventeen, but such positions are only attained by working *up*. As Miss Carey said, it was a problem because I do not look like an underling, nor in fact at all like a servant in any way.

"It is not that you lack proper deference or obedience to rules," she remarked one night. "It is simply that anyone knows at a glance you are no hedgerow brat. We'll never know the circumstances; there must not have been any family remaining to your parents, for we advertised," she interpolated. "All over the British Isles, the trustees authorized the expense because there must have been some background. You had a few dresses, sadly outgrown but all of the finest quality, and there was a christening robe— the sort of thing handed from one generation to the next. I have it safely put by for you—but there was no clue, no clue at all." She shook her head sadly. I held my breath, *willing* her to continue. . . .

"Luckily the neighbor who found your mother dead was an honest soul," Miss Carey said after a moment. "She hid the wedding ring, or it would have been sold to pay for the burial." Miss Carey pulled herself from her chair, puffing slightly, and rummaged in the breakfront desk. "You are old enough to have this, I think." She handed me a plain gold circlet, with a warning look. "Keep it out of sight, Silence! Gold is worth stealing—and it is all the proof you have of your identity."

I turned the ring in my fingers, awed by the thought that my mother had once worn it, set on her finger by my father. "There seems to be marking on the inside."

"It reads 'C.D.E. to L.V.M.—June 16, 1859—eternal love.' We put that in the advertisements, but there was no response. Believe me, child, I did try."

"It was very good of you," I said quickly. "I'm grateful."

"Are you?" she commented drily. "You're alive; I suppose that's something—but heaven knows what to do with you, Silence. I didn't know when Mrs. Hawkins brought you here in the first place, except that you didn't belong in an orphanage. Mrs. Hawkins knew it, too, but she couldn't help. She was only an illiterate old woman living on a few shillings a week for scrubbing offices, but she knew quality, and she said your mother was a lady."

"Did she say anything else?" I asked timidly.

"Yes and no," Miss Carey said slowly. "Nothing to help. She knew your name because your mother used it when she fed or dressed you, and when she became delirious she kept saying 'The rest is Silence.' There were names: Richmond and Atlanta—those are American cities in the South; I looked them up in the atlas—but in '64 they were fighting the War between the States. We didn't know how or where to advertise over there."

"Then I might not even be English. . . ."

"Perhaps not." She eyed me curiously. "I must say, you take this well, Silence."

"Why shouldn't I? I'm still a charity orphan, but at least I have a name. I'm probably legitimate; my mother was English and a lady; and I have her wedding ring, even if I don't know where I was born or exactly who my parents were. L.V.M. and C.D.E.," I murmured. "The E is Eddington, but I can pretend his name was Charles, and perhaps my mother was . . . was Lucy Victoria."

"Perhaps," she agreed. "There's no harm in pretending so long as you don't start to think it's true, Silence, but you're a sensible child. I'm glad I told you. Generally, we say nothing." She grimaced. "And usually when we know, it's nothing a child can be proud of! There's one more thing," she added suddenly. "*Alison Castle*—I'd forgot that. Mrs. Hawkins thought it was a friend, but I always felt it was a ship—either the one that took your mother to America or brought her back after your father's death.

"And I always thought she must originally have been born or raised near Belliston," she finished soberly, "or why did she come *here?* The rector—old Dr. Barton—kindly undertook to search local records for any family with a name beginning with M that had died out at that period. He wrote to a number of outlying parishes as well, but nothing was found."

We stared absently at the flickering flames for a while. As a family background it was not much, but better than nothing. I'd assumed I was a by-blow like most of the other orphans, except with a name pinned to my blanket when I was left on the doorstep. Miss Carey was always happy when relieved of the responsibility for

SILENCE IS GOLDEN

a name. She had long since solved the problem by standard names followed by number of arrival, which explains Tommy Six. Currently we were up to Henry Ten, Edward Nine, and John Five. The girls were always Mary, Margaret, Elizabeth, or Catherine. When she reached Twelve, Miss Carey started over again. She was not personally superstitious, but she thought Thirteen might upset future employers of orphans.

Now I had not only my own name, but a few clues. Mine is not a romantic nature—I was not given to fancying myself a duke's daughter stolen from my cradle by gypsies —but here were some facts. Perhaps in time I could discover whether there had been a ship named the *Alison Castle*, a Confederate soldier named Eddington, or any record of the marriage and my birth in those cities. It seemed unlikely that I had any unknown relatives, or why should my mother have left America? Still, it was fun to think about. . . .

It was the next day that Catherine Twelve panted into the storeroom where I was listing supplies. "You're to dress *quick* and take tea to Miss Carey," she announced. "Millie's readying the tray with the best cups and *two* kinds of cake. It's a strange gentleman. What d'you suppose he wants? Aren't you 'cited, Silence?" She danced alongside me as I went hurriedly to my room.

"Why should I be? It's my duty to wait on Miss Carey," I told her repressively, "and I don't suppose he wants anything but his tea."

I was completely wrong.

Perhaps if I'd guessed the stranger's reason for visiting Belliston Parva I would have taken a sharper glance—and if I'd had the least idea of what lay ahead of me I should certainly have dropped the tea tray.

"Ah, Silence, set it here, please." I could tell by Miss Carey's voice that the visitor was important. When I had handed his cup and presented the sandwiches and cake, I retreated to my unobtrusive corner. I tried to fix my gaze on the stark branches of the trees outside, but I sensed his eyes flicking over me again and again during the low-voiced conversation, and inside I trembled with a prescience that this man would change my life—not that he was young.

When I stole a glance at him, he looked like a trustee, although considerably more handsome. His hair was black, powdered with snow at the edges of the thick waves capping his head and the neat side whiskers. At second glance, I revised my estimate. Everything about this man was vital and vigorous; his movements were quick and assured. The body was erect, broad shouldered and muscular beneath the fine broadcloth coat. No, despite the hair, this was a man in the full prime of life, as accustomed to command as our trustees, but far younger.

Apart from his appearance, he apparently had charm. There was a humorous tone in the deep resonant voice; he laughed readily, with every indication that he was thoroughly enjoying his visit. So was Miss Carey, laughing and twinkling at his remarks, perfectly at ease in a way I'd rarely seen. Could he be a relative or old friend? I was absorbed in watching the tea party, when he turned suddenly and his eyes met mine in a brilliant blue flash that was like the swoop of the first kingfisher of spring. I felt hot color rising in my cheeks to be caught peeping, yet I could not look away from that frank appraisal, until at last he turned back to Miss Carey with a few words.

"Silence, come here, child." Miss Carey summoned me with a smile. "Mr. Ffolliott, this is Silence Eddington—Mr. James Ffolliott, Silence. You are to be companion to his stepdaughter."

I hardly know what I said as I curtseyed respectfully and took the hand he extended. To leave Belliston Parva? I had thought it my dearest wish, but now a tide of loneliness swept over me.

"It seems all too sudden and confusing, does it not?" Mr. Ffolliott smiled kindly. "But I think you will be exactly right for my Amy. She is in delicate health, Silence, but little older than yourself. I must go away for several months on business, and it is my thought that she will survive the separation better with someone young and cheerful. She is too grown to be left with servants; she must have a . . . a *dame de compagnie*," he said humorously, "if you understand me?"

"Yes, sir. I speak French," I told him politely. "Madame Dubois, who escaped from Bismarck, liked to come here to teach such of us as wished to learn."

"And you wished to learn, Silence?"

"Yes, sir. It is such a pretty language."

His eyes surveyed me keenly. *"C'est vrai,"* he said deliberately. *"Vous pouvez peut-être persuader Amy à continuer ses études?"*

"Il sera mon plaisir de faire mon possible, monsieur."

Mr. Ffolliott's eyebrows rose slightly. "The accent is excellent," he murmured approvingly. "You were fortunate in your teacher, Silence." He rose as he spoke, turning to Miss Carey. "Mr. Chisholm was right that you would be able to help me," he said cordially. "I am most grateful. You will set Silence on the coach two days hence, then, and she will be met at Chelmsford. Good-bye for the present." He nodded and smiled at me, while I curtseyed again, and then he went away with Miss Carey. When they had disappeared, I ran to the front window. In the drive stood a carriage with a pair of matched bays finer than any owned by our trustees. A footman sprang to open the door, a coachman controlled the snorting sidling horses, and the tall figure of my new employer strode forward. Then the door was closed, the footman swung up to his seat, and the equipage was dashing away to the outer road for Belliston Magna.

I straightened the curtains and began to collect the cups onto the tea tray. "Set that aside for a moment, Silence." Miss Carey sank heavily into her chair, gesturing to my usual stool, but when I had taken my place, she stared at the fire for so long that I thought she'd forgotten me. Finally she drew a long breath. "It is exactly the situation I would have hoped for you: a genteel private home with a young lady; you will have a room of your own, be treated as a member of the family, and be paid twenty-five guineas a quarter."

She nodded at my gasp. "Yes, you may well be astonished. It is a munificent sum for your start in life, is it not? Perhaps *now* they'll agree it was not 'educating you out of your places' to take advantage of Madame Dubois. Margaret Three, gone to Paris as ladies' maid to a duchess . . . Henry Seven in the finest hairdressing establishment in London because they can call him Henri . . . and now yourself as companion in a gentleman's home!"

I tried to find the right words of gratitude for settling me so well, but she only smiled faintly. "Have I?" she murmured. "You should rather thank Mr. Chisholm; it was he who arranged it."

That explained much, for I knew he disapproved my continued residence. Months ago he'd told Miss Carey she was selfish to keep me. "You are using her like an unpaid crutch, madam! She must earn her living; it's unfair to delay. She should be assistant in a nursery school, or working under a head nannie, gaining experience and references to qualify for full charge."

And now he had found me a situation superior to anything any orphan had ever had. Why should it disturb Miss Carey so deeply? I knew she would miss me, not merely my work, but our companionable evening chats; yet I sensed it was more than parting. In the next days, she said repeatedly that it was the perfect post, but I felt it was more to reassure herself than me. I'd no time to ponder; every minute was a bustle of delegating my duties, preparing my meager wardrobe, and packing the dilapidated wicker basket that was all we could find in the storeroom.

The last dinner was cooked for Miss Carey; for the last time I sat on my stool beside her, conscious of mingled melancholy and anticipation. She was unwontedly silent, and again I sensed it was more than the parting from me. Involuntarily I asked, "What troubles you, ma'am?"

"I mislike it, somehow," she said after a moment, and shrugged impatiently. "I suppose I'm only an old hen with one chick, but . . . it's *too* good, and if it proves otherwise, you'll be the other side of England. It'd be different if you were nearby, or if I knew aught of Mr. Ffolliott, but all Mr. Chisholm can tell me is: the man's a rich widower, a brilliant financier with widespread interests overseas. He didn't even know the girl was a *step*daughter or in poor health."

"Why should he?" I asked confusedly.

"Because you're not a nurse, Silence. You've neither the knowledge nor the physical strength, although I can't believe. . . . The man's a gentleman, well able to pay . . . yet why should he take an orphan from the West Riding when London is at his doorstep?" With sudden decision, Miss Carey went to her bedroom and returned with a small chamois bag secured by a pin. Within were three paper twists. "Those are guineas, Silence, enough to return you

SILENCE IS GOLDEN

to Belliston. Keep them by you at all times—pinned to your bodice by day, to your nightdress when you sleep—and let no one know you have them."

"Yes, ma'am," I whispered tremulously. "But why?"

"I don't know," she said helplessly. "But I can't have you ... trapped. Do as I bid you, Silence: put up the money safely, and *tell no one you have the means to leave Hazelhurst Grange.*"

For the last time I looked about the cubicle that had been my home for so long. I felt terrified at the thought of leaving it. Miss Carey feared I might not be equal to the tasks of a nurse—but suppose Miss Amy didn't like *me*? It was all very well to say I should have my own room and would not be a servant, but as I blew out my lamp and crawled into bed, I realized I was eighteen years old—*and I had never in my life been abovestairs in a private home.*

For the first time ever, I cried myself to sleep.

It was full dark before the coach pulled into Chelmsford. I was numb with weariness, and so stiff I feared my legs might buckle when at last I reached the ground. The other passengers went into the inn for hot tea and buns, while I tried to flex my cramped muscles, feeling dazed by the commotion about me. Mr. Ffolliott had said I would be met, but by whom, and how would I be recognized? Compared with Belliston Magna, this town was bewildering. People dashed in and out of the inn, back and forth from the stableyard, shouting hoarsely and indistinguishably. There were private carriages as well as the coach, which stood stolidly in the middle of the yard, so that everything had to detour around it.

I looked about uncertainly, retreating step by step from the surge of people. Should I go into the taproom to inquire for Mr. Ffolliott? One glance at the turmoil, and I shrank into the shadows, engulfed by panic, until a middle-aged man in neat livery approached. "Miss Eddington?"

"Yes!" I half sobbed with relief, and he grasped my elbow, leading me away from the flambeaux and lanterns.

"This way, miss. I'm Herbert Dawson, coachman," he said. "Mr. Ffolliott's apologies, miss—he meant to meet you himself, but Mr. Beltane came unexpected-like—he's Rector of Hazelhurst. Here we are." He helped me into the carriage I'd seen from Miss Carey's window and tucked a rug about my knees. "It's no' but a half hour, with a good dinner at the end. We'd be halfway home if I could ha' seed you when the coach came in."

"I'm so sorry you had the bother," I quavered.

" 'Tis no bother. You'll be the young lady to look after Miss Amy?"

"Yes—"

"Well, then." He shut the carriage door as if all were explained.

In a way it was, I realized as we bowled along through the darkness. No effort for her was too great—how wonderful to be so loved and willingly served! Mr. Ffolliott had sent his own carriage, meant to have me in person ... if only Miss Amy would like me. ...

Suddenly the carriage slowed, turned through lighted gateposts into a long curving drive, and stopped before an imposing mansion that seemed to glow with light. Now that the moment was here, I was trembling so that I could hardly grasp the strap to pull me from the seat. Dawson helped me out, leaned in for my basket, while I stared fearfully at the opening front door: a plump elderly woman in decent black ... a young man running down to take the basket.

"Don't be scared, little miss," Dawson said quietly. "There's naught but kindness and help for you at Hazelhurst, you'll see. Go along with Alfred—and that's Mrs. Davenport, the housekeeper."

Unsteadily I mounted the stone steps and faced her. "You poor child!" she exclaimed. "You look exhausted, but you shall have a cup of tea directly and time to freshen. The master's still with Mr. Beltane." She put a motherly arm about me, and led me up broad stairs, talking all the while until we reached a bedroom larger than Miss Carey's parlor.

A fire crackled in the grate, a figured china lamp stood on a table beside the bed, another was on the bureau. Frothy white curtains veiled the windows, and Alfred was just setting my humble luggage on a stand. "There you are, miss." He grinned cockily, swaggering off to the hall. Mrs. Davenport turned up the lamps. "Sarah, bring hot water for Miss Eddington," she commanded, "and mend the fire."

SILENCE IS GOLDEN 15

"Yiss, mum."

Startled, I whirled to find a chambermaid bringing in a tray with teapot and cup.

"Now take off your cloak and bonnet, and sit by the fire, my dearie. Have your tea and warm yourself. Sarah'll be back directly—why, whatever is the matter, miss?"

I'd sat down—and burst into tears. "You're all so *kind.*"

"That's as may be," she muttered cryptically. "There, there—you're overtired, that's all. You ought to be in bed, but Miss Amy's anxious to meet you—that's her room." She nodded to a door beside the fireplace. "She'd have come to welcome you, but she can't leave the master and Mr. Beltane. Have the tea; you'll feel better."

"It's not that." I sternly suppressed the tears. "You don't understand, Mrs. Davenport. It's . . . everything: this lovely room, someone bringing tea and hot water. I expect you know"—I strove for dignity—"Mr. Ffolliott hired me from an orphanage."

"Aye, so he said." She sighed. "I hope it will answer, for you're no bigger than a cricket."

"Oh, please," I cried fearfully. "I'm really *very* strong! Don't let Mr. Ffolliott think I can't do the work."

"Bless you, it's not that sort of work. It's only to stay with Miss Amy. You'll read or play games, whatever she wants to amuse her and keep her . . . cheerful. Drink your tea, child. Here's Sarah with the water, and when you're tidy I'll be back to take you down." The housekeeper went away with Sarah, but I sensed her final glance was troubled despite the smile.

Alone by the fire I shed a few more tears. I knew it was principally weariness, but I felt utterly forlorn. Already Mrs. Davenport doubted my suitability. So did I, when I looked about the room. Was this how *people* lived? Flowered china instead of tin on the washstand, violet-scented soap and monogrammed linen towels, a gilded clock chiming softly on the mantel shelf, a pomander ball in the closet and lavender in the bureau drawers. . . .

Even the tea was a delicate blend finer than Miss Carey's most treasured private stock.

Mechanically, I washed and put on my "best" dress, which was only someone's brown poplin made over to remove a scorched breadth. When I was ready I studied myself anxiously in the mirror. The best that could be said was that I was clean and neat. Otherwise I was insignificant: no more than five feet tall, with brown hair dressed in a plain bun, a snub nose, a mouth too wide for beauty, and a pointed chin without a dimple.

Did I look like my father or my mother? I would never know—but if Lucy Victoria had been English, perhaps my brown eyes came from Charles Eddington. I set the wedding ring on my right hand, and felt a tiny surge of my natural optimism. I might be alone in the world, but I wasn't a bastard. Whatever lay ahead, I must do my best for their sakes.

"You look better already!" Mrs. Davenport nodded approval. "Not but what brown is a bad color for you, my dearie, but Miss Amy will choose something better. Come along; they're in the library."

Sedately we went down the stairs and to the right, where double doors stood half opened. Mrs. Davenport pushed them apart. "Miss Eddington, sir." I glimpsed book-lined walls, a great mahogany desk in the window niche, lamps everywhere, and joyous flames leaping in the fireplace. Mr. Ffolliott rose from an immense wing chair and came forward with a smile. "Silence, welcome to Hazelhurst!"

Behind him another man arose courteously. I had a confused impression of *blackness:* jet-black hair in thick waves above a high forehead, inky brows straight as a pen stroke, onyx eyes, a curly black mustache. The effect was completed by the black suit of a rector. He seemed to be studying me thoughtfully, but my eyes went beyond to a young girl leaning forward eagerly: Miss Amy.

"Silence," she said, holding out her hand, "such a lovely name—but I hope you *aren't*—silent, I mean. I like people to laugh and talk, don't you? Come over here; let me see you."

I went to her as a bee flies to honey. She was so very lovely! Palest blond hair, dressed to frame her cameo face in feathery curls, clear blue eyes in a thicket of lashes, skin translucent as Limoges china, straight little nose and curving rose-petal lips. . . . She wore a dress of sapphire blue with a stiff pleated edging that stood up like a ruff behind her slender neck.

When I put my hand in hers, it was gypsy-brown against

the ethereal softness of her fingers. "I am nothing to look at, Miss Amy."

"But you are!" she exclaimed, squeezing my hand gently. "Look, Papa, Silence is like a darling little fawn—such beautiful brown eyes and hair, and look at her lovely delicate hands! Oh, Papa, I *knew* you'd find exactly the right person this time. Sit down, Silence. What fun we're going to have, getting to know each other!"

Mr. Ffolliott laughed. "Tomorrow, Amy! First, Silence must know our rector, Mr. Beltane. Hugo, Miss Eddington will be Amy's companion while I'm in the West Indies."

Miss Eddington? As though I were a real person, a young lady like Miss Amy? I felt my hand grasped warmly as I curtsied. "How do you do, sir?" Mr. Beltane surveyed me keenly, then he smiled and nodded in the most friendly way. "Miss Eddington—Silence," he said. "Welcome, indeed!" He handed me toward the chair beside Miss Amy, where I sat down thankfully. So much courtesy set me trembling again.

It is hard to recall that first evening clearly, for all was new and strange, and I nearly disgraced myself later. I remember Miss Amy pouring tea, the grace of her white hands, her wrists clasped by enameled gold bracelets. While the men talked together, we frankly studied each other. In the whirl of leaving, I'd not considered what my mistress might be—as well, perhaps, for certainly to know only that one would companion an invalid could not have cheered the spirits. But although Miss Amy was pitifully small and frail, there was none of the peevishness of ill health nor any lines of pain. Her smile was mischievous; her eyes sparkled with gaiety. Even her whisper was musical; her full voice was a soft delight.

It appeared as Mr. Ffolliott had said: I was simply another girl to keep her company. Miss Carey's fears were groundless, although I blessed her repeatedly that night! It was the first time I had ever seen a formal dining room, but after the initial hesitancy, I found myself able to handle everything as correctly as Miss Amy. All that was really different was the food itself. There was a bewildering amount of it, beginning with the first oysters I'd ever seen—not that I knew what they were, but an orphanage teaches you to eat whatever is set before you. I did have to peek, then I boldly copied Miss Amy. They were delicious!

The crisp slice of fish between soup and roast mutton was new, too, as well as the side dish of some cold white spear-shaped vegetable. By the thin tart dressing, I thought it must be a salad. Alfred and Sarah supplied butter, hot rolls, and refilled wine glasses for the men. Miss Amy and I had tall tumblers of lemonade. Finally there was cabinet pudding and a savory of broiled mushrooms—but although I'd often made these for Miss Carey, nothing at Hazelhurst tasted like anything I'd ever cooked.

Miss Amy took no more than a few mouthfuls of each dish. I felt uneasy at that—perhaps I should leave something, too—but I was frankly hungry after the long trip. Mr. Ffolliott reassured me by his concern. "Amy, dear, you must eat! I've given you such a small slice of mutton, surely you can manage it to please me, dear?"

"I'm sorry." Her eyes filled with tears; her chin trembled. "I do try. You *know* I want to please you, Papa, but I'm not hungry."

"Tchk, Dr. Robinson must change the tonic—this is useless," he said impatiently. "Look at Silence: she's eating her portions like a sensible girl."

I could see Miss Amy beginning to weep sadly. "I'm afraid I'm only a greedy girl tonight," I said apologetically, smiling at her. "I've been traveling since five this morning, with only a packet of sandwiches at noon. I can't promise to do this well every day, sir—after all, Miss Amy and I are only girls," I added merrily, "and there is not so much space in us as in you."

Mr. Beltane chuckled deeply. "I think she's made a point, James."

"A definite *touché*," Mr. Ffolliott agreed, while Miss Amy blinked away the tears and eyed me with horrified interest.

"Since *five?*" She picked up her fork automatically. "Poor Silence, how tired you must be!"

"Yes, and no," I said cheerfully. "It was all so interesting. We went through Nottingham, you know, and Melton Mowbray."

Miss Amy laughed. "Did you buy a pie?"

SILENCE IS GOLDEN

"There wasn't time—but I saw a hunt," I told her impressively.

"What was it like?" she asked eagerly. By the time I'd finished describing the horses, the pink coats, the dogs and hunting horns, her plate was half emptied, the salad finished—and Mr. Ffolliott's face was inscrutable.

I was suddenly aware that I was talking alone. My voice trailed away; I trembled inwardly for my boldness. How could I have so forgotten my place?

"Go on, Silence," Mr. Beltane said calmly. "You are just reaching the interesting part. You went through Cambridge, did you not? What did you think of it?"

"It was . . . inspiring, sir," I quavered.

"A good word," he smiled. "You passed Queen's and Clare—that's my college; James's is Magdalene—Trinity, Westminster . . . you'd not see much of the others, I'm afraid, because of the trees."

"Yes, sir, but they were lovely, as well as the river."

"So it is! James, we must drive up before the snows. It's a long while since we've renewed acquaintance with the Cam . . . which reminds me," Mr. Beltane launched smoothly into some personal reminiscence, and I could hide my embarrassment by looking at my hands. I was suffused with gratitude for his extrication, but still appalled by my behavior.

At long last dinner was over. "Amy, say good night and take Silence upstairs—nearly time you should be abed, too." Mr. Ffolliott held out his hand affectionately. "It's been an exhausting day, expecting her, but now she's *here,* and you must have your rest or you know what will happen tomorrow! Come, kiss me." He smiled.

Miss Amy fluttered forward, bending to hug him. "I'll go to bed as soon as Silence is settled. I promise! I don't want to miss a moment of tomorrow—but I feel as if I shouldn't, as if I'll be completely strong and well in the morning." She kissed his temple. "Good night . . . good night, Mr. Beltane. Come, Silence."

I went forward to curtsey, and Mr. Ffolliott's hand closed unexpectedly about mine, pulling me toward him, until it seemed natural to bend and brush my lips to his temple. "Good night, my dear." He patted my cheek. "Sleep well."

"Thank you, sir." I curtsied to Mr. Beltane, who smiled at me—but his eyes, like Mrs. Davenport's, were troubled.

I began to know Miss Amy as soon as we reached our rooms. She flung open the connecting door. "It shall never be closed again! Oh, Silence, Silence, how wonderful to have someone to talk to, laugh with!" She hugged me, moving about lightly to pat the counterpane, stroke the curtains, run her hand along the bureau. "It's a pretty room, isn't it, Silence? Do you like it? You must tell me if you lack anything. Oh, you have no flowers," she cried angrily. "How came they to forget? You must have some at once!" She started impetuously for the bell.

"I expect they thought flowers would be dead before I came—and truly, I'm so tired I'd scarcely be able to appreciate them."

"That is no excuse." Her eyes glistened with tears. "There are *always* to be flowers in every occupied room; it is a *rule*. And Papa has three greenhouses—there are always flowers; I wish you to have some. . . ." She went swiftly to her room, and I followed anxiously. I had no idea why Miss Amy should be so agitated; I was a servant, not a guest, after all.

Luckily, Sarah was just bringing a small tray of coffee, with Mrs. Davenport behind her. "There you are! Davenport, *why* are there no flowers in Silence's room?" Miss Amy cried. "Go and get her some immediately, do you hear? No, I won't listen to you, Silence—it doesn't *matter* if they didn't know when you were coming and thought flowers would die." She caught the bedpost and broke into sobs, while Sarah shakily set the tray on a table.

Mrs. Davenport hastened forward. "Now, now, my dearie, Miss Silence was right." She cuddled Miss Amy's shuddering figure, with a warning glance at me. "Of course we wouldn't leave flowers in the empty room—we put them here for you to enjoy until she arrived. See—the pansies in the pretty pot, and white roses on the sill. Sarah, take them into Miss Silence's room at once. How could you have forgotten? Shhh, Miss Amy, you see? It's all right. Let Nana help you to bed."

I sped forward. "Let me help." Between us, we got Miss Amy undressed and tucked into the high bedstead, and finally the tears ceased. She leaned exhaustedly against the plump pillows. "Oh, Nana, you *won't* tell Papa I was naughty, please?" she whispered pathetically.

"Of course not, my dearie. It was only the long day and the excitement, but now all's right." With another warning glance, Mrs. Davenport went to the washstand and shortly returned with a glass. "Take your medicine, my dearie, and Miss Silence will bring coffee."

Instinctively I poured it black. Miss Amy would have rejected it, but I said, "This is medicine, too; when it's gone you shall have a cup to enjoy." Obediently she sipped, until a faint color tinged her waxen cheeks. "Ah, that's better! Now"—I refilled her cup, adding sugar and cream, and poured one for myself—"I'll sit here, but let's not talk very much, because I'm so tired I can scarcely keep my eyes open."

Somehow I was confident again. Mrs. Davenport hung away clothes, while I coaxed Miss Amy to look at the lovely fire, to think about sleeping until we would both be rested to start tomorrow. Her eyelids drooped as I talked; I was just in time to catch the cup from her hand. Swiftly I mended the fire, placed the screen, took the coffee tray to my room; Sarah could get it later. Mrs. Davenport gently removed the extra pillow and the cashmere shoulder shawl, but Miss Amy was fast asleep, cuddled sideways beneath the quilt. I opened the window an inch, and tiptoed after the housekeeper into my room.

"Eh, Miss Silence, you were grand with her! For a moment, I thought we were in for a night of it." The housekeeper half closed the door and sank wearily into my fireside chair. "Make ready for bed, child. I'll sit for a moment to catch my breath, but she'll not wake."

Automatically I mended my fire, lowered the lamps to softness, wiped my cup carefully, and poured the last of the coffee. "Medicine for you, too."

"How d'you know so much, child?"

"Miss Carey said black coffee was good for the heart."

Mrs. Davenport nodded. She sipped slowly, staring somberly at the fire, until I said timidly, "I'm undressed." With a long breath, she finished the coffee and rose.

"Into bed then, and let Nana tuck you in." When the quilt was up to my nose, she stood looking at me wonderingly. "Eh, you *were* clever with her—perhaps it'll answer, after all. Sleep well, child."

I was too drowsy to ponder the strangeness of words and glances, tears and sobbing exhaustion of my mistress. The softness of *bed* was seducing me. If I opened my eyes I could glimpse the final fire glow of my grate, the dim flicker outlining Miss Amy's door—then, suddenly, I didn't see it.

I sat bolt upright, staring into blackness. Who had closed the door? Had Mrs. Davenport returned? Was there something I should do for Miss Amy? I scrambled from the bed, pulling on my bathrobe, and softly opened the door. To my surprise, I saw Mr. Ffolliott bending to add coal to the grate. He wore a dark red velvet dressing gown, and he'd closed the window as well as the door. As he straightened up he saw me, and beckoned me to the hall.

"How long has she been abed? You had no . . . trouble?"

Remembering her plea, "Don't tell Papa," I shook my head. "No, sir. She was very tired; we helped her undress at once and I drank my coffee with her, but she was asleep almost before she'd finished. We left the door open in case she should wake and call me."

"Well, that is good news," he murmured in surprise. "I quite expected . . . unusual difficulty, and to find complete peace instead—I think you must be a good fairy, Silence! I'm sorry to have awakened you."

"I wasn't really asleep, sir. Should I not leave the door open?"

"Yes, though it's not necessary. But night air is unwise."

"I'm sorry," I faltered. "Miss Carey thought fresh air healthy; I'm accustomed to it at night."

"But you are a strong little person, Silence, and Amy is not," he said kindly. "You must never allow her to do too much. She will try—she has no estimate of her limitations—but the result is exhaustion and collapse. I'm afraid it will be a very quiet life for you, to restrain your natural energy to the small amount of activity Amy can endure." Mr. Ffolliott sighed. "But already I think you will be the solution." He eyed me with a sort of amused incredulity. "Perhaps it's what she always needed: a healthy *young* person. She's been too much alone, but we find she cannot lead the normal social life of a young lady." His lips tightened briefly, then he sighed again. "Silence, back to bed— and you are to sleep until you wake!" he ordered with mock severity. "You must be entirely rested, or Amy will try to take care of *you*. Good night, child."

"Good night, sir—and thank you."

"Why, it is I who thank you." He patted my cheek gently. "You must learn your own worth, Silence." He went down the hall and through the door at the opposite front corner; the master's suite must be above the library. Returning to my bed, my mind was a confused, sleepy jumble.

Fortunate Amy to have a father who loved her so dearly . . . lucky Silence to have such kindness about her . . . how pleased Miss Carey would be . . . how hard I would work to keep Miss Amy happy. Most of all I wondered if my father had been as strong and handsome as Mr. Ffolliott. Would Charles D. Eddington be the same age? Had he ever worn such an elegant dressing robe, or smelled so deliciously of wine and good cigars mixed with bay rum on his cheeks?

I decided that he had—that he was twenty-one in 1859 and my mother was eighteen—that he didn't look at all *like* Mr. Ffolliott, but would have been just as kind to an orphan hired as company for his daughter . . . who would have been *me*.

Then I was asleep.

CHAPTER TWO

I awoke at six-thirty; after years of Belliston Parva, I needed no rising bell. Outside, the light was filmy gray, but when I'd heroically slid from bed to close the window, I saw it was a thin mist rolling away as the sun rose behind the low tree-clad hills. I lingered despite shivers, fascinated by the landscape emerging like a fairy tale. Somewhere out there lay the sea. To one from the West Riding, who knew no water but ponds and streams, the very word *sea* was enchanted. How far away was it? What did it look like?

Last night I'd realized only a gracious home; now I saw the house was the least of Hazelhurst Grange. Lawns spread in every direction—to the right was a tennis court; to the left I saw the edge of a greenhouse. A flagged terrace extended around the corner of the house. It was edged with clipped box and furnished with white iron tables and chairs. Straight ahead, the lawns sloped down, and as the final wisps lifted, I saw a lake! It was half hidden by trees; I couldn't guess its size, but the farther shore at this end was a considerable distance. My heart bounced happily, for one thing we all learned was skating! Even with wooden runners, I proved so proficient that a trustee gave me his daughter's outgrown skating boots. They were left behind for another orphan, but surely I could buy a new pair from my munificent salary.

It was going to be a lovely clear day. I could hardly wait to explore—to say nothing of breakfast, which raised a question: what was the morning schedule at Hazelhurst? I quickly learned! Miss Carey had been so pleased I'd be treated as one of the family, but she could never have envisioned a tweeny to make my fire, Sarah with a tea tray and hot washing water, or breakfast in bed! At Belliston Parva we had jam on Sunday, muffins for Christmas and

SILENCE IS GOLDEN

the Queen's Birthday, and a single boiled egg on the anniversary of our arrival. At Hazelhurst I was asked what I would "fancy"—and the menu included kippers, grilled kidneys, hothouse fruit, sausages and bacon, omelet or boiled eggs—and already I saw I must not be too humble.

As always, it was "know my place"—and the old question of what *was* my place?

Miss Amy still slept heavily beyond the half-opened door. It was nearly nine before I heard a faint moan from her room, and went in to smile at her. "Good morning! Shall I ring for you?"

"Who're you?" she asked thickly, her eyes half closed.

"I'm Silence, Miss Amy."

"That's right—I forgot. Yes, ring the bell." She sighed. "My head aches."

I wasn't surprised; between closed windows and a brisk fire, the atmosphere was stifling. "You're not awake yet," I said cheerfully, helping her into the bed jacket. She sank back dully against the pillows, while I went about the usual routine—but apparently it was not usual for Miss Amy. She looked dubiously at toothmug, comb, and dampened face cloth.

"Now? I do this when I get up, don't I?"

"If you like." I was taken aback. "But it freshens you to taste your breakfast."

"All right." She gasped faintly at the coolness against her face, but when I'd patted her dry, she murmured, "Yes, it does feel good. If only my head didn't *ache*...." Docilely, she sat forward while I plumped pillows and gently combed back the wisps of hair, but all her movements were lethargic. When Mrs. Davenport puffed in with a pot of chocolate instead of tea, she cast a practiced glance at Miss Amy, and mixed a powder with water.

"There—you'll soon feel better, my dearie."

Miss Amy opened her eyes slightly. "Is that you, Nana?"

"Yes—drink the medicine, and have your chocolate while I fetch breakfast."

"Ugh!" She grimaced with distaste. "Why must I think of food when I feel so horrid?" Her eyes filled with tears. "I won't get up today. Go away, Nana."

"Coffee will help the headache," I suggested. "Mrs. Davenport, why not bring it first, with some fruit, and later Miss Amy might like something more."

But when the tray arrived, it was loaded with covered dishes, and Miss Amy's face was rebellious. "I can't eat a thing," she declared tearfully. "I shall be sick if I try. Take it *away*, Sarah! I don't want to look at it—my head aches—I'll stay in bed. . . ." By their faces and coaxing voices, this seemed a daily problem—nor did I wonder. Delicious or not, there was simply too much food; it took away the appetite. While Mrs. Davenport pleaded and cajoled, I set aside everything but coffee, a single piece of toast, and an orange peeled as Miss Carey had taught me.

"Try this," I said quietly. "Coffee first—and you can have sugar to dip the orange, but it's so sweet you may not need it."

Tentatively, Miss Amy took a section. "I never had an orange like this before. Isn't it good?"

"Yes. Would you like jelly or honey on the toast?"

"Oh . . . jelly, I think. Honey drips." Slowly, a small portion at a time, she ate her way through a light but adequate breakfast. I inspected the plants and flowers, added water, pinched off a dead leaf, made a few casual remarks. . . . The result wasn't lost on Mrs. Davenport, even though most of the dishes went out untouched. Sarah's eyes widened when I handed her the tray. "However did you do it, miss! She never eats so much."

"Because you bring too much," I told her, "and for me as well. After this, tell cook to give us half-servings," and remembering last night, "for *every* meal."

"Yes, miss," she said after a moment. "Maybe you'd send a note-like to Mrs. Potter, with suggestions? She'd be grateful; she's at wit's end to tempt Miss Amy—and the master insisting on 'a good start for the day.' But like you said"—her gray eyes twinkled—"there's not so much space in girls."

I laughed at her grin. "Mrs. Potter can see for herself. And Sarah, tell her I never ate such food in my life. I'd be grateful to learn her secrets, if she'll part with them. I love to cook."

"She'll part with anything, Miss, if you can send back a tray like this."

Miss Amy cuddled dreamily against her pillows. "Mmmm, I feel better, Nana. I think I'll get dressed after all."

SILENCE IS GOLDEN

"That's good, my dearie," but when Miss Amy really *looked* at me, it was extremely bad!

She was horrified by my scanty wardrobe. I could not blame her; I knew it was dreadful, too, but within seconds we were plunged into a maelstrom of sobs rapidly mounting to vehement demands for the carriage. It took me so completely by surprise that for a moment I could only stand, open-mouthed with fright, while she twisted from side to side in Mrs. Davenport's arms.

"No! I can't stand to look at her in that horrid dress! Davenport, order the carriage. We'll go to Chelmsford at once, *at once,* do you hear me, Davenport? How could they send you here like this, Silence? Everyone knows I must have harmony around me."

It was worse than the previous evening's insistence on flowers. Miss Amy's deep gulping gasps for breath interspersed with soaring screams were terrifying. Instinctively I took my mistress away from the housekeeper and spoke as to one of the orphanage babies. "There wasn't time to get anything new before I came. Don't cry, or you won't be able to decide what I should buy."

"Buy? We'll buy *everything,*" she cried, but already the gentle pressure of my hands was holding her more steady.

"Shouldn't we plan first? Decide what's needed, write it down—and tomorrow we'll make no mistakes." Her sobs diminished, and I smiled at her wistfully. "If you want to go today, we will, but you'd have to choose everything, Miss Amy. I'm still so tired from yesterday that I couldn't tell red from blue."

By then, Mrs. Davenport had thrust the smelling salts under Miss Amy's nose, and with a final gasp she was quiet. "Oh, poor Silence! Of course you're too tired—forgive me? Yes, we'll make a list and go to Madame Raimond tomorrow. Where are the fashion books? Oh, I know: they're in the morning room. Come look with me, Silence."

"A wise idea!" Mr. Ffolliott's deep voice made us whirl to the door where he regarded us gravely.

"Papa!" Miss Amy hung her head penitently. "I didn't mean to be naughty," she whispered, "but such ugly clothes—I can't bear it! We're going to plan for tomorrow; Silence is too tired today." She went toward him hesitantly. "Please? I promise to be good all day!"

For a second his face was impassive, then he smiled tenderly and drew her against him for a kiss. "I shall ask for a report from Silence," he warned, "and *if* it is satisfactory, Dawson will be ready at ten tomorrow morning. Davenport, you will go with them, and make certain nothing is overlooked."

"Oh, Papa, you're so kind!" Miss Amy rubbed her cheek against his lapel like a kitten. "I promise *faithfully*—you'll see."

But it was I who saw, and throughout the day it took all my ingenuity to prevent another crisis. She could not be restrained in her determination that my wardrobe should equal hers, yet even happy anticipation unnerved her and she became feverish in the difficulty of decision. "You are to have *everything*—Papa said so," she insisted.

I thought Mr. Ffolliott would certainly disagree on the propriety of clothing an orphan in silk and velvet, but I dared not say so. Instead, I said, "It will take a long while for Madame Raimond to make so many dresses. Why not buy materials, and I will sew the first ones here?"

That caught her fancy, and in finding the pictures, considering colors and fabrics, debating the sort of trimming and writing everything down, the morning raced away. We were both astonished when Sarah said, "Luncheon, Miss Amy. The master has already gone in."

"Oh, we must wash our hands." My mistress quivered anxiously. "Papa likes me to be prompt."

"He'll understand. After all, *he* approved the magazines."

Her face cleared. "Yes, that's so."

Mr. Ffolliott did look grave, but she ran forward to kiss him remorsefully. "I'm sorry we were late, Papa, but Silence says you'll forgive us. We were choosing dresses for her, and you did say we should do so."

He softened at once, patting her cheek. "Silence was right. Have you found what you like, darling?"

Lunch was bouillon, creamed fish on toast, roast quail, and stewed pears, but Mrs. Potter had taken my advice. Mr. Ffolliott frowned at the sight of the half bird on our plates, but he made no comment, and Miss Amy ate it all, in between a full recital of our morning. I couldn't suppose him to be particularly interested, although he listened indulgently, nodding approval at the home sewing. "Well, it sounds most satisfactory."

SILENCE IS GOLDEN

Her face clouded. "But we haven't decided what Madame Raimond is to make."

"This afternoon—it's only to look once more and write it down."

She was still uncertain, her eyes tearful. "But can we do it all in one morning?"

"We can get the fabrics and do the rest another day when Mr. Ffolliott can spare the carriage. It wouldn't matter when, because I'd be working here all the time."

"That's so." Her face cleared. "I long to see you cut and fit, Silence. Papa, that will be fun, won't it?"

Mr. Ffolliott's face was thoughtful. "Yes . . . but," he smiled, "I will back your needlework against hers."

"A competition! Papa, you must offer a prize."

"I shall, although if you win, Amy, I shall give a duplicate to Silence for being a prize." He laughed, tossing aside his napkin.

Miss Amy tripped away happily with a final fond kiss for him, and he followed to the hall, watching her run upstairs, calling to Mrs. Davenport who waited at the top. Again I had that impression of amused incredulity as he moved aside for me to pass.

"Be certain she rests. She hates it, but it's essential." Mr. Ffolliott's smile broadened. "I wonder how you'll convince her to endure it." With a nod, he disappeared into the library.

Already I knew his meaning! I reached Miss Amy's room just in time to avert sobs. "I don't need a rest. Go away, Davenport! You know we must finish choosing the dresses."

"Couldn't we do it later?" I feigned weariness. "I thought I'd read to you, and perhaps have a little rest myself."

"Oh, poor Silence! Of course you must rest—forgive me?"

When we'd tucked her on the chaise longue, Mrs. Davenport measured drops into water. "Medicine, my dearie." I ran to my room and hastily threw off my dress, returned to settle down with the book from the night stand: *Ben Hur*. It was new to me. "How far had you read?"

She was astonishingly drowsy. "I don't think I'd begun."

"Then we'll start together." But in three pages she was asleep. I felt my own eyelids drooping, which was ridiculous.

I'd done nothing to make me sleepy. It was the overheated room, lack of exercise, and big luncheon. I opened a window in my room, breathing deep of fresh air until I'd shaken off lethargy. When I came back, I fancied Miss Amy's room was less stuffy, too, although she slept like one drugged....

I stared at her, half frightened. Why had that simile come to mind? But she was inert as Margaret Three when Miss Carey gave her toothache drops. Instinctively I sniffed Mrs. Davenport's bottle: laudanum! It might have properties I didn't understand aside from pain killing, but I was still uneasy. Why was it necessary for an afternoon nap? Miss Amy would be sluggish when she woke; in only an hour the effects couldn't wear off.

It was not my place to question a doctor's prescription, however. Resolutely I put it out of my mind, and wrote to Miss Carey. She must learn at once of my safe arrival, my room, Miss Amy's beauty, Mr. Ffolliott's kindness . . . but I said nothing of weeping spells or medicine. Until I understood more clearly, discretion was the better part of valor. But when Miss Amy was awakened, I felt confirmed in my distrust.

She turned about like a bisque doll while we dressed her. She'd completely forgotten we were to finish the fashion plates, nor did I remind her. "A walk?" I suggested. "We've had no exercise all day."

"I don't know," she said listlessly. "I think I'm too tired, and I might take a chill. Papa wouldn't like that."

"Nor I. But the sun is still high. If you put on a cloak, we might walk to the greenhouses and look at the flowers."

That drew a faint spark. "Yes, I could do that, couldn't I? Perhaps Macdonald would give me a buttonhole for Papa."

"I'm sure he will." I opened the closet. "Which cloak?"

"The blue goes best with my dress," she said automatically, and stood motionless while I fastened it about her.

Shortly we were down, out the front door, turning right along the flagged path and around the corner of the house. Oh, the air felt good! "Breathe deeply, Miss Amy," I urged. "Like this. . . ." I made her stand still, inhaling and exhaling, until she laughed suddenly.

"What a funny game! How do we know who won?"

"You did," I said promptly. "You took deeper breaths than I."

By the time we reached the greenhouses, she was bright-eyed and animated. Macdonald was a square, stolid Scotsman with a strong burr, and a dour impassivity. He nodded to me curtly, and ignored me while Miss Amy flitted from one plant to another. There was a small forcing house at Belliston Parva, but I'd never seen anything like the Hazelhurst succession houses! One for flowers, one for fruit, a third for vegetables—all furnished with hot pipes, thermometers, adjustable windows . . . and Macdonald.

He stood at the end of the aisle, watching Miss Amy's delighted inspection—*and intuitively I knew he hated her!* I could scarcely *believe* it; nevertheless the impression was firm and could not be suppressed in my mind. He gave her the buttonhole and cut some freesia for her; he was terse but not impolite, yet there was no warmth in the man for my mistress.

As we left the greenhouses, his taciturnity altered to the curled lips of contempt, looking at Miss Amy's retreating figure. He'd forgotten I was there until I passed him. Then his eyes blazed at my courteous, "Thank you, Mr. Macdonald. Good day."

"And a good day to you, mistress," he said deliberately, "but a better day to be keeping Miss Salford away from here. The atmosphere is no' healthy for her, ye ken?" Without waiting for an answer, he stepped back and firmly closed the door in my face.

I had no time to think. We were already at the house and found Mr. Ffolliott in the library with Mr. Beltane. They swung toward us in surprise, while Miss Amy slipped her cloak into my hands and went lovingly to slip the flower into her stepfather's lapel. I left her recounting our walk and took away the wraps, but when I returned with a vase for the freesia, there was still astonishment.

"Silence, you are a clever girl to get Amy out of the house for some fresh air." The rector smiled.

Mr. Ffolliott was less enthusiastic. "I trust Amy will not suffer for a walk so late in the day."

"Pooh, nonsense, James!" Mr. Beltane scoffed. "Look at their bright eyes and rosy cheeks."

"The sea air is damp even at midday. Dr. Robinson says it's not advisable for Amy's chest." Mr. Ffolliott sighed. "I suppose I ought to sell Hazelhurst, move inland to dry air, but it would be a wrench to leave everything dear and familiar."

Both Amy and Mr. Beltane protested, while my heart sank. *Why* had no one told me she had a weak chest? I sat silently beside Miss Amy, controlling tears of discouragement. If I continued to make mistakes, I wouldn't need Miss Carey's escape guineas—Mr. Ffolliott would pay my fare back to Belliston Parva. "Silence," Miss Amy's voice recalled me, "this is Papa's cup and that is Mr. Beltane's—and there are crumpets!"

Mechanically I handed the teacups, plates, napkins, and food: four sorts of dainty sandwiches, three kinds of cake, with a jam pot for the crumpets. I had scant appetite, but Miss Amy ate three crumpets lavishly piled with jam and was eyeing the cake, when Mr. Ffolliott said genially, "I have business to discuss, my dear. Run away until dinner."

"Yes, Papa." As always, Miss Amy kissed him tenderly before leaving the room. Upstairs there was a flood of heat; I wondered if I should ever become used to so much warmth, grateful as I'd have been for a bit more at Belliston Parva. Miss Amy looked about undecidedly. "What shall we do now, Silence?"

"I could read to you, or you could teach me a game."

"They're in the morning room," she began, and brightened. "I know! We'll finish the magazines!"

That occupied us comfortably until we were called to dinner, which was as ample as I'd feared. Miss Amy did not do quite so well as at lunch, due to those crumpets and jam, but Mr. Ffolliott withheld comment—to my deep relief—and we got through with no incident. Tonight we were not dismissed, but went to the library with the coffee tray while Mr. Ffolliott drank his port. It was a half hour before he strolled in with a fragrant cigar, but I had been studying the books with delight. Novels, biographies, history; names familiar and unknown; English, French, a peculiar curly script—I longed to be made free of these shelves. Would Mr. Ffolliott permit it?

"I expect so," Miss Amy said uncertainly. "He often gives me books, but I get so tired. Do you *like* to read, Silence?"

"Very much. And you won't be tired if I read to you."

She glanced about, half scared. "Must we read them *all?*"

"Only those we'll enjoy. I know you'd like *Ivanhoe* and *Pride and Prejudice.*"

"What are my girls plotting now?" Mr. Ffolliott asked jovially.

"Only think, Papa: Silence likes to read!" Miss Amy filled his coffee cup. "She has read a number of your books already, so she's sure to know what I shall like, isn't she?"

"Yes"—he smiled—"but consult me first, please, Silence?"

"Of course, sir. Miss Carey allowed me to read"—I pointed them out—"but you have others by the same authors . . . and there is Victor Hugo and Dumas. Madame Dubois often spoke of them, as well as Balzac."

"Yes, they are great authors." Holding the demitasse in one hand, Mr. Ffolliott came to stand beside me. "Here is Daudet, Verne—you'll enjoy him, Silence! Trollope, Scott. . . ." He moved along, caressing his books gently, while I memorized what was approved, conscious of an odd bond between us. Dimly I felt he was pleased I should love books, and was almost excited to introduce me to new ones.

The poetry was forbidden, whether French or English, without express permission. The curly script was German; another shelf held books in Italian; and there was a section that was incomprehensible. "These are Persian, Arabic, and Hindustani. You cannot decipher them, but you may enjoy the illustrations."

Miss Amy exclaimed with delight at the strange figures and lovely colors, but I was awed. "Sir, do you *know* all these languages?"

Mr. Ffolliott's face closed suddenly. "I was in the diplomatic service before I married Amy's mother." He thrust back the books with finality. "There—you will have more than enough to read, Silence. And if you can hold Amy's interest for half of it—" He shrugged, extending his cup. "More coffee, please."

We all had more coffee. Mr. Ffolliott lighted another cigar and listened indulgently to Miss Amy's fluting report of our fashion decisions, until Alfred appeared with a decanter and glass. "Ah, thank you, Alfred." Mr. Ffolliott poured an inch of liquid, settled back, and comfortably swirled it in one hand. "Well, Amy, that will do. Bed—or you will be too tired for Chelmsford tomorrow."

"I don't feel as though I should ever be too tired again," she protested. "It was such a *good* day, wasn't it?"

"Yes, but tomorrow must be equally good—and I am tired, if you are not," he said affectionately. "Off to bed, darling!"

Obediently, we kissed him good night, but in our rooms Miss Amy was fretful. "I don't feel one bit sleepy."

Neither did I. It was the coffee. Miss Carey rarely let me drink it at night, and took only one cup herself—and we had had two. With Miss Amy's nerves, I wondered it was not entirely forbidden her. Mrs. Davenport looked hopefully at me, while Miss Amy flatly rejected her nightdress. "Why not let her make you ready, so she can go to bed?" I suggested artfully. "Then we will read or play a game."

"Oh, poor Davenport! Of course you must be tired—*forgive* me?"

By the time we'd decided on dominoes, and I'd found them in the morning room, Miss Amy was in bed with extra pillows and a lap board. She was smiling and expectant, ready for some fun and enchanted when I set the little vase of freesia on her night table, "Where you can smell it all night long!"

Mrs. Davenport rustled forward with a glass. "Your medicine, my dearie."

"Shouldn't it be taken when she's ready to sleep? Leave it for me to give when we've finished." Did Miss Amy take *two* doses of laudanum daily? A repetition of this morning's headache would defer Chelmsford, would certainly cause a crisis of disappointment—she was so looking forward to it—and there was no doubt I must have a couple of dresses that pleased her, or *that* would be equally bad. . . .

Throughout two games, both of which she won, I debated internally: what best to do? "Poor Silence, this is no fun for you," she said tenderly. "Get us another game, something you can win."

"Why not let me read aloud instead?" I picked up *Ben Hur* and began at the beginning. I knew she'd scarcely heard me earlier. Tonight she was absorbed, lips parted with anticipation. We finished three chapters; I continued, and in a few pages she was asleep. Gently I removed extra pillows, pulled covers securely about her. When I'd mended the fire and turned out the lamps, I took the "medicine" into my room and emptied it into the slop jar.

CHAPTER THREE

My day was not ended. My mind was weary, but my body was not because of the coffee. It felt good to sit quietly thinking beside the fire. Before I could put my thoughts in order, there was a tap at the door. When I opened, Alfred grinned at me. "The master'd like to see you in the library, miss, if you're not abed—which you ain't. Can you find your way, or shall I light you down?"

"No, I can manage. Thank you, Alfred."

"A pleasure, miss. G'night."

Automatically I smoothed my hair, and picked up the letter to Miss Carey—perhaps Mr. Ffolliott would give me a stamp for it. The library door was ajar; he wore the dark red velvet robe of last night, but on his head was an odd round cap brightly embroidered in gold, with a bobbing silk tassel. On the floor beside him, next to the table holding decanter and glass, was the strange squat piece of furniture I'd vaguely noticed in the corner beside the fireplace. Now I saw that it was a small stand of inlaid wood, and on it was a curious bottle of brass encrusted with bits of colored glass that winked in the firelight. It was equipped with a long tube, on which Mr. Ffolliott drew and exhaled into the air already pungent with smoke.

"You wished to see me, sir?"

He closed the book on his lap, laid aside the tube, and rose to his feet with a smile. "Come in, Silence. Sit here." He gestured to the ottoman before him. "I shan't keep you from your bed; I expect it's been a long day."

"Yes, sir, but very pleasant." I settled at his feet, feeling oddly shy. I knew he meant to ask for that "report" on Miss Amy, and I could honestly say it was good—yet might he not think I was concealing the truth for desire of new clothes?

Mr. Ffolliott picked up the tube once more, caught my glance at the bottle, and laughed. "You wonder what I am doing?" he asked. "That is a hookah, Silence. It is a way of enjoying tobacco familiar in Eastern countries. See—the smoke passes through water and is cooled. . . ." He bent forward to demonstrate. "In India, it's called a narghile."

"You love the East, do you not, sir?" I asked impulsively. "Why do you not return? I understand it's a dry climate; it might be healthy for Miss Amy."

Mr. Ffolliott's face closed as earlier when he showed me his books. "Too late," he muttered. "There's too much to be done here. I shall never see the East again. Well"—he smiled broadly—"tell me of the day, Silence."

"It was a good day, sir, truly, aside from that first moment."

"So I gathered. I wish I knew how you managed to control her! No one else ever has," he snorted, "and it grows worse all the time. Dr. Robinson says it's a nervous condition that will correct itself with rest and a quiet life. Quiet life!" Mr. Ffolliott repeated bitterly. "What else is possible? Well, continue. What was your day?"

"In the morning we looked through the fashion plates and listed what we'll buy for me to make up. Miss Amy told you at luncheon, sir."

"Did she?" he murmured. "She always has so much to tell me. . . . Go on. How did you persuade her to take a nap?"

"I said I wanted one, too."

Mr. Ffolliott eyed me sardonically. "And after tea?"

"We chose the rest of the dresses," I said tremulously, "and when we left you after dinner, Miss Amy got ready for bed so Mrs. Davenport could be finished, and then we played dominoes and I read aloud until she fell asleep."

His face was inscrutable. "You make it sound so simple," he remarked, and suddenly threw back his head with a deep laugh. "Oh, Silence! We should have had someone like you long ago, I see that. If you *knew*—the first day without screams." His lips twisted and he drew deeply on the hookah. "Well, you've worked a miracle! I confess I didn't expect . . . but perhaps it was not so ignoble, after all," he murmured half to himself. "Two children together, and the servants are devoted—if it answers, I can leave with an easy mind; and it's only a few months before it's finished, after all."

I sat silent while he drew leisurely on the tobacco, staring somberly at the fire. "One swallow does not make a summer; we must see what tomorrow brings," he murmured, "but it should be another good day. She's always happy when she's looking at patterns and silks."

"Yes, sir, but. . . ."

"But . . . what?"

"She's chosen so much," I whispered desperately, "and all as though for herself, sir. I'll try to restrain her to what I can sew for myself, but I fear even those will take a long while for me to repay you, and if she insists on ordering from her dressmaker— Please, sir, can you countermand it?"

"Why should I?" he asked after a moment.

"Because I could never pay for such clothes, and in any case they would be improper for a servant."

"Miss Amy Salford's companion is not a servant, my dear, nor can she appear in garments out of a poor box." Mr. Ffolliott's blue eyes blazed at me. "The cost of a wardrobe will be trifling if it keeps Amy quiet, I assure you! Of course you will not pay, and the longer you can amuse her with trips to Chelmsford for forgotten fringe or reels of thread, the better!"

My face must have shown my uncertainty, for he laughed harshly. "You do not understand, but you will. My dear Silence, Amy is to have whatever she wants, *no matter the cost*. Only let me have peace at Hazelhurst—let me finish the business with a clear mind." Mr. Ffolliott stood up as he spoke, and mechanically I rose also. "You are to consider yourself a full member of the family," he said deliberately. "You are to have whatever pleases Amy, and you are to ask me for anything else you want. Money is unimportant. D'you understand, Silence? *Anything!*"

I was aware of the envelope in my hand. "Yes, sir. . . . May I have a postage stamp?"

Mr. Ffolliott's face stilled. "To whom do you write?"

"To Miss Carey, of course, sir," I said, surprised. "I must let her know I arrived safely, and send an occasional letter on my welfare." As he stood frowning, I struggled to explain. "She—the trustees, too—like to know how we go on. It would be a poor return for all these years if I failed to write. Mr. Chisholm would rather hear of me by a letter to Miss Carey than through a chance meeting with you, sir."

"I see," he said slowly. "It is a very proper thought, Silence, but I should like to see your correspondence, if you please."

"Certainly, sir." I handed him my letter apologetically. "I hadn't thought— The envelope is sealed. I'll write another."

"No, no. I'll write it myself, and tell Miss Carey all you were too modest to say, eh?" Mr. Ffolliott's eyes twinkled kindly. "There, I have kept you long enough. Go to bed, child."

"Yes, sir, but"—I hesitated—"have you any instructions? . . ."

"No." He shook his head, and chuckled suddenly. "Or yes, I have one: you are to have a dozen, two dozen new dresses, as many as your nimble fingers can make, Silence. It is not only Miss Amy who wishes to look at a pretty young woman!" He threw back his head and laughed heartily at my involuntary blush. "Go to bed, my golden Silence. . . ."

Thus began my life at Hazelhurst, and in retrospect I marvel at my temerity. It was a case of "fools rush in," and the wonder is that it was so nearly successful. The crux, of course, was Miss Amy's tendency to hysteria.

Almost anything—happiness as well as dolor—filled her eyes with tears that, if unchecked, became sobs soaring into a piercing soprano flood of imperious commands and demands. Once started, she was literally unable to stop until she was shaking with exhaustion, yet it was possible to deflect her by introducing a new thought. Miss Amy herself asked nothing better than to be calmed. She dreaded Mr. Ffolliott's learning of a crisis. "Don't tell Papa I was naughty!"

"You weren't really, and anyway it's over. Why tell him?"

"The others always did." She sighed. "Not Davenport or Sarah unless he asks, but all the others ran straight downstairs. . . ." Her blue eyes fixed mine compellingly. "You truly won't tattle, Silence?"

"I truly won't," I promised firmly, and I never did. Instead I was at hand every waking moment, alert to provide the diversionary topic, and with each day it became easier, although I moved only by instinct and the limited experience of the orphanage. Slowly I amassed a piece here or there in the puzzle that was Miss Amy, but as it emerged, my picture began to look entirely different.

Then I was really bewildered: how could I question established views? The Hazelhurst servants quite evidently considered Miss Amy "not quite right," although (with the exception of Macdonald) they loved her dearly. The neighbors we met at church spoke kindly, as to a simpleton. The Chelmsford tradesmen thought she was a lunatic; they brought out their finest goods, but with a wary eye for "fits." Mr. Ffolliott called it "ill health." I had no idea what he really thought. In any case, he could know no more than the doctor told him—and five minutes with Dr. Robinson was enough! He was a pompous, rotund old man, who clearly resented my timid questions, and whose only answer was a new prescription. We had a dozen tonics, elixirs, pills, and powders—plus laudanum. Every room contained smelling salts, although Miss Amy never swooned.

In fact, I thought her body as sturdy as mine. She had very fine, small bones, but her figure was fully mature. Because it was hidden by her elegant clothes, she looked as though a breath would blow her away—but so did Lady Lester, who regularly exhausted any trustees' meeting. The nerve storms were different. I might think Miss Amy's physique could withstand them, but they were certainly debilitating. How long had she had them, and most of all, *why?*

That was the major mystery, for there was always something hidden, something that hovered over Hazelhurst like a Sword of Damocles. I thought at first that it was only Miss Amy's constant nerve storms, which were as much a strain to the household as to her, but as they diminished and day succeeded day in relative peace, I realized the shadow had not gone. I could tell by the behavior of the staff: they breathed sighs of relief, but they did not relax. Today was good, but it was no guarantee for tomorrow. I came to feel that all my efforts were superficial. I made life easier by quelling the hysterical screams, but these were only a surface manifestation of some buried thing that troubled my mistress. The staff was aware of it, but not what it was. I had not exorcised it; it merely slept for a time. . . . The household was grateful for reprieve, but fatalistically awaited the moment of awakening.

What was this lurking terror? I dared not ask. I felt myself to be a servant; the servants considered me a young lady. They firmly called me Miss Silence, served me as willingly as my mistress. They gave me snippets of information, mostly by indirection, but they never *gossiped*. Any probe would have convicted me of vulgar prying, with consequent damage to my unquestioned status. Of what use to ask questions, in any case? Already I had more than I could interpret.

Unlike everyone else, I felt that Miss Amy was neither insane nor an idiot. Her interests were limited, and the fluting prattle enhanced the impression of feeblemindedness, but she was capable of total concentration and was far quicker than I at the immense stock of games and puzzles. That was point 1: books wearied her, aside from romances, but her fingers were incredibly deft.

Handwriting, embroidery, drawing, or painting—anything Miss Amy could do with her hands was exceptional. Colors, designs, fabrics entranced her, and *clothes* were an absorbing passion. The closets of bed and morning room were filled, plus a huge armoire in the hall. She changed her dress twice, sometimes thrice, a day, although we went nowhere but to church or Chelmsford. Aside from Mr. Beltane, we saw no one. The few guests were Mr. Ffolliott's male business associates, when Miss Amy and I did not descend for dinner.

I blessed the suggestion of sewing for myself! Miss Amy was fascinated from first cutting to final button, insistent on perfect fit, patience itself in picking out a crooked seam and resetting the stitches. She never wearied of *creating* my wardrobe—and that was point 2; for after the initial dress was done, Miss Amy studied the style selected for the next effort, and swiftly sketched it with alterations. Thereafter, she made innumerable fashion drawings, not merely for me, but to amuse herself, while I sewed or read aloud.

One day as I finished the final page of *David Copperfield*, she was still engrossed by her painting. "I'm nearly through," she said absently. "Come look."

It was—unmistakably—Dora Copperfield!

Miss Amy laughed at my amazement, reaching to her art folder. "They're all here: Micawber, Mrs. Gummidge, Steerforth, Little Em'ly. . . ." Wide-eyed I went from one to another, while she looked at me slyly. "Why d'you act so surprised, Silence? You've seen them before; you go through everything when I'm asleep." I could only stare at her, dumbfounded, and shake my head . . . until her eyes clouded with uncertainty. "Don't you? Don't you try on my clothes and furs and jewelry, Silence, to see how you'd look?"

I roused at that. "I couldn't get into your clothes, Miss Amy—you know I'm a full size bigger around—and I go to bed when you do. I wouldn't dream of touching anything of yours!"

"Wouldn't you?" she murmured vaguely. "The others always did—I think. . . ." In one swift movement, she shuffled the drawings together, tore them across, and tossed them on the fire.

"Oh, *why* did you destroy them!"

"We've finished the book, haven't we?"

"Yes—but they were so well done. I'm sure Mr. Ffolliott would have liked to see them."

"No, he wouldn't," she said flatly. "It would remind him of Mama. Put everything aside, Silence, and let's work on the new puzzle. I'm anxious to see what it will be."

Miss Amy's mother was certainly part of the mystery. Mrs. Davenport warned me never to mention the dead woman. "Six years it is, come Christmas, but the poor lamb's not got over it, nor's the master, for that matter."

Already I'd discovered Miss Amy could speak *of* her mother, but the most innocent question brought instant tears. I put Mrs. Ffolliott with the other puzzlements, and concentrated on today—for that was where Miss Amy lived. She spoke of yesterday, became vague for anything previous, and made no plans beyond tomorrow, yet she loved stories of *my* childhood! The exploits of naughty Tommy Six or Miss Carey outwitting stuffy trustees held her spellbound. My ring entranced her; I think she believed in Charles and Lucy Victoria far more faithfully than I! She made up innumerable stories about them, and shed gentle tears over the fragile christening robe, but she never spoke of her own early days.

From Mrs. Davenport I knew Miss Amy had been born in India. Perhaps that explained her terror of the autumn gales sweeping over Hazelhurst. She shuddered at the rain sheeting the windows, screamed at the wind buffets, and went to bed with a migraine, until I had the morning room shutters nailed fast and drew tight the curtains.

SILENCE IS GOLDEN   43

Then she worked away contentedly and said, "Isn't it lovely to be safe?"

It seemed a strange word to use. What could Miss Amy fear that made her choose it? Had she been badly frightened in some way as a child?

Solitude she found insupportable; even ten minutes *alone* was too much, but Mrs. Davenport gave me an innocent cue. "If you could get her back to the piano, Miss Silence— But the empty salon disturbs her." The housekeeper sighed. "For a time she'd practice and play for the master after dinner, the way her mama used, but then suddenly she seemed to take against it. I'd not know how you'll manage to get her back. 'Tis a pity."

That afternoon I said—wistfully, because that was infallible; Miss Amy always wanted everyone to be happy —that I had never seen the grand salon. At once she was leading the way. "Such lovely paintings, Silence, and the furnishings are so elegant." I could sincerely admire the long silent room, until we ended by the great piano. I patted the inlaid rosewood case with yearning. "How much I wish I could play!"

"You cannot?" Her voice was oddly intense.

"Not a note," I shook my head ruefully. "Orphans do not have 'advantages,' Miss Amy."

For a moment she stood beside the Bechstein, eyeing me keenly. Then suddenly she opened the instrument, seated herself, and set her fingers on the keyboard. "Tchk, it must be tuned," she murmured, and rippled through some experimental chords and arpeggios, while I sat in a chair beside her. I've no idea what she played, wincing at sour notes and finger mistakes, but I sat breathless until she ended and silently leaned her forehead against the piano.

Presently I said, "We must have the instrument tuned at once, and you must play every day, Miss Amy. How could you let this go!"

"Because of her," Miss Amy muttered, twisting her head against the polished wood, "always down here, playing when I'd been put to bed." Her voice was so low I could hardly distinguish the words.

I thought she was recalling Mrs. Ffolliott, and trembled for fear I'd unwittingly begun a crisis, but it was not so. "Come, sit beside me, Silence. Play a scale," Miss Amy commanded. Obediently, I drew a chair beside the music stool, and tentatively set my fingers to the keys. Slowly I struck one note after another, while she observed with a growing smile. "No, no. You have begun with A; it should be C."

"I'm sorry, Miss Amy," I faltered, "but I don't know one note from another."

"Then I'll show you. . . ."

It was that simple!

Thereafter we went down to the salon every afternoon after her nap, and I labored faithfully to learn a Haydn minuet by rote. My fingers were wooden compared with hers; she played beautifully. All her tender sensibilities were easily expressed, but although she often brought tears to my eyes, Miss Amy never cried. She would repeat and repeat a few bars until they flowed perfectly; she was tireless, completely absorbed while I sewed beside the piano.

It became usual, on the days Mr. Ffolliott went to London, for us to have tea in the salon. I took a tender pleasure in waiting on my mistress while she rested her back in the cushioned bergère by the fire. These moments were always calm and serene. Then she might return to the piano, not to practice but to play or sing for our amusement—and great was the excitement on the day we discovered I could take a correct second to her lovely soprano!

"We must practice secretly, and when we're perfect we'll invite Papa to a concert . . . . But"—her face clouded—"someone will tell him."

"Not if we explain it's to be a surprise—and why shouldn't we ask the staff to stand in the hall to listen?"

Mrs. Davenport readily promised secrecy. "Eh, 'tis good to hear the lamb playing again! And you've a lovely voice yourself, Miss Silence."

We were still nearly undone when the rector arrived early for tea and quietly entered the salon while we were finishing "Flow Gently, Sweet Afton." His hearty applause startled us.

"That was beautiful! May I have an encore?"

"Mr. Beltane! It must be later than I thought." Miss Amy quickly fluttered to the door. "We must wash our hands."

I lingered briefly to say, "Please don't tell Mr. Ffolliott you heard us singing together."

"Why not? James loves music."

"Because it's a surprise." I looked at him earnestly. "It means a lot to her, sir. The servants will stand in the hall; we're to wear our new dresses; there'll be a formal invitation and program card; Mrs. Potter plans a special dinner; and Alfred means to suggest one of the bottles of Napoleon brandy. So if you *could* simply say we were here without saying what we were doing," I pleaded, "it wouldn't exactly be a lie."

Mr. Beltane's broad smile became a chuckle. "Oh, Silence, if you could see your worried expression at tempting a Man of God to mendacity!" He laughed and patted my shoulder. "When is this momentous occasion?"

"Next week, if we can be certain of an evening Mr. Ffolliott will be at home."

"Tuesday!" The rector's lips curved with amusement. "It's James's birthday. I shall invite myself to dine on the excuse of parish business, which will ensure his return from London and prevent other guests."

In the event, however, we did have a completely unexpected guest, who began the changes at Hazelhurst that brought fear and final tragedy.

I wondered that Miss Amy had not mentioned such an auspicious moment, but when I spoke to Mrs. Davenport, she exclaimed, "There now, if we hadn't all forgotten! But the master makes naught of it since Mrs. Ffolliott's death. I mind she would invite friends; but there was always so much entertaining, I doubt Miss Amy ever realized the day. How did you learn it?"

"Mr. Beltane—he is going to invite himself to dinner," I said absently, "but I think we won't tell Miss Amy beforehand, Nana."

The housekeeper nodded briskly. "Leave all to me and Mrs. Potter. Should we have a birthday cake?"

I debated. "Something very plain that would accompany brandy for the gentlemen after the music—a single candle, perhaps—and fruit punch for Miss Amy and myself."

"Evening refreshments." Mrs. Davenport beamed. "Eh, it'll be like the old days."

My secret fear was overexcitement from anticipation, but I'd been right that Miss Amy could control herself for a desired goal. It required only a reminder that there could be no surprise without her; she must not risk migraine or a backache. Our dresses were ready—hers of gentian blue velvet matching her eyes, and mine of the deep amber taffeta she'd chosen for me. There was time for me to mark two linen handkerchiefs J.F. in threads of her golden hair, while she worked on carpet slippers, innocently unaware of their purpose. I'd persuaded her to choose ruby red velvet with a design of gold poppies, and they were so nearly ready that I set the final stitches while she rested on Tuesday.

I had long since daringly reduced, or abandoned, the doses of laudanum, and felt justified by Miss Amy's improved breakfast appetite. Today I gave her a single drop to ensure sleep. Then I wrapped slippers and handkerchiefs in dainty paper provided by Mrs. Davenport, and there was still time for a short walk. Lack of exercise was a major problem for me, but unless the weather was really stormy, I went *out* while Miss Amy napped, leaving Nana or Sarah to be at hand if she waked. Today, when I had made the tour of driveway and terraces, it occurred to me I would ask Macdonald for the corsages Miss Amy had bespoke.

He was always dour when I saw him at a distance, although he ducked his head to my hand greeting. Flowers or pot plants filled all the rooms of Hazelhurst; when the plants drooped, they were removed to the greenhouse where he nursed them back to health. I often thought it a pity he could not take Miss Amy with them, but of course the atmosphere would be bad for her chest. Macdonald's words that first day were to protect her from my ignorance. We had never returned; Miss Amy left the house only for the carriage to church or the Chelmsford shops.

Today I ran along the path impulsively. "Good day, Macdonald. You have the corsages?"

"Aye." He jerked his head unsmilingly at the tissue-wrapped bundles. "For what are they wanted, mistress?"

"Mr. Ffolliott's birthday. Did they not tell you?"

The gnarled fingers paused in pressing soil about roots. "Nae, I hold no converse wi' them." His eyes held mine authoritatively. "And how had ye knowledge of Master Jaimie's day, mistress?"

"From Mr. Beltane. It's a surprise. You'll not give it away?" I begged, unstrung by the implications of "Master Jaimie." Who and what was the gardener to use so intimate an appellation?

"Tell it me," he commanded, his fingers working once more but still regarding me.

I'd no wish to tell him anything. If he was no part of the indoor servants' hall, there must be good reason—but I'd not the courage to refuse those cold gray eyes. Haltingly I explained the evening's plans, taking heart by the slow softening of his face at the new dresses, songs selected, simple gifts to accompany the cake with a single candle; then in a twinkling he was stern again, gazing at me almost with hatred.

"So, he'll be at that again," he muttered, tight-lipped. "Not bad enough he lost all he loved last time wi' an auld 'un, but he'll dazzle a child."

"I don't understand," I faltered. "What have I done, or Miss Amy? It's only a surprise for the master."

"Ane ye thought of yourself, mistress," he grunted. "Yon lassie's too daft to know her ane name."

"That's not true!" I cried indignantly. "There's *nothing* wrong with Miss Amy. Don't you *dare* to think so, you— you ignorant old man!" I snatched up the flowers and whirled to the door. "Just you join the staff this evening, if they'll permit it," I told him arrogantly, "and perhaps they won't if you 'hold no converse with them.' But *if* they will, you can stand in the hall with them and see for yourself." I pulled open the door militantly. "And good day to *you!*"

Surprisingly his expression softened once more. "And a good day to yourself, mistress," he said deliberately. "Eh, ye're a proper termagant, are ye no'?"

I wasn't sure what the word meant, but instinctively I raised my chin. "Yes," I said, and whisked out to the path, closing the greenhouse door with insulting care.

Automatically my feet turned toward the lake; there'd be time to brush Macdonald from my mind before Miss Amy would wake. I ran impetuously down through the formal shrubbery, holding the flowers protectively within my coat; and rounding the final bush, I caromed into a sturdy male figure: the rector.

He caught me in strong arms with an involuntary "Oooof!"

"Silence!" he said, concerned. "What's wrong, child?"

"Macdonald," I panted, catching my breath. "Please, sir, what does 'termagant' mean?"

"A sharp-tongued woman—and where heard you this?"

"Macdonald. He said Miss Amy was daft, and I called him an ignorant old man," I confessed.

"And he called you a termagant." Mr. Beltane smiled amusedly, turning to walk beside me toward the house. "Tell me, Silence, what do *you* think of Amy? You have accomplished miracles at Hazelhurst; you brought peace with you; James calls you his 'golden Silence'—but you are as self-contained as your name. What do you *think*, I wonder?"

I was suddenly flooded with trust in this black-a-vised man. Compared with my master, the rector was almost ugly, but in the past weeks I'd learned the beauty of his voice, the wisdom in his sermons, the warmth of his smile. "Miss Amy is *not* daft, sir," I said earnestly. "I'm not wise enough to know what is wrong, and Dr. Robinson is useless—he just writes another prescription, because he doesn't know the answer, either." Once started, I poured out all my puzzlements in a despairing cataract. "Prevention is not cure, sir, and I don't know why the nerve storms occur, nor when they began—but there is no *mental* deficiency. I would recognize that, from the orphanage. Miss Amy cannot control her emotions, but she is perfectly intelligent."

Mr. Beltane nodded. "What does Mr. Ffolliott say of your opinion?"

"I haven't told him, sir. He's so occupied with business that we rarely see him, but in any case I promised Miss Amy I wouldn't tattle. I did ask him the first night if he had any instructions, but all he said was that she was to have whatever she wanted, no matter the cost. I was to have as many dresses as would keep her contented, and he liked to look at a prettily dressed young woman, too." Mr. Beltane's heavy brows flicked up and down, but I scarcely noticed. "I can't help feeling I might do better for Miss Amy if only I understood a bit more, but there's no one to ask," I finished unhappily.

"What is it you want to know?"

"I'm not sure," I said slowly. "Perhaps . . . her mother?

Miss Amy can speak of her—we spent two mornings cleaning her jewelry and Miss Amy described the costumes with which it was worn—but if *I* mention Mrs. Ffolliott, she goes into a nerve storm. Were they very devoted? From chance words, it seems Miss Amy was a delicate but normal child, and these nervous attacks are more recent."

"True," Mr. Beltane pondered. "Amy's mother was Helen Ormond; her father owned Hazelhurst and was a friend of my father—that was how I got the living—but there was no mental instability in any of the Ormonds. I don't know about Salford, but it's unlikely. He was a Nabob, very rich and much older than Helen. When he died, she brought Amy home. I recall Helen worried over the climate; she was apt to keep Amy indoors whenever the wind blew"— he frowned with the effort of memory—"but now you mention it, I don't recall more than an occasional cold. Of course I rarely saw the child—she was in the nursery—and I was not so free of the house because the older Ormonds died within the year. Helen married James a while later. He'd been a protégé of Salford, almost a son—he was younger than Helen, too, but they were extremely happy. He's never cared to remarry."

"He said he'd been in the diplomatic service."

"Chargé d'affaires for both Lord Elgin and Sir John Lawrence. . . . When he came home for reassignment, it was generally expected he'd serve a few apprentice posts and be Viceroy of India in ten years." Mr. Beltane's voice held affectionate pride.

"Then . . . what happened?"

"Oh, the first assignment was Kabul." The rector shrugged. "James was eager to try his hand on the Afghans, but Helen was terrified—couldn't blame her; the Fuzzy-Wuzzies' national sport was killing the British residents— but the alternative was Damascus, and she was afraid for Amy's health. It was a real problem," Mr. Beltane agreed. "The child was too young for boarding school, no grandparents or responsible relatives with whom to leave her, and on top of all, there was Hazelhurst and Salford's importing firm. In the end, James resigned from foreign service and took over the management of Helen's affairs."

We had reached the rear terrace. "I must go up to Miss Amy. Thank you for telling me this, sir."

"But it doesn't really explain . . ." Mr. Beltane muttered

absently. He went along the terrace and disappeared, while I ran hastily through the kitchens to the back stairs—but Mr. Beltane was right: he had given facts, but they did not explain Miss Amy.

I'd no time to consider them now. More than ever I was determined this evening should be a triumph for my mistress. I wanted Mr. Ffolliott to be surprised, to enjoy his birthday, but mostly I wanted everyone to realize Miss Amy was not a feebleminded idiot!

She was just waking as I came in, and I was encouraged by her clear eyes, her mischievous smile. *"No* aches and pains," she said happily. "What d'you think of *that?"*

"I think you're a clever girl, and it's going to be a delightful evening," I returned promptly. "Here are our flowers—but I think Sarah should put them in the stillroom to keep them fresh, don't you?"

All continued smoothly. There was anticipation, certainly; she went over every detail while Mrs. Davenport dressed her in the soft velvet, but nothing caused a sob. I could hear them chatting while I dressed myself, and when I returned, Miss Amy was standing calmly before the cheval glass, adjusting the bracelet at her wrist. "How beautiful you are!" I said involuntarily.

She turned to inspect me. "So are you," she said wonderingly. "Such lovely dark eyes—I can really see them. How good we chose that color, Silence! But"—she frowned faintly—"there must be something at the neck. Davenport, bring the jewel box again." I stood, dumb with surprise, as she sorted through various pieces, until she said, "Of course! Mama's yellow diamonds."

"Diamonds? Oh, Miss Amy, no!"

"Don't be silly, Silence." She set the collar firmly about my throat. "The dress is lovely, but you must always complete the effect. There"—she studied me with pride—"you look perfect, Silence."

"That you do! A pair of little beauties you are, my dearies." Mrs. Davenport sighed sentimentally.

Hesitantly I turned to the mirror. Was that small elegant girl in silk and diamonds really the orphan from Belliston Parva? Miss Amy smiled at me. "Hold your head up!" Automatically I raised my chin. Why not? Miss Carey had said my mother was a lady. Lucy Victoria would have worn a crinoline, but she would expect her daughter to

SILENCE IS GOLDEN 51

manage a bustle and diamonds with grace. "That's better," Miss Amy approved. Her eyes were sparkling with excitement. "How surprised Papa will be!"

The surprise was common to us all, for when we entered the library there was not merely Mr. Beltane and Mr. Ffolliott, but a third figure turning to us as we halted on the threshold. It was a young man in dinner clothes as finely tailored as my master's. He was of middle height, with waving chestnut hair and eyes more gray than blue.

"Amy, dear! Come in! Here is a surprise for you: Robert Ormond, the son of your dear mother's favorite cousin." Mr. Ffolliott smiled.

It was potential disaster; her eyes filled with tears and her lips quivered. I leaned to her ear. "Tears will spot the velvet, and we have our own surprise!"

She glanced at me wildly, but with a gulp she was controlled and moving forward. "Cousin Robert?"

Mr. Ormond had a pleasant tenor voice. "You won't remember me, Cousin Amy"—he bent gracefully over her hand—"and to be truthful, all I remember is that you consistently beat me at spillikins."

"Did I?" she asked wonderingly. "I haven't played spillikins in a long time."

"It's not a very grown-up game," he agreed humorously, "and you are very grown up indeed, Cousin Amy."

"Oh, yes. I'm twenty, you know—but I still like lots of nursery games, don't I, Papa?" She turned to kiss Mr. Ffolliott.

"Yes, darling, and you still beat all challengers," he said absently. "Who is this mysterious little stranger you have brought with you, Amy?"

Startled, I took my eyes from my mistress—to find myself the center of attention. Mr. Beltane's black eyes smiled approvingly, which enabled me to meet Mr. Ormond's frank admiration, while Miss Amy trilled, "Silly Papa! It's Silence, of course. Isn't she lovely?"

My cheeks were warm with agonized embarrassment, suddenly aware of the diamond collar. Mr. Ffolliott would recognize his dead wife's jewels! What might he not think and be unable to say before a stranger? Oh, *why* had he brought Mr. Ormond on this evening? I looked at the inoffensive young man and very nearly hated him!

"She's breathtaking," Mr. Ffolliott was saying. "You must look to your laurels, my dear, if she is not to outshine you. And now that we have admired you, Silence, come in." He laughed, stretching out his other arm. "Robert, here is my second 'daughter': Amy's companion, Miss Silence Eddington."

Hesitantly I went forward to curtsey, feeling my hand warmly grasped by Mr. Ormond. "Miss Eddington," he murmured formally, and laughed at Mr. Ffolliott. "What a lucky chap you are, Cousin James! *Two* beauties: one 'a daughter of the gods, divinely fair,' and one who's 'all that's best of dark and bright.'"

"Very apt, Robert. Indeed, my golden Silence 'Walks in beauty like the night.'" Mr. Ffolliott's lips brushed my temple and I was released with a gentle hug. "Tea!"

I felt reprieved, but new anxiety arose. While I served my master and the rector, Mr. Ormond drew a chair beside Miss Amy and began talking with animation. *Please let him not mention her mother!* Never had Mr. Ffolliott taken so long to select his sandwiches and cake, or so it seemed; but when I returned to my seat, I breathed more easily. Mr. Ormond was speaking of his life at Oxford, home in Wales, position with a London firm that appeared to be part of Salford, Limited, and required a great deal of travel.

Miss Amy was intrigued, listening eagerly to his descriptions of Paris, Madrid, Lisbon, Rome. "But Berlin is best—so neat and clean. You would like it of all things, Cousin Amy."

Watching her deep interest, I felt confirmed that her life was too restricted—to the point of boredom. Surely, if she could be the gracious hostess tonight, an occasional guest would actually be helpful. Instinctively I glanced at Mr. Ffolliott—but his eyes were not on Miss Amy, they were fixed upon me, and involuntarily my fingers went to the necklet. My heart beat wildly, yet I could not look away from that intent blue gaze but sat transfixed, until his lips slowly curved into an infinitesimal smile. As Mr. Beltane raised his head from the papers he had been discussing, Mr. Ffolliott smiled with sudden easiness and extended his cup. "More tea, please."

"Yes, sir." But when I returned, Mr. Beltane's expression was grave. Did he, too, feel the impropriety of a bejeweled orphan? "Please," I faltered. "Miss Amy *would* have me wear these tonight to complete the dress. Mrs. Davenport saw no harm, but we had not expected a stranger."

Mr. Ffolliott's eyebrows rose. "What of it?" he asked lazily. "Amy is right; they do complete the costume. She had better give them to you. I doubt she'd ever wear them; they wouldn't display to advantage against her white skin, while they're perfect for you—eh, Hugo?"

I saw that Mr. Beltane was as startled as I, but he sensed my distress. "Yes, you look charming, child," he said kindly, and turned back to Mr. Ffolliott. "Then we're agreed on the extra shilling for the verger?"

Shakily I resumed my seat. Tonight it was I who needed help for composure, and amazingly it came from Mr. Ormond. Unaware of undercurrents, he bridged all gaps with a ready flow of conversation that held Miss Amy's attention and drew reminiscences from the older men. When we left them to cigars and port, I'd regained sufficient calm for disclosure of Mr. Ffolliott's birthday, but all was well.

"How fortunately it all comes about!" she exclaimed. "It is every way lucky we chanced to choose tonight, Silence: our dresses, the concert, Cousin Robert, and Mr. Beltane to make it a party—and we have gifts to complete the surprise. . . ." Her face was suddenly sharp. "How did *you* know it was Papa's birthday? And I hadn't finished the slippers. . . ."

"I didn't know until I met Mr. Beltane this afternoon," I fibbed, "and then I did the last leaf for you."

She was still intense. "Why didn't you tell me at once, Silence? Why did you keep it to yourself until now?"

"Because"—I faced her squarely—"I was afraid it *might* upset you." She caught her breath, staring at me wildly. "It was already your surprise," I said quietly. "Dear Miss Amy, I wouldn't risk anything that might lessen it. Please see I was right? There were always to be refreshments after the music—all I've added is to tell Mrs. Potter to put a candle on the cake and to wrap the things we were embroidering. It is only a tiny extra for your original surprise—and you see how they are enjoying themselves. Come, arrange the music in the right order. Alfred must be presenting the invitations by now.

They'll soon be here, and we must impress Mr. Ormond."

She drew a long breath. "Yes. Do you like him, Silence?" Her eyes slid sideways to me across the music. "He likes *you*. He could hardly take his eyes from you all evening."

"Nonsense!" I was astounded. "He's very pleasant, but it was you who captivated him."

She eyed me again with a knowing smile. "It would be a very good thing for you, Silence. The Ormonds are a most respectable alliance."

I stared at her, speechless, and simultaneously the men arrived from the dining room, laughing and curious to be formally received by Miss Amy; Alfred ushered them to chairs, gave them programs, and supplied them with brandy. Once more it was I who was unnerved, requiring all my will power to do my part after Miss Amy's incomprehensible words, while she herself was perfectly at ease.

Smoothly she progressed from one selection to another, pleased by the pleasure she gave, yet oddly indifferent to applause. It was as though she knew herself to be excellent, and if you did not recognize this, it was your loss. It was evident that Mr. Ffolliott loved music and was deeply moved by Miss Amy's accomplished fingers; he leaned back with half-closed eyes, repaid her with a smile when the others applauded. I took heart; all was well; I had achieved a private thanks for his kindness to me. I could glimpse the servants taking turns to peek through the rear salon door crack, and when it was my turn to sing with her, I managed it adequately. I was still devoutly thankful when all was ended!

Miss Amy bowed graciously, I curtseyed behind her, but she shook her head to requests for an encore. "This is intermission for refreshments!" With a tiny laugh, she skimmed across to Mr. Ffolliott, sinking onto the fauteuil and taking his hand. "Papa, you were surprised? You truly enjoyed it?"

I thought Mr. Ffolliott pulled himself back to our company with an effort. How much he must have missed such evenings! "I truly did," he assured her. "I thought you no longer played because of your back."

"Oh, Silence watches and will not let me sit too long without resting," she said blithely, "and it is so good to play again."

"It is good to hear you!" Mr. Ormond exclaimed admiringly. "You are as accomplished as Clara Wieck, Cousin Amy, and the blending of your voice with Miss Eddington —superb!"

Mr. Ffolliott threw back his head with a sudden bark of laughter. "Secret practice for weeks? A pretty pair of minxes! I knew I had a canary, but a lovely brown thrush as well? It is too much; *je suis comblé de richesses*." He leaned to refill his brandy glass, still chuckling to himself . . . but something in his amusement made me anxious. Had he not liked to hear Miss Amy compared to a concert artist? I stood uncertainly, watching him—and the servants advanced ceremoniously with the tray.

He stared thunderstruck at the round cake with its flickering candle, while Miss Amy squeezed his hand and crowed with laughter. "Here is the real surprise: Happy birthday, dearest Papa." Unobtrusively I slid the parcels onto the tray, while Mr. Ormond exclaimed, "By Jove, what a party it is! But I call it shabby not to tell a fellow— I'd have filched a box of Turkish Delight, or a packet of latakia for your Own Sort." Beaming, Alfred placed the tray and stepped back. "Me and the staff wish you all the best, sir."

"Thank you, thank you." Mr. Ffolliott nodded automatically, but I sensed that a surprise it had been, and somehow not a happy one. Mr. Beltane's face was austere . . . but it was *he* who'd told me. . . .

Slowly, Mr. Ffolliott opened a parcel. "Slippers!"

Miss Amy leaned against his knee. "Try them on, Papa. Silence had Dawson call the bootmaker for the forms, but we were still not just sure," she confided anxiously, "or if you would like the pattern. I wanted roses, but she thought gold would show to better advantage."

With a snort of laughter, Mr. Ffolliott slid one foot from its boot and into the slipper. "A perfect fit!"

"A perfect design." Mr. Beltane tossed off his brandy. "Poppies, James, for Nepenthe—a clever choice, Silence."

"It's not my gift, sir. Mine is nothing so fine."

Mr. Ffolliott would not agree. He removed his pocket kerchief, and replaced it with one of mine. "A sweet thought, Silence, but you must mark two more with your hair, so both my girls will go with me," he said deliberately, and again I sensed some hidden meaning . . . as though Mr. Beltane disapproved and my master was defiant.

"Make your wish and blow before the candle dies," Mr. Ormond warned cheerfully. "It's burning fast, Cousin James."

"A habit of candles," Mr. Beltane remarked. "Choose wisely, James, you've only the one."

"One is enough." Mr. Ffolliott held Miss Amy's hand and reached to clasp mine. For a second he closed his eyes dramatically, then with one tremendous puff the candle was extinguished. "Now! That's a fairy cake, and you may all have a piece of my enchantment. Slice it, Amy, and give the largest piece to Hugo. He needs it most."

Miraculously, the constraint vanished—if it had existed at all. We ate and drank, laughed and chatted, until Mr. Ormond said gaily, "Now this is long enough for intermission! Back to the piano, Cousin Amy, and I will turn the sheets so Miss Eddington can give us a solo."

"Oh, I couldn't," I protested, but Miss Amy insisted, "Of course you can, Silence. Here"—she drew out the music—"you do this *beautifully*. Quiet, everyone, and listen." She rippled through a few arpeggios, began the simple introduction, and said "Now!"

> "Greensleeves was all my joy
> Greensleeves was my delight,
> Greensleeves was my heart of gold,
> And who but my Lady Greensleeves."

My voice wobbled disastrously at the start. I heard a sharply indrawn breath which further unnerved me, but softly a voice joined mine: Mr. Ormond!

It was the last of the surprises, and almost best of all. Miss Amy was delighted; Mr. Ormond modestly disclaimed, the while he was eagerly examining her music. "We must have a *singfest*. It is the common thing in Germany after dinner, you know, but in general we have nothing so fine in England. The young ladies play their 'pieces' "—he wrinkled his nose—"but you are a true musician, Cousin Amy. Mr. Beltane, Cousin James, you will join us?"

"With pleasure," said the rector. "Stop admiring your slippers, James, and sing for your supper."

"Do, Papa," Miss Amy pleaded lovingly. "You haven't sung with me for so long."

Briefly, the master's lips tightened. Then he pulled him-

SILENCE IS GOLDEN

self erect, and crossed to stand beside me. "Very well. What shall we have, Robert?"

It was exhilarating! I was no match for any of them; they all must have been trained like Miss Amy to take their parts effortlessly, while I quavered along as best I could—until Mr. Ffolliott's arm about my shoulders drew me gently against him, his fingers lightly indicating my part. Unconsciously I leaned against him, and my heart sang as joyously as my throat. Oh, fortunate Silence—to share such beauty and loving kindness!

From song to song we went, oblivious of time. As we began the next, I was aware of movement in the outer hall: a single figure, motionless in the shadows: Macdonald.

For a moment he stood at the doorway, observing, until his eyes met mine; and he glared at me with such malevolence that I shrank, shivering, against my master. Then Macdonald stumped away, and simultaneously the song was ended.

CHAPTER FOUR

So was the party.

"Do you realize the time?" Laughing but inexorable, Mr. Ffolliott closed the piano and swept everyone out to the hall. "Robert, you can find your room? The carriage will be ready at seven for the London train. Now you know your way, you'll make yourself free of Hazelhurst every weekend, eh? Amy dear, sleep well."

"Yes, Papa. Wasn't it a happy evening?"

"Very happy, darling." He kissed her cheek affectionately, shook hands with Mr. Ormond, smiled, and nodded as they went up the stairs. "Hugo, a nightcap before your carriage is brought around?" He stood looking after Miss Amy and her cousin, while Mr. Beltane disappeared into the library. I stood in the shadows of the salon, feeling suddenly forgotten, but without turning he said softly, "Where's my golden Silence?"

"Here, sir."

"You're too little," he complained, his eyes twinkling at me. "Stand on the stairs so I can see you."

Laughing, I went up two treads and faced him. "Many happy returns of the day, sir."

"Why, as for that, you couldn't be so cruel as to make me wait a whole year! Let's do it again tomorrow and tomorrow and the next day."

Involuntarily I chuckled. "I couldn't possibly make so many handkerchiefs, sir. We'd have no hair left."

"My practical Lady Greensleeves!" He bent forward to kiss my cheek. "Good night, my golden girl, and sleep well."

"And you, sir." I ran upstairs and found the reaction I'd feared. Miss Amy was determined not to go to bed until every detail was discussed.

SILENCE IS GOLDEN

"No, I won't undress. I'm not tired, Davenport. Build up the morning room fire. Isn't there some punch and cake left?" The voice was rising, the tears beginning to spill. "Silence, *make* her bring the refreshments."

"Not tonight. Our voices would keep Mr. Ormond awake, and you know he must get up very early."

"Oh, poor Cousin Robert. I'd forgot." She sighed wistfully. "But I hate to have it all over, Silence."

"We'll enjoy it more when we're rested tomorrow and can begin at the beginning—and Mr. Ormond spoke of new music for the weekend." I rapidly loosened hooks, while Mrs. Davenport trotted about silently to prepare the bed and set the fire screen. "What a good voice he has, and how much he knows of music," I murmured admiringly. "You sounded beautiful together, Miss Amy."

"Did we? He's going to bring songs from the London operettas." She yawned drowsily, crawling into bed. But when I started to tuck the covers about her, the blue eyes suddenly were clear and she put out her arms to pull me toward her. "Oh, Silence, you're so good to me. You make everything different. I love you . . . shan't we be sisters?"

"I'd like that, Miss Amy," I said tremulously. "It would be so good to have a sister; and I love you, too." Gently we kissed each other; my eyes were blurred with tears. "Now, to sleep, and be ready for tomorrow!"

I fumbled with the unfamiliar catch of the necklet. I ran to the door, but Mrs. Davenport was gone. The back stairs were dark—was anyone awake, if I felt my way down to the servants' rooms? Hesitantly I went forward along the hall, past the night lamp, and heard voices in the library—better to disturb Mr. Ffolliott and Mr. Beltane than to wake Miss Amy. . . .

"If you please, sir, I don't know how to unfasten this, and Miss Amy's asleep."

"So soon and so easily?" Mr. Ffolliott laid aside the hookah tube. "Well, well! Bend down, Silence."

"Yes, sir." Obediently I knelt, presenting my back. "We are going to talk tomorrow, when we are rested and our voices will not keep Mr. Ormond awake." In a second, the diamonds were freed and dangling from his fingers before my eyes. "Thank you, sir. I'm sorry to have disturbed you." I scrambled to my feet apologetically, but Mr. Ffolliott's blue eyes were very bright as he took up the hookah.

"A pleasant interruption! It's like old times to unfasten the jewels at evening's end, although these never graced so lovely a throat before, eh, Hugo?"

"Stop it, James!" Mr. Beltane's voice sounded angry, but he smiled at me. "Good night, Silence. It was a delightful party. Thank you for inviting me."

"Yes, sir. Good night, sir." Hastily I went to the hall, but after the light in the library, I had to move cautiously, feeling with my toe for the bottom step of the stairs. Behind me, Mr. Ffolliott's deep voice held reckless laughter. "Are you disapproving of me, Hugo?"

"Unworthy, James! Stop flirting with that . . . *sweet child!*"

The laughter ceased. I had finally touched the newel post and could see the faint night lamp above me, when Mr. Ffolliott's voice remarked thoughtfully, "But . . . *am* I flirting, Hugo?"

"Good God, James"—the rector's protest was vehement—"are you out of your mind?"

"Perhaps, but at the age of forty-one—*forty-one*, Hugo!" My master's voice was anguished. "Half my life in years and all of its purpose— For God's sake, Hugo, let me have something!"

The voices were dying away into fragments as I reached the upper hall. "You *know* what will happen!" Indistinct murmurs, finally a name: "Mrs. Langley meant . . . means . . . *nothing*, Hugo."

She meant nothing to me, either. I stumbled down the hall to my room, somehow stripped off my clothes, and was asleep almost before I crawled into bed.

Later, I dated everything by that concert. It was as though I had served an apprenticeship and been promoted to a higher grade. We could all speak more freely, even Miss Amy. The next morning, when each detail was thoroughly talked out, she suddenly said, "I started to be naughty, didn't I? What happened, Silence?"

"I reminded you we'd disturb Mr. Ormond."

"And that stopped me?" She sighed. "Thank you, Silence. It makes Papa so sad."

SILENCE IS GOLDEN

"Doubly sad on his birthday night, but"—I nerved myself—"if only we could find the *reason,* so I could help. . . ."

"You always do." Her eyes filled with tears. "And you never shake me or hit me, because I never have any bruises. I always look at my arms first, to make sure. . . ." I sat appalled while she babbled on. "They said it was to prevent my harming myself. But I never do, do I, Silence? And I don't hurt you or Davenport, do I?"

"Never!" I said pitifully.

"They said I did. But Mrs. Langley scratched *herself* with a nail file. I saw her!"

"Mrs. . . . Langley?"

Miss Amy wiped her eyes and sat up. "She was the worst." Her voice was vicious. "She kicked me and beat me, Silence. She wouldn't let Nana into the room because she knew Nana would tell Papa." Her tone was rising. "And when I showed him the marks, she said I'd made them and I ought to be put away! What d'you think of *that!* It was because she wanted to marry Papa—he's very rich, you know—but"—she laughed shrilly—"he didn't love *her*. He doesn't love anyone but me. And as soon as Davenport made him listen, he discharged her."

"But you need never worry again," I soothed. "Neither Nana nor I would hurt you, nor will you hurt us. But if you could tell me what happens, perhaps we could think of a way to prevent it."

"I don't know," she murmured helplessly. "It's like the picnic at the sea on Mama's birthday, and the wave broke over my head." She choked and closed her eyes with a shudder. "Papa saved me, and we never went back. But it's like that, Silence: as though everything drains away under my feet and rises up behind me in a great curve over my head." She screamed faintly and threw herself from her chair into my arms, sobbing wildly. "Then I forget everything until Papa comes—but he isn't always here."

"But I am, and Davenport and the others." I held her protectively. "There'll always be someone to save you, Miss Amy. But when you feel the water draining away, why don't you run toward shore? You must make a picture in your mind of me and Mr. Beltane and—and your cousin Robert. We'll be sitting under an umbrella with a picnic basket, and the servants will have their umbrella and basket. You have only to call us, and long before the wave breaks, we'll have reached you."

She lay trembling against me. "Oh, if it could be like that— But you're so small, Silence. Papa is so big and strong, he can pick me up in his arms and carry me, and even if the wave broke, he could swim."

"Why should we not learn, in the lake?"

"Oh, no!" She shuddered convulsively. "It is too dangerous; it is worse than the sea. There are deep springs and places the ice will never form." She closed her eyes sickly and shivered.

"But we will not be skating. We'll stay safely at the edge, and there are no waves in the lake."

"No, there are not," she said after a moment, "and Papa could teach us. He often swims in summer. We could be with him, couldn't we?" She pulled away from me. "What a good plan, Silence! You must make bathing dresses. There was a design in one of the books."

In the next days Miss Amy was more calm than ever before, as though revelation had dispelled fear. The weather broke sharply; my exercise had to be limited to breathing fresh air in the vestibule, or the gale would blow me over, yet she seemed unaware of the torrential rain gusting against the long salon windows. Daily she practiced against the weekend when Mr. Ormond would return. We saw nothing of Mr. Beltane and little of Mr. Ffolliott. Alfred said he went only to Chelmsford where there was both telephone and telegraph to London, but apparently he dined at his club when business was done, for we ate alone each evening.

Miss Amy was undisturbed! All that troubled her was the possibility of delay on the Saturday train bringing her cousin from London, and whether the tempest would subside sufficiently for the rector to join us.

For myself these days were difficult. I had all too much time to think, and far too much to think about. Each apparent solution merely brought a fresh enigma, until I felt I walked through a forest on a downward trail that grew ever darker. There were always alternatives; where was Truth?

Did Miss Amy's "wave" explain her fear of storms in the morning room, when she was entirely composed in

SILENCE IS GOLDEN 63

the salon? I'd thought the shadow over Hazelhurst was Miss Amy's hysteria, but was that the result of the picnic accident, or of Mrs. Ffolliott's death?

From the Winterhalter portrait in the morning room, she had been equally fine-boned, but (to my mind) even more beautiful than Miss Amy: masses of chestnut hair, brilliant greenish eyes, a warm golden skin enhanced by a ball gown of apricot velvet baring smooth shoulders in the fashion of 1856. Sarah told me it was formerly in the library; the master had not liked to give it up, but Miss Amy had begged for it. "Sobbed something terrible, she did, until he agreed."

Then why was it hung *behind* Miss Amy's chair? Why had she never said "That was Mama" when we were cleaning the magnificent emerald parure of the portrait? From my sewing seat, I viewed the lovely woman over Miss Amy's shoulder, and thought it not strange Mr. Ffolliott had found no one to succeed her. Helen Salford looked all vibrant *life* and luxurious enjoyment compared with her daughter. What a handsome couple they must have been in the days of Hazelhurst entertaining—but had she loved him as he loved her? From the rector's words, she had placed her child before her husband, and in so doing, had robbed him of a glittering career.

I remembered the tone of his voice, "I shall never see the East again," and my heart ached for the master. Instinctively I knew he'd have gloried in Fuzzy-Wuzzies, enjoyed every dangerous moment, cleverly charmed local potentates into the Empire. How had he felt that it was Lord Lytton instead of Sir James Ffolliott who proclaimed our Queen the Empress of India nearly four years past? Of course a small child would be a problem, but surely something might have been contrived. Not all of the Orient held native assassins, and Amy had survived six years of infancy in India. Why fear to take her back? . . . Or had Helen Salford really feared the loss of her second husband?

Perhaps. For all its beauty, that chin was as determined as Miss Amy's! An intelligent woman, certainly, but willful, older than he, the widow of his beloved friend. . . . Yes, I could imagine Mr. Ffolliott: young, impetuous, deeply in love, unable to resist her persuasion to stay home "for her sake." But when she died, why had he not reentered the diplomatic corps? Miss Amy was fourteen then, of an age for boarding school.

"Aye, she'd already had a full term." Mrs. Davenport sighed. "But 'twas that Christmas the mistress died of a chill, and when the master sent her back—a fine academy it was, near Cambridge—she fretted herself sick until she was home again. It was in her mind she must look after him in his loneliness, poor child."

"I didn't know she'd ever been to school."

The housekeeper nodded. "Mrs. Ffolliott chose it. The master traveled a lot in those days, and of course he wanted the mistress with him. I mind they went abroad twice, and they were going to South America in the January, but he sent someone else because Miss Amy was feverish." Mrs. Davenport looked at her toes and said no more, but I sensed there was more to say, if she knew how.

"Nana, you must help me a little," I said gently. "Miss Amy says the others . . . beat her, and said she hurt *them*." Mrs. Davenport drew in her breath, staring at me unhappily. "I can't believe Mr. Ffolliott would permit it, but please . . . tell me?"

She sighed. "It was never that bad, Miss Silence, but some of the nurses did try to bring her out of the fits with a slap or a shake. They said it was the right thing with hysterics." Her eyes misted with tears. "Dr. Robinson said so, too—but it was never brutal, Miss Silence! I'd not have stood for that, and in any case it didn't answer; it only made her a wild thing. She'd round on them, and throw whatever she could reach or scratch with her nails, until it'd take the master or Alfred to hold her still.

"It's why I feared for you, my dearie, so little as you are—but you've a knack. And at first, one of us was always at hand," she said steadily. "There's still always one of us listening."

"I see. Thank you, Nana," I murmured absently, "but I've promised she needn't worry. We'll never harm each other: you, and I, and Miss Amy."

"That's as may be," Mrs. Davenport muttered involuntarily, and shuffled her feet nervously, making up her mind, until suddenly she faced me squarely. "Grand as you are with her, Miss Silence, I tell you truly I don't know how you'll manage when the master goes on this trip. Twice it's been put off since last September, so all will be ready

SILENCE IS GOLDEN

and he'll not be delayed, but go he must, for it's to do with Miss Amy's trust that ends in June when she's of age. I'd not know the details, but he'll not be guardian after that."

"Is he really going, then?" I asked in surprise. "Miss Amy says it's only a joke to tease her, that Mr. Ffolliott often talks of traveling but never leaves her."

"Aye, in the past—but this is different. He cannot send a substitute, and how she'll take it, I don't know," the housekeeper said grimly. "It disturbs her most of all to be apart from the master. I mind he took her away from the gales to Italy some years ago, to a villa in the sun, but he couldn't stay from his business, and in a week the nurse had to bring her home. Eh, she was in a state!" Mrs. Davenport drew a long breath and stood up. "But this time, bad as it may be, you'll have all of us to help, Miss Silence."

"Thank you, Nana." I had long since understood Miss Carey's distrust, and my master's reference to "ignoble motive." In desperation, he'd hired an orphan who would be unable to leave Hazelhurst—for where could I go? That was why he supervised my letters, willingly paid for anything, and called me his "second daughter"—but after my first startled comprehension, I felt rather set up than otherwise. No one had had much hope of me, and I had surprised everybody, including myself. In time, I'd do better and it would be an achievement I'd value as much as my salary, although that was exciting, too, and I had no fault to find with it.

On the Friday, Mr. Ffolliott summoned me to the library. I went in some agitation. Did he wish a report on Miss Amy, or had the rector told him of our conversation? I had not exacted secrecy, but might not my master be angry that I should discuss his ward with an outsider, no matter how close a friend?

He seemed only now to have returned home. Alfred was helping him into a velvet robe and slippers—deep blue with silver embroidery this evening. His face was certainly tired, but he smiled at me kindly. "Come in, Silence. Thank you, Alfred. That will be all for tonight."

"Beg pardon, sir, but Mrs. Potter's left sandwiches and coffee."

Mr. Ffolliott sighed. "I want nothing, but you may as

well bring them." He turned from me, warming his hands at the fire for a moment, leaned to pour brandy into the balloon glass, chose a cigar and lit it. I stood uncertainly by the door, making way for Alfred with the tray, but with his final dismissal, Mr. Ffolliott said, "Where are you, Silence? Why are you lingering in the shadows?"

"I thought you had forgot me, sir."

"I never forget you," he said deliberately, looking at me over his shoulder. "Do you forget me?"

"Of course not, sir." I went forward into the lamp light. "It is good to see you, but you are so weary. . . ."

He raised his eyebrows. "You have missed me, my Silence?"

"Very much, sir," I said warmly. "Hazelhurst comes alive when you enter the door. We would know you are here, even if we did not see or hear you."

"Fee, Fi, Fo, Fum," he remarked. "The ogre is home!" I chuckled irrepressibly at his terrible grimace, and he laughed. "Well"—he sank into his chair with a long breath—"sit at my feet, Scheherazade. Tell me how you go on—and for heaven's sake, eat a few of Potter's sandwiches, or she will be hurt."

Reluctantly obedient, I settled on the corner of the ottoman, and took the plate thrust at me; I wanted nothing, but at least I could disarrange the neat piles. "All goes extremely well," I said earnestly. "Miss Amy has been so occupied at the piano that she has scarcely noticed the rain. She looks forward eagerly to Mr. Ormond tomorrow—I hope nothing prevents! Otherwise, the week has been without incident." Looking up from the sandwiches, I saw Mr. Ffolliott's eyes were closed. "Forgive me, sir, but are you not too tired?" I asked anxiously. "Truly, all goes well."

"So they tell me," he nodded indifferently and opened his eyes. "And I am less tired already. Do you know what day this is, golden Silence?"

"Why . . . it is Friday, sir."

"What Friday—or do I mean which?"

"It is the Friday after your birthday, sir." I felt bewildered. "I think it is November thirtieth—or perhaps the thirty-first—I have not looked at the calendar."

Mr. Ffolliott's expression was . . . curious. I could not interpret, but sat transfixed by his gaze. "You really

SILENCE IS GOLDEN

do not know," he murmured incredulously.

"Know what, sir?" I faltered, but he only laughed.

"Bring me the small sack from my desk." And when I'd obeyed: "Hold out your hands." Wonderingly, I did so, and within them he placed golden guineas. "Your salary, Silence. It is three months this day."

I stared at the money open-mouthed; it quite filled my hands, and in my surprise, I dropped a few coins. "Has it *really* been so long, sir!"

"Yes, *really*." He laughed amusedly. "But you must not scatter your wealth so recklessly."

"Oh, no, sir." I blushed, and quickly knelt to retrieve the money, unconsciously counting. "But you have given me too much, sir. It was to be twenty-five, and this is thirty."

"On the contrary, I have not given you nearly enough for all you have done, but we will begin with a token of my satisfaction."

I was confused by pleasure, stammering my thanks for his generosity—although when was he not? With sudden memory, I asked, "Please, sir, how does one forward money by post? I should like to return the three guineas Miss Carey gave me."

"Three guineas?" he repeated harshly. "A large sum! Why did she give it you?"

Too late I remembered, but I could not bring myself to equivocate. "She thought I might not be . . . quite happy," I replied quietly, "and wished me to have sufficient to return to her."

"Ah, the excellent Miss Carey," he muttered drily, hauling himself to his feet and adding a log to the fire. "I might have known. Well, I will give you a bank draft, but"—there was a reckless flash of blue eyes—"think well before you burn your bridges, Silence. Are you 'happy' at Hazelhurst?"

"Very happy, sir," I told him steadily.

"I really think you are," he said after a moment, "but your wages would always provide the escape route henceforth, would they not? Or shall I withhold them on some pretext, and search your room to remove whatever coins you have secreted?"

I saw that he was furiously angry, bitterly humiliated that Miss Carey should have understood so clearly, but I could not resist a twitch of the lips. "Please, sir, this is not a gothic tale by Miss Edgeworth, neither are you Mr. Rochester to my Jane Eyre," I assured him innocently, and waited . . . until his lips began to curve into a rueful grin.

"Then you would never leave me, my Jane?" he quoted.

"No, sir."

"What if I should send you away?" he enquired dramatically.

"My heart would break," I replied promptly, "and I should be found dead in the nearest snowbank."

Mr. Ffolliott threw back his head in a roar of laughter. "Oh, Silence, my golden girl! There you stand: a small, submissive Griselda—and all the time you are a witch! How you coax everyone into good humor!"

"Yes, sir." I smiled. "But I truly would not leave you or Miss Amy so long as I can be of use, nor would you constrain me to anything distasteful."

"I wouldn't?"

"No, sir. You might wish to, but it would be impossible for you. I know you better," I said simply.

Mr. Ffolliott's jaw hardened. "Do you?" he remarked sardonically. "I wonder." He moved away from the fire and threw himself into the master's chair. "Go along with you—you have your wages. I'll send a draft to your Miss Carey," he said impatiently, and picked up the newspaper.

Silently, I set three guineas beside the brandy decanter, and went away with the rest of the money.

It was true that I knew Mr. Ffolliott too well to fear the least unkindness—which is not to say I *understood* him at all.

He was always fond and indulgent. Miss Amy doted upon him; she kissed him every time she entered or left a room, and loved to hold his hand, fingering the great onyx intaglio seal ring while she recounted details of our day, or she would settle on a cushion at his feet, leaning her head against his knee. She lavished affection upon him, with smiles, gentle hugs, gossamer kisses. Miss Amy talked constantly of "Papa," everything in her life centered about Mr. Ffolliott: what he liked her to do, eat, wear.

It seemed he studied her equally. He brought "sur-

SILENCE IS GOLDEN

prises" from London; all showed his knowledge of her tastes, but perhaps he was an unusually observant man. Whenever Miss Amy had a gift, there was a trifle for me also; each was always exactly right, as though he'd noticed me as different from Miss Amy.

And yet . . . an odd impression grew within me that *he disliked Miss Amy,* and forced himself to endure her caresses.

It was a shocking thought, yet I could not rid myself of it—and now that I had Mr. Beltane's words, I saw that it was logical. It was not Miss Amy's fault, yet because of her, Mr. Ffolliott had lost his shining chance . . . and for what? A mess of pottage not of his own making! He'd lost his lovely wife, been left with a ward who must be an exasperation of dullness even when she was not screaming with hysterics. It was the more to his credit that he never gave her a harsh word and was constantly alert for her health and happiness.

What would happen next June, when, according to Mrs. Davenport, his legal responsibility would end?

On Saturday the gales had subsided, the storm had dwindled to a dismal drizzle, and Mr. Ormond arrived, laughing and shaking himself from the raindrops that had escaped Dawson's huge umbrella. He handed an immense package to Alfred. "Unwrap it in the pantry, we mustn't spoil pretty dresses!" He came smiling into the library, rubbing his hands together. "Cousin Amy, I won't make my proper bow until I've changed, but I knew you'd be in a fever to see what I've brought! Miss Eddington, how are you? Cousin James, same room? No need to show me, then—ah, here's the package for you to examine, Cousin Amy. By Jove, it's good to be here again!"

"Good to see you, lad." Mr. Ffolliott clapped him lightly on the shoulder. "There's no haste, we're *en famille* tonight."

"But the ladies are as pretty as ever. What a lucky dog you are, Cousin James!" Mr. Ormond went away, laughing lightly as Alfred set the pile of music beside Miss Amy.

"There y'are, miss. I warrant that'll keep you busy, and fine we'll like to hear it."

"Oh, thank you, Alfred." She eyed the stack with

trepidation. "He's brought so much! How can I play it all? But if I don't, he'll be disappointed. Oh, Papa, I *can't!*" she wailed.

"You're not supposed to do it all at once," I said, leaning to pick up one piece after another. "He's brought enough to amuse you for weeks while we're alone, and you know how long it takes to teach me my part. *Look at the shore, Miss Amy . . . walk forward, I'm waiting for you . . . there's plenty of time . . . come along, darling.*"

"What did you say?" Mr. Ffolliott looked up from the newspaper.

"Nothing, sir. I didn't mean to disturb you." I stared straight at Miss Amy, holding out my hand with a smile, until she drew a long breath and laid her hand in mine. "All safe!" I whispered, and with a nod, she began to look over the music with increasing interest. By the time Mr. Ormond joined us, she was all eager anticipation for the treats ahead. I saw that Mr. Ffolliott had observed the bad moment, but without comprehension. Would it be "tattling" if I explained Miss Amy's wave? Perhaps I could tell Mr. Beltane and let him pass it on. There was no doubt in my mind that it was vital; although she never spoke of it again, her instant response to my command showed its reality to her.

There were only minor ripples until Mr. Ormond left for London, promising to return next Saturday. Miss Amy was charmed by his taste, and entranced by the unfamiliar composers and Mr. Ormond's knowledge, for he also played the piano. "I'm not to be compared with yourself, Cousin Amy, but duets hide a multitude of wrong notes," he said cheerfully.

Watching them together, I remembered her words on the night of our concert, and swiftly dismissed them as absurd. Mr. Ormond was unfailingly polite to me, included me in their conversation by a word or glance, as though I were a friend rather than a hired companion. He abandoned "Miss Eddington" for "Miss Silence," and we were perfectly at ease with each other, but there was no doubt of his romantic interest in Miss Amy! Inexperienced as I was with love, I yet instinctively recognized courtship in his compliments to her, the tiny excuses for touching her hand or leaning gently about her to turn the music.

Nor was Miss Amy displeased. She had a very pretty

dignity that neither invited nor rebuffed, but showed awareness of wooing. She blushed and glanced away shyly, but without coquetry. It was new to her to be admired and flattered by an attractive young man; she evidently liked it, but in general she was entirely natural—which only increased Mr. Ormond's ardor.

I was not the only observer. Mr. Ffolliott's eyes were on them as well, and I thought he had introduced Mr. Ormond with this very possibility in mind and was pleased that it went on so well. No doubt of its being a good thing! Miss Amy needed someone to love; a third cousin was not forbidden by consanguinity; Mr. Ormond shared her deep interest in music; there was certainly money, if her trust required Mr. Ffolliott to take this long trip in order to end it. My role was clearly marked: it would be my responsibility to help my mistress to serenity until her husband could take charge.

For the first time I felt the shadow lifted from Hazelhurst. I ascribed it to Mr. Ormond, who brought laughter and life to my mistress. Between study of the chosen pieces in preparation for weekends and the approach of Christmas, Miss Amy was literally too busy for nerves! Mr. Ormond and Mr. Beltane would be with us; great surprises were planned. We worked early and late in an aura of secrecy. Mysterious boxes were carried up to Mr. Ffolliott's chamber; our completed parcels were hidden in a guest room. Miss Amy's eyes occasionally filled with tears, but they were of happy anticipation. There was no wave!

"It's always easiest at Christmas," Mrs. Davenport told me, "but this year is the best since Mrs. Ffolliott's death. Eh, the things she has for you, Miss Silence!"

"Oh, dear! I have so little in return," I fretted.

"Don't worry, my dearie; you've already given more than can be repaid by *any* of us! To see the master enjoying his home, Miss Amy happy at the piano, to hear singing and laughter again—" She drew a long breath. "It puts heart into us, that it does."

It heartened me, as well. The weather continued inclement, with threatening gray skies when it was not actually raining, but never so wildly stormy as the week of my master's birthday. He was with us daily, sometimes for luncheon and always for dinner. We grew used to his walking into the salon, warming his hands until Alfred brought the house slippers. I served tea, while Miss Amy rested her back, but there was always time for songs before we dressed for dinner. Mr. Beltane nearly always joined us, and although I was adamant about the length of time Miss Amy sat at the keyboard, we were no longer dismissed after dinner.

Instead, we read aloud in the library. Taking turns, we worked our way through *Emma, Alice in Wonderland,* and *The Rose and the Ring.* On the night we finished it, Miss Amy sighed and said, "What a nice story! If only Silence's ring were enchanted, so she could know who she was."

Mr. Ffolliott eyed my hand sharply, and I slid the ring from my finger to hand him. "It was my mother's. Inside it says C.D.E. to L.V.M.—June 16, 1859. I pretend they were Charles and Lucy Victoria. The trustees advertised, but I might be American."

The rector got up and together the men bent over the ring with a magnifying glass under the desk lamp. Slowly Mr. Ffolliott returned to his chair. "Why? Tell me what you know, Silence."

I repeated Miss Carey's story, and he made notes on a page of the book from his breast pocket—but I sensed some deeper significance lying between my master and Mr. Beltane, as though Mr. Ffolliott were triumphant in some way. I thought I understood: they'd thought me a by-blow, and the rector had doubted the wisdom of entrusting Miss Amy to me. His face was still vaguely troubled when Mr. Ffolliott closed the notebook.

"Lloyd's Registry, and Pinkerton, of course," he murmured, while Miss Amy clapped her hands delightedly.

"I *knew* you'd know what to do, Papa! Isn't it romantic?"

"Very. But after so many years and the confusion of war, I would not hope too greatly," Mr. Beltane warned.

"I know, sir. It's only a story," I agreed, "except that probably my parents were married. It makes it easier to be an orphan, somehow."

"But I'm an orphan, too," Miss Amy remarked unexpectedly. "Papa isn't my real father, Silence. I call him so because he married Mama, and takes care of me—but he takes care of you, too."

"It's not at all the same," I protested tenderly.

"Yes, it is," she insisted. "He calls you his second

daughter; you should call him Papa. I'll share him until he finds your real family."

There was a dreadful pause, until Mr. Beltane rescued me. "That's very generous of you, Amy, but I suspect Silence is used to being an orphan and would find it hard to pretend. Your ring, Silence." He extended it quietly.

"But don't you *want* a father, Silence?" Miss Amy asked tearfully.

"I suppose so. But you see, I have a sort of picture in my mind, and—and my father doesn't look at all like Mr. Ffolliott," I said shakily.

"He doesn't?" she asked incredulously. "What does he look like, Silence?"

"Let her tell you upstairs," Mr. Ffolliott said harshly. "It is time for bed. Say good night, Amy."

But for the first time, he and I did not kiss each other. It was long before we did, and by then it was entirely different. In the weeks between, there was no constraint, merely a tacit recognition that we were master and employee. If Miss Amy noticed the omission of night and morning hugs, she said nothing, and seemed to have forgotten the whole thing in the excitement of presents.

The finest of these (to my mind) was her decision to send a bank draft to Miss Carey, with instructions to *spend it!* I was touched by the thought, and amused by her impracticality: new suits for all boys, enough silk for all girls—these were the least of her suggestions in the letter she insisted on writing personally, "to thank you for sending my sister, Silence." I had no fears; Miss Carey would get out of it somehow, and a hundred pounds would go a *long* way at Belliston Parva.

"Will she like it, d'you think?" Miss Amy asked anxiously, setting the sealing wafer on the envelope.

"Indeed she will." I was near tears at such generosity, unable to restrain a gentle hug and kiss on her forehead. "How kind you are! If we were really sisters, how happy I should be."

"Well, as for that," she remarked unexpectedly, "we might easily hate each other, Silence . . . like Miss Babbington and Mrs Forster at church. Mr. Beltane has a terrible time keeping them apart. I think perhaps it's better this way."

"Perhaps it is," I agreed, disconcerted—but when she'd

gone for her nap, I chuckled. I was right, Miss Amy was no fool!

Outside was the first tentative snowfall; within was peace as I worked contentedly on my surprise for Miss Amy. With Mrs. Davenport's connivance I was copying four fashion plates for four delicate French bisque dolls, using scraps of fabrics secretly obtained from Madame Raimond. "Oh, *quelle idée charmante*," the Frenchwoman sighed sentimentally. "They were Madame Ffolliott's, *vous comprenez?* She designed her gowns on them for us to copy, but I have not seen them in a long while"—her forehead puckered in memory—"since Madame Langley."

That name again! Before I could ask "Who was she?" the dressmaker had added some bits of Lyons velvet to my pile "for a cloak— *Oui, j'y viens!*" and gone out to a customer.

Who and what was this Mrs. Langley, who meant nothing to Mr. Ffolliott, but whom Miss Amy detested for ill treatment? Was she in some way responsible for the shadow at Hazelhurst Grange? I dared not ask Mrs. Davenport. For all her new confidences, I sensed we were not yet at a point of questions. If only I could speak again with Mr. Beltane! But often as I walked hopefully toward the lake, I never met him, and although he was so constantly with us in the evenings that I wondered if his housekeeper were ill, I had no opportunity for private speech.

Furthermore, I felt a peculiar strain between Mr. Ffolliott and his friend. It was not identifiable; it was as though Mr. Beltane felt required to be at hand when Mr. Ffolliott was at home, and as though Mr. Ffolliott understood his presence and secretly laughed at it. Perhaps it was something connected with parish business, in which the master was deeply concerned. Tonight he dined in Chelmsford to attend the annual business meeting. Miss Amy and I would be alone.

"That's so! Let us have dinner in the morning room, Silence, and really *work* to finish up. Oh," she quivered, "the letter for Miss Carey—we must have a stamp and post it at once, or it won't arrive in time."

"Give it to Alfred. He can leave it on the library desk, or Dawson will take it tomorrow."

But somehow the envelope became pushed aside, and going into the morning room for a reel of silk after Miss

Amy was asleep, I saw it still on her escritoire. I could have rung for someone to take it down to the library, but it seemed unfair to ask Sarah or Mrs. Davenport to climb up and down stairs at the end of a long day. Hastily, I ran down the rear stairs, but all was still and shuttered for the night. There were lighted lamps to the front, and voices. Mr. Ffolliott must be home. I went forward to tap on the library door, glimpsing Alfred trotting upstairs with outer boots and coat.

"Yes?"

"Excuse me, sir...."

"Silence! What's wrong?" Mr. Ffolliott strode toward me anxiously.

"Why, nothing, sir, merely that we need a stamp for Miss Amy's letter to Miss Carey with the bank draft. I'm sorry to trouble you, but if it does not go tomorrow, it may not arrive before Christmas."

He exhaled deeply, releasing my shoulders and turning to the desk. "Here you are. You had better have stamps of your own; Dawson will get them."

"Yes, sir, but...."

"Your correspondence with the excellent Miss Carey?" He raised his eyebrows in amusement. "I trust you implicitly, my dear Silence. She—and you—understood me painfully well, but I feel no further need to scan the outpourings of your girlish heart."

My cheeks burned; involuntarily my chin went up. "It was never necessary, sir," I agreed evenly. "Miss Carey trained us in the concept of loyalty to an employer. She would have been as distressed as yourself had I made any private disclosure."

"What are *you* doing here?"

I turned with a jump of surprise—Miss Amy was leaning against the door jamb, her hair fallen free of its plait and her eyes staring at me wildly. "I *knew* it!" she cried, catching the velvet peignoir untidily about her and stumbling forward in the trailing folds. "*I knew it!* You put me to bed, and then you sneak down to be with Papa . . . telling lies about me, so he'll love you best." Her voice soared in a sobbing scream. "Papa, whatever she says, it's not true! *Don't* believe her!"

Mr. Ffolliott's face was ghastly white, tight-lipped. His hands clenched the edge of the desk as though he would tear it in two. I went swiftly to put my arms about her. "Shhh, it's not so, Miss Amy. Don't you remember?" I held up the envelope. "Your letter to Miss Carey with the bank draft—you wanted it to reach her before Christmas, and we forgot to give it to Alfred, so I brought it down for a stamp."

She grasped my arm with such painful strength that I winced. "I don't believe you," she panted, sagging against me. "It's just an excuse to be alone with Papa, because he's rich and handsome. *But he doesn't love you!*"

"Amy, for God's sake!"

"No, of course he doesn't, darling," I assured her affectionately. "I'm only a little girl, and you offered to share your papa with me because I don't have one—remember?"

The glitter slowly died in the eyes searching mine. "Did I?" she asked dully. "I don't remember." She looked about vaguely. "What am I doing here, Silence?"

"I think you must have had a bad dream that waked you," I said gently, "and when I wasn't in my room—because I'd come for the stamp—you followed me, looking for company."

"Yes"—her breath caught with a shiver—"that must have been it."

I straightened the robe more securely about her. "You're still fuddled with sleep, and you've forgotten your slippers!" I scolded tenderly. "Come, sit by the fire to get warm while I run up to fetch them."

She let me lead her forward a few paces, leaning heavily on my arm. "Oh, Silence, why are you so good to me?" She sighed.

"Because we're pretend-sisters, silly, and we love each other more than real ones because we chose each other."

"Yes, that's so. I'd forgotten—but I do love you dearly." She caught sight of Mr. Ffolliott. "Papa!" she exclaimed in happy surprise, and went past me with her arms outstretched. "I thought you were in London."

"That is tomorrow," he said with an effort, while she patted his cheek and stood tiptoe to kiss him. Automatically his arms went about her. "And what are you doing out of bed at this hour, you naughty Amy?"

"Silence says I had a bad dream," she confided lovingly,

"and she is going to fetch my slippers, but I'm not cold. Papa, hold me the way you used?"

"You're too big for that, Amy. You're a young lady, now."

"But I'll always be your little girl, Papa—you promised!"

I left them together and ran upstairs to straighten the tumbled bedclothes, mend the fire, find the slippers. There was not time to consider the scene in the library, although it must mean something. Did it hold a clue to Miss Amy's hysteria? Was she more conscious of being an orphan than we knew? The wave had not overtaken her tonight, yet she had quite certainly been unaware of what she said or did. Could it be a form of sleep walking? The two somnambulists we'd had at Belliston Parva never talked until awakened. Perhaps it *was* what I'd said: a nightmare from which she'd fled, and not finding me, had desperately sought reassurance elsewhere.

I couldn't think now—I ran back with the slippers, and found Miss Amy curled like a kitten, sleeping on Mr. Ffolliott's lap, her head against his shoulder and braced by his arm. Gently I slid the slippers onto her tiny feet. "Shall I take her back to bed, sir?"

He shook his head. "She'll sleep the night through," he said deliberately. "I've drugged her." I stared at him uncertainly, and he snorted. "That shocks you, doesn't it? You think me callous and indifferent, but a man achieves peace however he can, Silence. In time you'll learn to be grateful for that 'medicine'—I do not know how you have managed for so long without." He laughed harshly at my confusion. "Oh, *I* can tell, my dear. But after tonight's display, and I assure you it was mild—though I hardly believed my eyes at the way you handled it—you do see it won't be wise to omit the sleeping draught again?"

"If you say so, sir," I faltered. "I'm very sorry, but she seemed so much better."

Mr. Ffolliott held out his hand with a warm smile. "She is! Never doubt my gratitude for these past weeks." He held my hand against his cheek for a moment. "How did I live before you came?" he murmured half to himself.

"Is she not too heavy for you, sir?" I asked anxiously. "Would you not be more comfortable if I placed the ottoman for your legs ... and couldn't I bring the hookah?"

"You could, and be damned to Grundy!" He laughed shortly. "Do you know how to prepare it?"

"No, sir, but you can tell me." I adjusted the ottoman, shifting until his long legs seemed comfortably placed. I brought the small table and bottle. "I'll get some water, sir. Would you like more brandy?"

"Yes, thank you, Silence."

I poured what looked to be the usual amount and gave it to him. In the pantry I found Alfred polishing boots. "Oh, could you get the master's slippers—and how much water does he need for the hookah?"

"Fill that pot." Alfred gestured mechanically, staring at me. "What's afoot, miss? Why does he send you?"

"Because Miss Amy had a nightmare, and now she's asleep so he can't move to ring the bell."

"Nightmare, is it?" Alfred thrust aside the boots and stood up anxiously. "She didn't hurt you, did she, Miss Silence?"

"No," I said steadily. "Bring the slippers."

By the time he came into the library, I had the hookah readied for the match, but I couldn't miss the exchange of glances. "Shall I carry her up, sir?"

"No, I'll manage, thank you, Alfred."

"Very good, sir. If you need me, you've only to ring."

"It's not necessary. Go to bed, Alfred."

"Yes, sir." But I knew by Alfred's expression that he wouldn't; he'd be waiting *in case*....

In case of *what?*

"You, too, Silence. You must be tired."

"No, sir. I'm perfectly awake. I'd rather stay until Miss Amy's abed—unless you don't want me?"

"I shall always want you, my golden girl!" He emptied the brandy glass and refilled with a reckless splash. "Moon of my delight," he muttered, "read to me? Fourth from the left on the third shelf...."

"Yes, sir." I found the book, tossed the sofa cushion on the floor beside his knee, and settled to read softly for fear of waking Miss Amy.

> "Awake! For morning in the bowl of night
> Has flung the stone that puts the stars to flight.
> And Lo! the hunter of the East has caught
> The Sultan's turret in a noose of light."

SILENCE IS GOLDEN 79

On and on I read, lost in the magic of the words, unconsciously shifting until my head rested against my master, feeling his hand lightly on my hair before he resumed the hookah.

"Ah, Love, could thou and I with Fate conspire
To grasp this sorry scheme of things entire,
Would we not shatter it to bits—and then
Remould it nearer to the heart's desire?"

I sensed the quatrains held meaning for my master; to me they were only lovely sounds, although I felt a yearning to read each verse alone and ponder on its meaning. The final page—I hated for it to be ended, it was so peaceful and yet so exciting.

"Ah, Moon of my delight who know'st no wane,
The moon of Heav'n is rising once again.
How oft hereafter rising shall she look
Through this same Garden after me—in vain!

"And when Thyself with shining foot shall pass
Among the guests star-scattered on the grass,
And in thy joyous errand reach the spot
Where I made one—turn down an empty glass!"

I closed the book with a sigh, turning my cheek and feeling Mr. Ffolliott's hand beneath it. "How lovely it was," I murmured. "What is the name of it, sir?"

"The Rubaiyat. But I should not have let you read it to me, Silence, although it was never so beautiful before." He laughed softly. "Neither Hugo nor Miss Carey would approve."

"I expect it has a meaning I don't understand," I said finally, "but I thought it was . . . truthful. Life *is* a checkerboard of nights and days. It *isn't* possible to erase what the moving finger has written, is it? And I expect everybody at some moment would like to shatter the sorry scheme, and be remembered with an empty glass."

"Yes." He was silent for a long while as I leaned dreamily against his knee and stared at the flames in the grate. If I could remold the sorry scheme, what would I choose? As if he read my thoughts, Mr. Ffolliott asked quietly, "What is your heart's desire, Silence?"

"I scarcely know, sir. I have so much already."

"Have you? Pretty clothes, food, and shelter—with a nervous invalid," he said sardonically. "Is that the limit of your ambition: mere creature comforts? Do you envision no future beyond this dull routine?"

"I don't know; I hadn't thought," I said after a moment. "That was foolish of me, wasn't it? It's so pleasant to be in a real home with kind people—but I forgot it can't be forever. When you return from your trip, you won't need me any longer."

"On the contrary," he muttered, "I shall always need you—but time is slipping underneath my feet." He drew a deep breath, laid aside the hookah, and patted my cheek. "Bed!" In one smooth motion, he swung down his legs and stood up, holding Miss Amy in his arms. He went up the stairs easily and laid her on her bed. She was as inert as a rag doll while I stripped off the peignoir and tucked her beneath the covers. Mr. Ffolliott stood looking at her impassively for a minute. Then he said, "Good night, Silence," and went away.

CHAPTER FIVE

I knew by the expressions of Sarah with my tea tray and the unaccustomed appearance of Mrs. Davenport with my breakfast that Alfred had told what he knew of last night. I saw they were deeply worried, almost unable to believe my cheerful smile, and I knew the shadow had descended again—but whatever it was, I meant to fight it. In the face of my serenity, they asked no questions, and when Miss Amy finally waked, she had evidently forgotten the entire episode.

Heaven knows how many drops Mr. Ffolliott had given her, but we were back where we started on my first day. "Silence?" she murmured thickly, groping aimlessly for my hand.

"Yes, darling, I'm here."

"It's a bad day; I think I'll stay in bed. You won't leave me?"

"No, but you'll feel better when I've bathed your face and brought a cup of coffee."

She didn't, although she was docile over the freshening of teeth and hair. The sight of Sarah with the breakfast tray produced the nearest to a crisis we'd had in many weeks. "Take it away! It makes me sick to look at it!"

"Then you needn't. Put the tray in my room, please, Sarah." It wouldn't hurt Miss Amy to miss a meal; she'd make it up at lunch. But in the end, she was intrigued by the old trick of peeling an apple in one continuous strip. When I'd fixed one for myself, she said, "Do it again, Silence. That looks good," and ate nearly all the slices.

I let her take the day at her own pace, with no pressure and very casual conversation, but I noticed that either Sarah or the housekeeper lingered in my bedroom behind the connecting door. Unnecessary! Miss Amy was as weak as cambric tea, and no danger to anyone, poor girl! I told myself a setback must be expected, Rome was not built in a day, and so on; but I could not repress some discouragement. There must be a way to conquer her nervous fears and suspicions without drugs; they were too easy a solution—for other people. What about Miss Amy? Did no one think of her? Surely these past weeks proved her capacity for living a normal, if limited, existence. Then what had caused the scene last night?

Going over it in my mind while she drowsed against the pillows, I had it: buttered crab! Knowing Miss Amy's fondness for the dish, Mrs. Potter had made it the main course, following a vol-au-vent of oysters and succeeded by a sherry trifle! Even without the usual fish course, I had been unable to finish my crab and had refused dessert entirely, but Miss Amy had eaten every crumb.

No wonder she had a nightmare!

But Mr. Ffolliott had "achieved peace however he could" without waiting for the simple explanation, and left me to cope with today's result, I thought indignantly. I was quite out of charity with the man, and happy to learn he'd gone to London, not to return until tomorrow.

"If Miss Amy asks, you'll not say the master's in London, miss," Alfred warned. "Just that the master is away for dinner, understand?"

"No, I don't."

His sharp face went grim. "After last night? Take my word for it, miss!" I stared after him as he went along the hall. Taking a key from his pocket, he unlocked the door to Mr. Ffolliott's room and entered. In the stillness, I heard the bolt thrown when the door closed. Curiouser and curiouser! Why should the master's room be locked in a private home? What lay within that must be secret from all but the valet's eyes? Wickedly, I wondered if Mr. Ffolliott were a Bluebeard with six corpses hidden in a closet.

I was sufficiently annoyed that I felt it possible.

Miss Amy reawakened in about an hour and was more herself, although still languid. I sent for fresh coffee and toast, and shared it with her, talking of nothing in particular until she said, "I think I'll get up now." Thereafter the day went somewhat as usual: we sewed in the morning room; we ate lunch (beef tea, plain omelets with broiled mushrooms, and a small blancmange); and I did *not* give any laudanum for her rest.

Mrs. Davenport prepared it. "Medicine, my dearie." Smoothly, I emptied the glass into the slop jar and refilled it with plain water. "The master said—" she whispered fearfully.

"No!"

I was right. Miss Amy listened to two chapters of *Kenilworth* and slept naturally. In my bedroom, I said to Nana, "You see?"

"Aye," she agreed somberly, "but it does not answer, Miss Silence. You've seen for yourself, by what Alfred says."

"Drugs are not the answer for a nightmare. Mrs. Potter must give her simpler food. I know she wants to please Miss Amy, but, Nana, think! Last night Miss Amy had an upset stomach from so much richness. Please, a very plain dinner tonight?"

She nodded, but the staff was not convinced. Throughout the day, someone was always at hand. When Miss Amy was dressed after her nap, we went down to practice carols, and Alfred was immediately polishing the brasses of the fireplace. When Sarah brought tea, she retreated no farther than the hall, where she made play with a dustcloth on the bannisters, and only departed to her regular duties when the rector walked in and cheerfully said, "I have come to learn my part." Nor was I surprised when he said, "The good Davenport says I am welcome for dinner, and perhaps later we can finish the music."

"Oh, that would be good, if you have the time, for we lost all this morning," Miss Amy confided. "I do not know why I waked in the doldrums, Mr. Beltane, but Silence cured me as always." She hugged me affectionately. "And I think after all we shall be ready when Cousin Robert arrives."

Aside from the master's empty chair, dinner was extraordinarily pleasant! The three of us laughed and talked in the most informal way, interrupting each other and changing subjects in midstream. For all his austere black garb, Mr. Beltane had a quiet thrust of humor that made it hard for the servants to keep their faces straight. I could see why my master was so attached to him. Mr. Beltane was a man any other man would value—or woman, for that matter. Deeply as I'd respected and trusted him these past months, tonight I viewed him differently. It struck me that hitherto he was always overshadowed by the commanding, brilliant presence of Mr. Ffolliott, but alone and unobscured, Mr. Beltane was a full personality in his own right.

It was a revelation to me, but Miss Amy took it for granted. "Oh, yes, Mr. Beltane is very good fun," she said at bedtime. "Papa says he's an unusual rector because he understands the worst in people, but never abandons hope of them."

I had my own hope—that he might still be in the library where we'd left him—but when I could leave Miss Amy, all was dark below. Retreating to my room, I wondered whether I dared ask Alfred to send word to the rector tomorrow. He'd take a note for me, of course, but he'd certainly be curious. Why should Miss Amy's companion write privately to Mr. Beltane? Remembering Alfred's attitude to Mr. Ffolliott, I didn't doubt whose man he was. Better not chance his discretion—nor Dawson's— and who else was there?

Macdonald? Climbing into bed, I snorted to myself. "Aye, he was always with the Ffolliott family; the master brought him down here when the estate passed to a cousin," Mrs. Davenport had told me. "He likes no one and nothing but his plants. You'd not know, Miss Silence," she added kindly, "but house staff never associates with outdoor help. I'm surprised the man would make so bold as to enter!"

"I told him to come. I didn't know any better," I admitted apologetically, "and from the way he spoke, I thought he was . . . oh, part of the master's family, like yourself with Miss Amy, Nana. But the way he glowered as though he hated us, I wonder why he came."

Mrs. Davenport shrugged. "Eh, all Scots are strange."

To my deep relief, Miss Amy regained her calmness after that single day. I do not know how long Mr. Ffolliott remained in London. Alfred *said* that he had already left each morning, but would not have Miss Amy wakened, and that he would not be home for dinner. She was saddened, faintly tearful that he was missing her daily progress, and worried that he would not know his part for the weekend. "I'm sure he's familiar with the carols, Miss Amy. It's I who needs the practice, you know. I'm so stupidly slow," I said artfully. "And don't you think he'll like to be surprised again? Almost more fun if he hasn't heard the music each evening."

For myself, I was glad not to see my master; I could not yet wholly forgive him. The staff continued uneasy, and by the rector's daily appearance from tea to evening's end, I suspected they had unsettled him as well. Let him see for himself, I thought proudly. Miss Amy was perfectly recovered from her nightmare, unaware she'd had one. I began to wonder how many previous incidents might have been due to indigestion. Miss Amy had to be coaxed to eat plain meat and vegetables, but add gravies or an unctuous sauce, and she ate with relish. Dessert plates were always cleaned; teacakes were her delight; and there was a standing order in Chelmsford for a weekly box of sweets in the morning room. She seemed never to gain any weight, and the translucent skin of her lovely face was always unblemished—and she took *no* exercise whatever! I had sometimes thought the weak chest and backaches were a subterfuge. Miss Amy was averse to physical motion, fresh air, and walking, but always in fine fettle for a carriage drive to Chelmsford.

On the Saturday, Mr. Ffolliott arrived in company with Mr. Ormond, and there was no cloud in his affectionate greeting for my mistress. To me he gave a nod and a smile and a "How are you, Silence?" but his attention was centered on Miss Amy. She sat beside him, patting his hand and pouring out the trivia of Hazelhurst, but I noticed with pleasure how she turned to her cousin, sharing the recital with him. When I had served tea, I quietly effaced myself into the far corner of the salon with my sewing—nor was I summoned to join the family group until we separated to prepare for dinner.

Throughout the meal I said little, from the last lingering spark of exasperation with Mr. Ffolliott. Let him see for himself, too! I thought he comprehended my faint defiance, and was amused by it, yet relieved at the way I had surmounted the difficulty he had created. Good! As we rose from the table, I was able to smile at him wholeheartedly once more; and by the rueful twitch of his lips, he was tacitly apologizing.

But he would not join the music. "I have time to listen to one piece, Amy, before I shut myself into the library. Robert, you must forego the port, but we will have cigars with the coffee—our ladies do not object."

"Oh, I say, what a shame we cannot practice, Cousin James!"

"Business, Robert—business. You are more important than I, in any event," Mr. Ffolliott returned jovially. "Amy must wait all week for you, while I am an old story. Ah, Hugo, there you are! I'll be with you when coffee is finished. Sit down with your cigar. What do you play for me tonight, Amy darling?"

"It is a Slavonic dance, Papa. . . ." But she seemed scarcely to notice his departure with a kiss at the end, Mr. Ormond's enthusiasm was so unbounded.

They spent every minute with music. "It is the last chance before Christmas; we *must* practice, Silence. Why must I have a nap?" she fretted tearfully. "I'm not a bit tired."

"You will be later, and I think Mr. Ffolliott wishes to speak with Mr. Ormond on business matters," I told her mendaciously, "so it will be exactly right: you can rest while they talk. It doesn't matter if you sleep, Miss Amy; what is important is to avoid the backache."

"Yes, of course you're right. . . ."

I did permit a full afternoon. "Let Mr. Ormond play the accompaniments while you sing from the chaise longue . . . and I am still unsure of my entries. . . ." Faithfully I labored, and patiently they endured my quavers and wrong notes. "I think I should not try to join; it will only ruin the whole piece." I sighed. "If I could read the music—but I keep losing a measure because I'm listening to you."

"Come, stand with me, Silence, and I'll pinch you when to come in!" Mr. Beltane laughed behind me. "James, do you join us?"

Teatime already! Sarah and Alfred were bringing in the service; Mr. Ffolliott was walking into the salon with a smile. "I shall sing better when I have wet my throat. No, no, don't disturb yourselves, Sarah will fix a cup. Let me hear some carols, eh?"

I needed little help from the rector for these; they were familiar from the years when the orphans of Belliston

Parva went a-wassailing. From one to another of the old favorites we went—and suddenly I was singing alone: "Oh, Come All Ye Faithful," with Mr. Beltane humming the *cantus firmus*. "Again!" he said softly as I finished, and this time sang it himself in Latin, while I added the descant.

It was not a moment for applause. In the minute silence after Miss Amy's final chord, Mr. Ffolliott said deeply, "Thank you, Hugo. Tea—before it grows cold. . . ."

Christmas would be Thursday, Boxing Day on Friday. "Cousin James has arranged I may have a holiday for Saturday," Mr. Ormond said gratefully. "By Jove, it'll be as good as a vacation to have four whole days with you, Cousin Amy!"

Monday, Tuesday, Wednesday—we worked feverishly to finish, wrap, and label. Mrs. Potter filled the house with delicious odors; the greens were looped over lintels and fireplaces; the tree was set in the corner of the salon, awaiting decoration—and Miss Amy was too busy for nerves. Mr. Ffolliott had ordered sleeping drops; I would not disobey, but I persuaded Mrs. Davenport to halve the dose. "She is so looking forward, I'd hate for a headache to diminish her pleasure. Most of all, we don't want her cousin to be disappointed."

The housekeeper darted a keen glance at me and compressed her lips. "No, we mustn't risk that," she murmured.

Insensibly, my own suspense heightened each day. Probably the trustees kept Christmas in this way, but I'd never known what occurred *within* the great houses we visited as waits on Christmas Eve. At the orphanage we had a pasturage seedling tree sparsely decorated with paper chains and crayon drawings. There was muffin for breakfast; we went to church, and after the sermon, we stood in our pews and sang a carol while the parishioners straggled out to carriages with heated bricks for cold feet (Miss Carey placed herself strategically to accept shillings or an occasional guinea as they passed). Then we went back to dinner, of which the most memorable was when a farmer had lost two lambs in a sudden freeze, and naught to be done about salting down because his wife was in childbed!

As for presents, we got an orange or a second slice of cake. Once in a while a local mill owner would send us lengths of cloth (in a pattern that hadn't sold well), or a trustee would give Miss Carey an impulsive five pounds "for crackers and fancy hats." She always bought books and games that would last the year round. I was agog to hear what she'd get with Miss Amy's hundred pounds—she would certainly squeeze each farthing until the birds screamed!

Mr. Ormond arrived, cumbered with boxes and laughing apologetically. "I am not expected so early, but knowing my plans, Mr. Hasworth kindly excused me from the office high tea. You do not object, Cousin Amy? If I am in the way, I can sit in my room—but I could not resist to be *here*."

"It is delightful to have you beforetime," she exclaimed, blushing prettily. "I feel Christmas has fairly begun!"

It had, indeed. From the storeroom, Alfred brought an immense box of tinsel, fragile colored balls, gaily painted tin holders for the wax candles. In a special box of its own was a shining, many-pointed star "for the top of the tree. The master always places that." Mr. Ormond placed nearly everything else, running up and down the kitchen stepladder under Miss Amy's direction, with great consultation on the most effective spot for this or that. I busied myself in stringing cranberries, the while I watched the cousins; they were two children, playing happily together and enjoying each moment. That tree could have been trimmed in half the time, but I was as sorry as they when the last ornament was set! Miss Amy was inclined to be tearful; I think she would almost have liked to take everything off again for the fun of replacing.

"We haven't enough trimmings; there are empty spots," she mourned. "Dawson must drive us to Chelmsford *at once!*"

Mr. Ormond looked startled at her imperious voice. "Why, I think it looks very nice as it is, Cousin Amy," he protested.

Oh, dear, her lip was quivering ominously! "You haven't hung my cranberries yet," I inserted swiftly, "and if they don't fill in sufficiently, we can get some oranges and apples from Mrs. Potter."

"I never heard of hanging fruit on a Christmas tree." She was intrigued. "How d'you do it, Silence?"

"I'll show you. Here"—I gave her the cranberries—

"think where to set these while I get the necessaries."

As always, her fingers were deft at tying the oranges into cradles of leftover Christmas ribbon, and by the time they were secured to the branches, she pronounced the decoration satisfactory. Thereafter, all was smooth, proceeding according to the tradition of Hazelhurst. At teatime the servants were summoned to stand at the doorway; Miss Amy and I stood up also, while Mr. Ffolliott ceremoniously set the star on the topmost twig and lit each candle. Then he shook hands with each person, calling them by name and saying, "A happy Christmas to you!" Along the line he went, with the same words for Mr. Ormond and myself, and finally a kiss for Miss Amy.

The hidden parcels were brought forth and piled enticingly about the tree, completely obscuring the trunk. By contrast, my gifts were paltry: monogrammed handkerchiefs, a fringed silk scarf, Miss Amy's dolls. I thrust them almost out of sight to the rear, and firmly reminded myself of Mrs. Davenport's amazement that I should *give* anything. "If you wrapped a tuppenny bit for the master, it'd be more than he's ever had," she said grimly. "The others only *took,* and grumbled it was never enough, while as for thinking of the *staff*. . . ." She shook her head incredulously at the small remembrances I'd given her to hand about below stairs.

"How could I forget you, Nana, when you're all so dear and kind to me?"

"Eh, 'tis our pleasure, my dearie"—she hugged me heartily—"for you've made all different for everyone."

It was still a poor return for the riches heaped upon me! I sat bemused, scarcely aware of the lavish plunder opened by the others, while another and another and yet another package came my way: furs, a gold watch and pin, books, soft French kid gloves, a silver-mounted hand mirror, walking boots, a gold-handled umbrella. . . . I knew these were rich people who could afford anything, but to be to them a *person* whose needs and tastes were studied from a wish to please? . . .

"If I try to thank you, I shall cry," I whispered tremulously, and felt a strengthening hand on my shoulder.

"Thanks are unnecessary between friends," Mr. Beltane said. "Cheer up, Silence, the best is always yet to come. Robert, I see more parcels lurking. . . ."

"By Jove, so there are! What a Christmas it is!" Mr. Ormond ducked beneath the tree to pull out my meager offering, but these were gracious people; they would admit no fault in the gifts.

"One can *never* have too many handkerchiefs," Mr. Beltane stated.

"No, by Jove," Mr. Ormond agreed feelingly. "I believe my laundress eats them."

Mr. Ffolliott studied his muffler with an odd quirk of the lips, a glance darted at the rector. "Is it the right length, Papa?" Miss Amy asked anxiously. "Alfred gave her one for measuring, but she was not sure about the fringe."

He wound it about his throat. "It is quite perfect; you can see for yourself," he said deliberately. "Thank you, Silence. I shall treasure this."

But the major success was the dolls. When Miss Amy opened the box, there was dead silence. She sat transfixed and staring for a long moment, until Mr. Ormond leaned forward to exclaim, "I say, what beautiful dolls, Cousin Amy! Finer than most of the ones in the royal nursery museum display."

"Yes." She roused herself with an effort. "These are very old. They were Mama's design dolls, inherited from her grandmother." She raised eyes swimming with tears to look at me blindly. "It's so long since I've seen them—I'd forgotten," she whispered disjointedly. "Where did you find them, Silence?"

"Not I—Davenport; she had them safely put away, and when I was at wit's end for your present, she suggested I should copy the fashion plates you liked best."

She drew a long shuddering breath, batting her eyes with a hanky, and took them up singly. "So this is what you have been doing behind my back, you sly Silence! How lovely they are! Look, Papa: such tiny stitches, such lovely fabrics—"

"Scraps from Madame Raimond," I admitted ruefully, "although I suspect she gave me from the bolts when I explained, and is hoping you'll use them again for your orders."

"Yes, I shall—I'd forgotten," she murmured. "It's such a . . . *surprising* surprise . . . after all these years . . . and you made them for *me!* Dear Silence"—she squeezed my hand with a sparkling smile—"you can't know! I shall have them copied for spring, and we will be thinking of each following season, until it is Christmas again."

Mr. Ormond groaned dramatically. "That's a promise of bills to come, Cousin James!"

"I'm accustomed to them, Robert," Mr. Ffolliott said drily. "I'd forgotten those dolls, too. Amy, that shade of rose is perfect. You must order it at once. Well"—he exhaled deeply and rose—"that is the end of Christmas for this year. Hugo, shall we sing a few praises to the Lord before you leave us for your dedicated life of sermons?"

Mr. Ormond was already at the piano. "Oh, I say, Cousin James, how amusingly you put things! I expect tomorrow *is* a busy day for a rector. What d'you give us, Mr. Beltane—the Gospel of St. Luke?"

"No"—the rector rose slowly—"the Beatitudes are more fitting this year."

"The meek shall inherit the earth?" Mr. Ormond glanced up from the music with a laugh. "One wonders what in heaven's name they'd *do* with it."

"Make a mess on 'Change," Mr. Beltane agreed smoothly. "But I was thinking more of the . . . pure in heart and the peacemakers, Robert. Come along, James, and let us 'make a joyful noise unto the Lord.' "

Miss Amy set the dolls on the mantel in the morning room, where they simpered into space for the remainder of the holiday while she was occupied in the salon with her cousin. She bade him good-bye on Sunday with a most encouraging show of regret. "It has been the nicest Christmas! If it were not that you return for New Year's, I couldn't bear to part with you, Cousin Robert."

"Nor I from you," he said fervently, smiling into her eyes. "The next three days will seem very tedious, I assure you."

They were boring to Miss Amy, too. After the pleasant bustle of preparation and constant company, she was decidedly moped and inclined to tears. Nothing really pleased; one puzzle was too complicated, another was an ugly color when pieced together. The new games were dull with only two players; she was bored by reading aloud, sick of the embroidery laid aside for the holiday, and in no mood to try the paint box. She practiced the chosen selections for Mr. Ormond's return, but her heart seemed not in it. I noticed she spent far more of her time dreamily playing over the pieces he'd particularly commended, and for once she was thoroughly out of patience with me. "What is the matter with you, Silence? I've shown you and shown you, and you *still* insist on coming in too soon. You'll ruin everything."

"I'm sorry, Miss Amy, but truly I'm doing my best." I allowed my voice to quaver artistically, and her eyes filled with tears.

"Of course you are; you always do. Dear Silence, forgive me? I don't know what's wrong with me to scold you." Impulsively she caught my hand and rubbed her cheek against it. "Forgive me?"

"Nothing to forgive, darling. After four days with a real musician, I know I must be exasperating, but Mr. Ormond comes again tomorrow."

"That's so . . . and we are going to Chelmsford in the morning for the crackers."

No trip to Chelmsford failed to include a glimpse of the newest modes! From warehouse to linen draper to milliner we went, and ended at Madame Raimond's, who was delighted to welcome us—with a wink for me. *"Alors, les poupées sont un succès?"*

"Very successful," I said gratefully, "thanks to your help, madame. Mr. Ffolliott particularly liked the rose silk."

"Oui, it is perfect for Mademoiselle Salford." Briskly, Madame Raimond brought out the bolt and tossed a length under Miss Amy's chin. "Yes, as I thought: *c'est charmante!* And you have liked the designs Mademoiselle Eddington copied?"

"Oh, they were my favorites," Miss Amy agreed. "But I must study them again. I am not sure I want that one in rose, and I think I may prefer ruching to bows, but please put aside enough silk for me, madame."

"Oui, oui, there is no haste for decision. Bring me the doll when you have it worked out for your taste." The Frenchwoman nodded, folding away the silk, and swiftly replaced it with a figured muslin. "Just received, ma'amselle —superb for the morning dress! It is so much easier for both of us to have the dolls once more; you change the lines with the fabric in mind, and there is no indecision for me. It is merely to copy, one fitting only is required, which is

less fatiguing. Your mother found it tiresome to stand—Madame Langley also—but when all is settled, *c'est tout à fait simple!*"

"Langley had no right to the dolls!" Miss Amy swept aside the muslin and stood up stormily. "First she said they were so valuable we must put them away safely, and I was too young to decide my clothes. And when I caught her sewing, she said her mother was Mama's dearest friend, and she knew Mama wouldn't mind her using the dolls until I was old enough! What d'you think of *that?*"

"I think she was *stupide*," I returned promptly, "and that is why Nana hid the dolls. How fortunate I caused her to recall them! And now we must go, Miss Amy, or we shall not reach home in time for lunch nor be ready for Mr. Ormond at teatime. *Au revoir*, Madame Raimond, *à bientôt.*"

"*Au revoir*, ma'amselle," the dressmaker said mechanically, while Miss Amy was retrieving her muff with a smile for the seamstresses peeping around the corner of the workroom door.

"*Au revoir*, madame. It may be some weeks before I can get back—we're certain to have snow—but please save the silk." Miss Amy waved her hand and departed, smiling.

Madame Raimond stared after her, shivering slightly in the crisp air of the open door. "*Mon Dieu*, what did I say?" she muttered as I passed. "The woman was a family friend—I thought. She came often with Madame Ffolliott—much younger, but they seemed *tout à fait sympathique*. Later there is the *carte blanche* from M. Ffolliott—one had even conjectured. . . ." She shrugged knowingly. "*Vous comprenez?*

"I have the same for yourself," she inserted absently. "Whatever you wish, he pays without question—but you order nothing privately. And I tell you, *moi qui vous parle*," she added vigorously, "for you I would make half price, ma'amselle! *Mon Dieu*, how you avoided!" She cast her eyes dramatically to heaven.

"Silence?"

"Coming! *Au revoir*, madame—but do not mention Langley again."

"What took you so long? What were you whispering to Raimond?" Miss Amy asked suspiciously.

"She was trying to persuade me to persuade you to order that muslin," I lied smoothly, crossing my fingers within the muff and asking God to forgive me, "but I told her you are the arbiter of Hazelhurst. You not only decide for yourself, you have to decide for me also, or I'd be a sad spectacle."

"Not really," she said. "Your *eye* for color is good, Silence, and you have an instinctive sense of *line*. If you've a fault, it's choosing simplicity, but I suppose that comes from inexperience and having to wear whatever they gave you." I saw that her interest was fairly captured, and listened with encouraging murmurs to her lecture on fashion until we turned into the drive for the Grange.

Miss Amy was sound asleep; outside the snow fell lazily, and I ran down the rear stairs. "Nana, I'm going to take a turn about the house. Listen for Miss Amy, please?" In the scullery I passed Macdonald with his rolling cart of house plants returning from their convalescence.

"Good day, Macdonald. You're very early, aren't you?" I frowned.

"The sna'," he grunted, lifting the protective tarpaulin with a contemptuous shake that sent a small shower over my walking boots. "Shortly I'd not get across to the house, and you'll not get far, mistress. 'Tis icing fast." He turned his back on me, stolidly transferring the bundles of cut flowers to the table beside vases, turning back to stoop for the plants. "For what do ye linger?" he remarked in sour surprise. "Go along wi' ye, do! Ye'll soon be in again, or I'll leave the pots and ye'll bring out the old to Davenport later. I suppose ye're capable?"

"I suppose I am," I replied with spirit, "and a happy New Year to *you*, Mr. Macdonald."

He straightened up, eyeing me impassively over the container of begonias. "I thank ye, mistress," he said deliberately, "but keep the wish for yourself—you've the greater need."

Two turns about the Grange, and the damp cool air calmed me somewhat. After this I would ignore the gardener! It was useless to attempt even the barest civility. Was it only myself, or did he dislike all Miss Amy's companions—such as Mrs. Langley? I *must* learn more of that woman, who was not an impersonal stranger but an intimate friend of Mrs. Ffolliott, ordering her own clothes from Madame Raimond with a *carte blanche* from the master. When had she been at Hazelhurst to supervise Miss Amy? It would seem a perfect solution: a widowed family friend (one assumed widowhood, for there was no mention of a Mr. Langley), accustomed to the household and the locality, well known to my mistress—who must originally have liked her, or Mr. Ffolliott would never have made the arrangement.

What had occurred to alter the matter?

Going up the rear stairs, I passed Macdonald with his tray of plants. "I've left yours in the morning room," he said, his eyes coldly sardonic, "and a proper mess it is." He descended a few steps. "And I'll gie ye ma own New Year's wish to reinforce yours," he said over his shoulder, and disappeared through the kitchen passage.

Without removing my coat, I ran to the morning room to stare aghast.

The design dolls lay on the stone hearth, limp and lifeless, their china heads shattered in a thousand pieces. . . .

CHAPTER SIX

"I thought I heard you, Miss Silence. I'll go along then, until you—" Behind me, Mrs. Davenport stopped abruptly, catching her breath in horror. "Oh, Miss Silence! What happened?"

"They must have been too close to the edge—one fell against another until they all came down," I said with an effort, because I knew it was no accident. If the dolls had toppled of themselves, the pieces would lie as they'd fallen —not be crushed and jumbled together. "Shhh, Nana, go back to Miss Amy while I sweep up. With luck, she'll be too busy to notice. If she asks, say you think I put away for safekeeping."

The housekeeper backed away, her eyes on the tragedy. "Yes, miss," she muttered somberly, "but she'll not ask."

I wished I could be so positive of Miss Amy's forgetfulness! Picking up the decapitated kidskin bodies in their scraps of satin and lace, I felt sick. I'd worked so hard to give her a pleasure; she'd so loved them, taking them out to the servants' hall and saying, "See what Silence did—just for me!" Only this morning she'd ordered the rose silk laid by, was planning the small changes of trimming, looking forward to bringing Madame Raimond the completed design—and now all was ruined by a clumsy, ignorant old man! I raged inwardly, knowing how it must have been: moving plants in and out of the room, Macdonald had inadvertently brushed the dolls, and once broken, he'd contemptuously finished the holocaust, thinking "yon daft lassie" too old for dolls. How could he be so vicious? All that calmed me slightly as I tidied the hearth and hid the remains in a drawer of my chest was the possibility that new heads could be fixed to the bodies.

It was a poor start toward 1881, and there was worse ahead. The snow had thickened and begun to stick, delaying the London train bringing Mr. Ormond and Mr. Ffolliott. Miss Amy was fussed and tearful that our festivities would not begin at teatime, and only partially soothed by the announcement that the rector had arrived and was waiting for final song practice. "It's not the same without Papa and Cousin Robert," she fretted.

"They'll soon be here. Alfred says Dawson sent word by a drayman that the train was at Calne Halt, slowed but not stopped," I told her. "Come, finish dressing, darling, for once they reach Hazelhurst, perhaps we'll be snowed in for a week."

"Would we have enough food?" she asked anxiously, twisting her head while I tried to brush the long golden hair.

"Well, we might have to break the pond ice in order to get a fish course," I returned judicially, "or send the men out to shoot some of the rabbits we saw this morning."

"Oh, Silence"—she laughed at me in the mirror—"how absurd you are!"

"So are you! You know Mrs. Potter has so much laid in that we'll never be able to eat it. Nana, will you finish while I dress? We mustn't make Mr. Beltane feel unimportant."

Miss Amy had decreed my amber taffeta, but when I returned, she inspected me with a frown. "I'm tired of that dreary bun," she announced. "Nana, plait her hair into a coronet."

"Aye, that's a fine style for Miss Silence! Sit here, my dearie." In the mirror my eyes met the housekeeper's, conveying an infinitesimal warning. Perforce I shook free my coarse brown mane, and let Mrs. Davenport arrange it atop my head with the gold-headed pins Miss Amy laid on the dressing table—but when she would have fastened the collar of yellow diamonds about my throat, I protested resolutely.

"No!"

She blinked in astonishment at my vehemence. "Why not? You must have them to complete the costume; you wore them before. . . ."

"Because I knew no better—but not again," I said simply, rising from the dressing chair and gently pushing aside her hands. The crisis warnings were clear: tear-filled eyes, quivering chin, quickened breath. But I would not give in. "Dear Miss Amy, you are not thinking! No matter if they complete the costume, you cannot lend me your mama's jewels even for an evening. Mr. Ffolliott recognized them at once; I think Mr. Beltane was shocked that you would so hurt him, no matter how graciously he turned it aside."

"What d'you mean? What did Papa say?" She clutched the collar violently, staring at me. "What did you tell him?"

"That you insisted on my wearing the necklet," I said steadily, "and he said you were right, Miss Amy. It did complete the effect, and you would probably never wear it yourself because it was not the right color for you, but that was only his kindness, and I will not wear them again." She drew a deep stormy breath, but before she could open her mouth I was in first. "Generous you are, Miss Amy, and appreciative I am, but you cannot be so cruel as to remind Mr. Ffolliott of his loss."

Over her shoulder I saw Mrs. Davenport's stricken face, hand pressed to mouth in terror for my plain speech, but Miss Amy's eyes were on the winking sparkles in her hands. "Are you afraid he'll think you stole them, Silence?"

"No, of course not, silly!" I reached to pat her shoulder, but she moved aside and away from me, still looking at the diamonds.

"What d'you want then? Mama's emeralds or sapphires?" Her eyes glittered at me intensely.

"I don't want anything. Dear Miss Amy, I'm only a little girl. Haven't you a plain gold locket, or a single chain—something you wore years ago?"

"You don't want Mama's jewels?"

"No, they are not suitable for me."

She smiled suddenly. "You are right and I am wrong," she said like a penitent child. "I forgot: you're not out yet, Silence! Davenport, bring the small box."

Decorously we went downstairs, with a gold locket tied to my throat by a bit of velvet ribbon. Mr. Beltane noticed at once, and I felt warm approval in his smile. "Good evening, Silence. How charming you look."

"A great come-up for an orphan, is it not?" I grinned at him. "But I am aware that pride goeth before a fall; I am not puffed up, for charity vaunteth not itself, and

SILENCE IS GOLDEN

after all"—I widened my eyes innocently—"I am being paid."

The rector laughed. "Oh, Silence, I should know better than to tangle with you! Do you know the Bible by heart?"

"When it is the one book you hear daily for fourteen years, you are apt to remember it," I said drily, "which does not make it the less valuable."

"Very true! Come and have tea. Amy, save enough for our wayfarers."

They were more than an hour behind time, and when they were finally changed into dinner clothes, Mr. Ffolliott rejected tea in favor of a concoction he called an Allahabad Aperitif. "Bombay Bombshell would be more accurate," Mr. Beltane remarked, "but yes, I'll have one, thank you, James."

Mr. Ormond had three, and told a very funny story about an illicit punch party when he was in school.

It was the gayest, most delightful evening. The older men were relaxed and amused. Miss Amy was sweetly flushed and sparkling with laughter, while Mr. Ormond was in uproarious high spirits. "Save the fine stuff for tomorrow, Cousin Amy, tonight is New Year's Eve. What's wanted is a touch of music hall." He seated himself at the piano, and gave us a program of popular songs from light operas in London, followed by polkas, galops, waltzes. "Cousin James—Mr. Beltane—why are you sitting still with two lovely partners available?"

Laughing indulgently, Mr. Ffolliott laid aside his cigar and arose. "Miss Salford, will you honor me?"

"Oh, *yes!* What fun to dance again."

"Silence, shall we follow them?" Mr. Beltane smiled at me.

"How I wish I could, but I don't know how to dance," I said regretfully, watching Miss Amy circling gracefully the length of the salon.

"It is really very easy. Come." He stood up and held out his hand. "The steps go like this. You have only to fit them to the music."

"So you say, sir," I gasped when we were halfway down the room, "but I don't seem able."

"Yes, you are," he said calmly. "Listen to the music."

It did go better then, although I still felt wooden. "Slide

your feet, Silence, and let yourself move as I guide you. That's better. You're going to be a beautiful dancer," he approved.

"Oh, I say," Mr. Ormond pleaded, "I want a turn. Cousin Amy, if I hum, will you dance with me?"

"I'll do better: I'll play while you dance with Silence." She would hear no objection. "Nonsense, you did very nicely with Mr. Beltane. You only need to practice."

Perforce I accepted Mr. Ormond's arm about me—but what had been relatively possible with Mr. Beltane was suddenly impossible. I did my best, hopping this way and that, but Mr. Ormond held me too tightly and instead of gliding, he *bounced*. "*One*-two-three, *one*-two-three," he chanted. "Don't be afraid, Miss Silence. *One*-two-three, and *around* we go."

We did, indeed, until I was breathless. To complete my discomfiture, when we'd made the circuit back to the piano, I saw my master and the rector nearly helpless with laughter. "Oh, poor Silence! Let her go, Robert! You are hauling her about like a sack of meal," Mr. Ffolliott choked. "For heaven's sake, take Amy and whistle the tune, while Silence recovers from this disaster."

"Sit down, child, and catch your breath," Mr. Beltane chuckled. "We should not laugh—forgive us? But the sight of your astonished face, and Robert capering about—"

"Amy is not doing much better," Mr. Ffolliott snorted. "Hoooo, he nearly lost her on the turn! Oh, I don't know when I've laughed so much, Hugo."

"Nor I," Mr. Beltane mopped his eyes with a sigh. "Robert dances in the German fashion, Silence," he explained. "It's different, more vigorous, than the steps I taught you. The result was hilarious"—his shoulders shook with amusement—"but not your fault."

"Why then, I am glad you were entertained," I said gaily, "and I wish I might have seen myself."

Miss Amy was as breathless as I, but intrigued by the new style. "If only we had a third person to play for us! Papa, you haven't danced with Silence, nor I with Mr. Beltane. Cousin Robert, please play once more."

"Not time enough." The master opened his watch case and stood up. "Give us 'Auld Lang Syne,' Robert, while I deal with the champagne."

We made a circle, holding hands and singing while the tall case clock sonorously struck twelve. Miss Amy was between her cousin and Mr. Ffolliott; I was between Mr. Ormond and the rector; and on the final stroke everyone cried, "Happy New Year!"

"This is the moment we've been waiting for," Mr. Ormond declared, "when we can kiss the girls, eh, Cousin James?" With a laugh, he squeezed my hand and kissed it heartily. "Happy New Year, Miss Silence! Cousin Amy, come and be kissed."

"Papa first!" She threw her arms about Mr. Ffolliott, standing tiptoe to press her lips to his and rub his cheek with hers. "Happy, happy New Year, dearest Papa!"

"And to you, darling." He gently detached her arms. "Give Robert his share. Silence?" He grasped my hand warmly between both of his. "Happy New Year, my dear."

"The same to you, sir."

"Thank you." He turned to the wine cooler, taking out his handkerchief and wiping his mouth. I had a curious sense of savagery in the gesture, but Mr. Beltane was saying, "Happy New Year, Silence." His lips lightly brushed my cheek, and involuntarily I kissed his in return. "Thank you." He smiled at me. "Robert, New Year's Eve or not, you're only allowed one!"

"Exactly so, sir, so it has to be enough to last the whole year," Mr. Ormond returned blandly, keeping his arms about Miss Amy, "and you've interrupted me. I forget where I was and shall have to start at the beginning. Say 'prunes,' Cousin Amy...."

I sat quietly, a bit to one side, and observed the salon with love. It was one more new experience to add to my store. We had 'seen the old year out,' pulled the crackers and laughed at the funny hats, drunk a champagne toast to the future. I'd sneezed miserably at the bubbles, which added to the fun. We'd sung and danced, exchanged kisses and good wishes. Miss Amy and her cousin were at the piano; my master and the rector talked comfortably in the fireside chairs. A new year lay ahead. No matter what it brought, I was expectant, eager, confident for the future.

At Christmas, Mr. Beltane had said, "The best is always yet to come, Silence." For the first time in my life, I did look *forward*. In the past four months, I'd learned much—of myself, as well as people in general. Wherever I went, whether or not I ever again so completely shared the household, the memory of Hazelhurst would be invaluable. I could bid 1880 Godspeed with no regret. It was a very good feeling.

Miss Amy yawned.

"Good heavens, it's half after one! To bed, all of you!" Mr. Ffolliott stood up with mock severity. "Tomorrow is a new day in a new year. We must be ready to face it."

"Oh, *yes!*" Miss Amy fluttered forward to kiss him tenderly. "I feel it's going to be the best of all years, Papa!"

"I am sure of it," he said after a moment. "Good night, all! Sleep well, Robert! We'll be lazy tomorrow and talk in the afternoon."

In a straggle, chorussing good-nights, we left the salon. Miss Amy and Mr. Ormond were going up the stairs; the rector stood in the hall where Mr. Ffolliott assisted him into his overcoat. I came last, because I'd run back to retrieve Miss Amy's handkerchief from the piano, and as on the night of his birthday, my master said, "Good night, Silence," when I slipped behind him to the stairs.

"Good night, sir—Mr. Beltane. . . ." I hesitated on the first step, for Mr. Ffolliott had turned and come toward me. "Is there something you wish me to do, sir?"

"No, only to say Happy New Year once more." He stretched out his hand, and I took it with a smile.

"And to you, sir!"

He leaned forward with a reckless flash of blue eyes, and Mr. Beltane was standing beside him, reaching for my other hand. "May every year be better than the one before, Silence."

"I would wish you both the same, but I think it's not possible," I said doubtfully, "is it?"

"No." Mr. Ffolliott drew back and straightened up. "But for every seven lean years, there must be seven fat— or so the Bible says. Good night, Silence."

I left them standing at the foot of the stairs and made my way hastily up to Miss Amy. I was nearly to the upper

SILENCE IS GOLDEN

hall when I heard the front door open, and Mr. Ffolliott's voice inquired softly, "Are you my chaperone, Hugo, or my competitor?"

"Both, James—both." The rector's voice was equally soft.

CHAPTER SEVEN

Mr. Ffolliott's departure took me by surprise. It had often been mentioned, and despite her earlier disbelief, Miss Amy now seemed to accept the trip as a reality. For this, Mr. Ormond was largely responsible. He got out the atlas, and spoke enthusiastically of the West Indies. "Oh, yes, Mr. Hasworth has often been there. He thinks of living in the Islands when he retires. It's always sunshine, you know, with such beautiful flowers; and the waters are so clear one can *see* the fish swimming about."

Mr. Ormond appeared to know the business that required my master's presence, and fascinated Miss Amy with his description of sugar plantations and natives. "They sing and dance in a special way. I confess the music sounds strange, but Mr. Hasworth says it is very gay, and one soon grows accustomed."

So did Miss Amy. From week to week, she spoke easily of "Papa's trip," the people he would meet, and the things we would do in his absence. "I shan't allow you to be dull, Cousin Amy! When the weather is better, Cousin James agrees I may escort you and Miss Silence to a Saturday theater, and," Mr. Ormond announced triumphantly, "there will be a new presentation of Gilbert and Sullivan: 'Patience.' The opening is already announced."

Occasionally her eyes were tearful at the thought of missing Mr. Ffolliott, but watching closely, I felt she was somewhat reconciled by her cousin. It was established Mr. Ormond would be at Hazelhurst each weekend, with Mr. Beltane in between. She would not be lonely. There were spring clothes to be chosen, pleasant weather to anticipate, music to practice, and a London treat. Why, Mr. Ffolliott might even return before it took place!

But in all this casual conversation, no definite *time* was mentioned, and from this and that, I had supposed the

SILENCE IS GOLDEN

voyage was to occur in March or April. Accordingly, I was unprepared when Mr. Ffolliott summoned me to the library on the Monday after New Year's during Miss Amy's nap, and said, "Silence, I am leaving tomorrow. I am placing you in full charge for all household decisions. There should not be any, but in the event of something unexpected, the staff will obey your instructions."

"*Me*, sir?" I swallowed in a dry throat.

"You," he confirmed impersonally. "Hugo—Mr. Beltane—will supply any money you require and will be glad to counsel you if you find yourself uncertain." He raised his eyebrows. "Why are you so astonished? The trip has been deferred longer than anticipated, but you knew it would occur. It is why you were hired originally."

"Yes, sir," I agreed, "although I had not realized you meant to set an eighteen-year-old orphan over well-trained servants twice her age, nor was I told any definite date for this. I confess I feel a certain . . . lack of preparation."

Mr. Ffolliott's lips twitched. "The majesty of your mouselike stance confronting the ogre!" he remarked with a deep chuckle. "Come in, Hugo, and protect me from Silence."

"What have you done to her, James? Good afternoon, Silence." The rector came forward, stripping off his winter gloves with a smile.

"I have failed to give her advance notice of my departure, and she is enraged—are you not, my 'Jane'?"

"I do think you might have warned me, sir." But I couldn't resist the blue twinkle of Mr. Beltane's kindly laugh. Reluctantly, I smiled, shaking my head. "I fear I shan't know how to go on, sir, and you'll find the staff in a pelter when you return, to say nothing of Mr. Beltane distracted by my demands."

"Nonsense! I shouldn't wonder if I find all is doubly comfortable from your commonsensible changes," Mr. Ffolliott returned bracingly. "But in reality there's little to do, Silence. It is merely that I must have someone authoritative *in* the house—a sort of court of last appeal—and Hugo cannot be at hand constantly."

I was still tremulous at such responsibility. "How long shall you be absent, sir?"

"Two months, more or less." He shrugged. "You will scarcely have time to miss me."

"Yes, sir. Does Miss Amy know you leave tomorrow?" I asked bluntly.

Mr. Ffolliott drew a long breath. "No. And you will not tell her until you must, Silence. I shall go to London as usual tomorrow morning, and take the boat train for Southampton. Alfred will say I shall be late, have left early, for as long as possible. Hugo will be here for tea or dinner; Robert will be here for weekends. It may be some while before she realizes my absence, and God knows what will happen then." He stroked his forehead wearily. "It's not fair to leave it in your lap, Silence, but I've no choice. All my dependence must be on you."

"Well . . ." I said, disconcerted, and pulled my shoulders straight, "well then, I expect I shall manage somehow. And I hope you have a pleasant voyage, sir. You will find time to write us, and say when to expect you for a welcoming dinner?"

"Yes," he said after a moment. "Yes, I shall send you word." I stood waiting for his dismissal, but he only looked at me intently. "I was wrong—you are no 'Jane,' but my personal David," he murmured.

"I don't understand you, sir."

"I fear you will." He sighed. "But what else can I do, Hugo?"

"Don't distress yourself unduly," the rector said quietly. "It must be begun if there is ever to be a conclusion, James. The way must be opened for withdrawal, or you'll never be free. We've been over and over it: there must be a period of preparation. I shall be here. Don't hesitate to call on me, Silence."

"Thank you, sir."

Mr. Ffolliott's face was reluctant, somber. "She's so . . . *little,* Hugo," he muttered. "Dammit, man—I'm afraid."

I sought for some reassurance; it *was* why I'd been employed; and what had size to do with it? I said so, adding, "and wasn't it a mouse that freed the lion in Aesop's fable, sir?"

They looked at each other silently, and Mr. Beltane remarked gently, *"Touché,* James."

"Out of the mouths of babes," Mr. Ffolliott agreed, and threw back his head in a roar of infectious laughter. "My golden girl! Go along with you. I don't know why I should worry. You are certainly no mouse!"

Going upstairs, I was torn between pride in his confidence, and dismay at my inadequacy. Mrs. Davenport took one look and said, "You'll not be anxious, child! You've all of us to help. And 'tis best for you to be in charge, my dearie, for you've the knack. She'd pay no heed to me."

"I suppose you're right. And I've Mr. Beltane to consult, as well, but you'll not hesitate to guide me, Nana? The rector's so busy, I mustn't bother him more than absolutely necessary. . . ."

But in the event, I needed him the following morning, and he was away in the hills at a deathbed.

What prescience waked Miss Amy—or was it the bump of Mr. Ffolliott's steamer trunk carried from his chamber by Alfred and Dawson? They were halfway down the staircase to the entrance hall where the master stood, pulling on his gloves and saying farewell to the others clustered at the rear, and suddenly above: *"What are you doing? What is that box?"* I ran forward, but the men blocked my way on the bottom steps, and Miss Amy was right behind them, clutching the bannister with one hand and pulling the robe about her with the other.

"What are you doing?" she demanded shrilly. "Papa, that is your trunk! Why are they taking it away? Tell them to bring it back *at once!*"

"No, no, darling. He'll need it." I slid past Alfred's back and caught her stumbling figure. "Don't you remember? He's going to those lovely islands for a little while."

Briefly, her eyes glittered at me, but this time I couldn't reach her. "Papa is not going *anywhere*," she hissed, and thrust off my hands with such force that I fell painfully against the newel post. "You lie! Papa, tell her," she panted, throwing herself against Mr. Ffolliott. "You *never* leave me. You promised Mama and me. You said I was your little girl, and you'd always take care of me—we'd always be together."

"And so he will. He's only going on this trip because of you," I said, trying to pull her away. "Don't you remember the sugar plantations, and your Cousin Robert is to amuse you while Mr. Ffolliott is gone? We are going to London to a theater, and we are to plan a special welcome party."

It was useless. Even Mr. Ffolliott could not detach her arms from their strangling grasp about his neck. As often as he got one free, she clung to his sleeve or lapel, or hung deadweight to prevent movement toward the door. She would listen to nothing; repeatedly she struck away my hands and nearly overbalanced me, while the servants cowered, weeping frantically in the rear hall.

"Amy, *Amy!*" Mr. Ffolliott pleaded hoarsely. "It is only for a little while. . . ."

Useless! She was quite beyond reason, kicking viciously when I tried to grasp her. His cravat was disarranged, his coat torn at one pocket. I saw that Mr. Ffolliott was unnerved, grim-faced at the need to fight her physically, but he *had* to leave or he would miss the connection for the boat train. "Alfred," I said quietly, "detach Miss Amy and hold her until the master has gone."

"Very good, miss."

I don't know how he managed it—he got a long scratch on his face in the process—but she'd gone into true hysterics by the time he had her struggling and writhing in his firm hands. The piercing screams had become laughter and babbling words directed to me. "What a fool I was to trust you!" she spat. *"You're* sending him away from me. I suppose you mean to go, too, but he'll not take you. He'll come back to me, you'll see. He loves me, *me*, do you hear?"

"Yes, I hear." I stepped forward steadily. "Forgive me, darling!" and I slapped her cheek full force, ignoring the gasp about me, and holding out my arms to catch her body sagging in Alfred's grip. "Shhhh. It's all right, you'll see. There, there, cry it out darling. Shhhh." I cuddled her against me, murmuring soothingly while she clung to me and sobbed normally.

"Oh, Silence, it's not true, is it? Don't say it was all for nothing! Oh, God, what shall I do?" With astonishing speed, she slid through my hands in a heap on the floor.

"She's fainted! Oh, Lordy me, where's the salts? Burned feathers are better. . . ."

SILENCE IS GOLDEN

"Dear God! Silence. . . ."

"Yes, sir?" I straightened up, releasing Miss Amy's pulse, and faced Mr. Ffolliott's agonized face. "You placed me in charge, sir," I reminded him quietly. "Alfred, carry Miss Amy to her room, please. Nana, make her comfortable in her bed. Sarah, bring hot coffee. And as for you, Mr. Ffolliott, will you please leave before she revives?"

"Yes," he muttered, his eyes on Alfred ascending the stairs.

"You will miss the train, sir."

He hesitated, unconsciously straightening his cravat with his gaze still upward, where Alfred had disappeared with Mrs. Davenport behind him. "What have I done?" He looked at me halfblindly. "Silence, my golden girl. . . ."

"The train, sir."

"Yes." With a long breath he stepped forward and caught me into his arms, his hand warm beneath my chin pulling it up until his lips met mine. "I pray God for your safety," he muttered.

"Why, so do I wish for your safety, sir." I looked into the deep blue of his eyes. "But you will soon be home again—and now you must *go!*"

For a moment I stood, bemused by his kiss and the strong arms, hearing the clop-clop of horses' hooves gaining pace until they were gone beyond the driveway into the main road. Miss Amy had feared to be without him, but with a shiver, I knew it was really I who was alone. . . .

Miss Amy was ill, twisting back and forth feverishly, growing worse from hour to hour. I sent for Mr. Beltane: "He's gone to a farm twenty miles away; there's no telling when he'll return, miss." I sent for Dr. Robinson: "He's abed with the bronchitis, miss."

I would *not* send for Mr. Ffolliott, despite panic in the household. "He must be on the boat train by now; we cannot reach him before Southampton; he could not return to Hazelhurst before tomorrow. And you know that he must take this trip. There *must* be another doctor in Chelmsford. Dawson, get him!"

"Yes, miss."

Dr. Albert Jermyn was a brisk, young, cheerful squirrel of a man. "How d'you do, Miss Eddington. What's amiss here?"

"Nothing—and everything," I said tersely. "Mr. Ffolliott has been forced to go away on business, and Miss Salford has suffered a nervous collapse. She swooned from the shock this morning. We had great difficulty in reviving her, and she is no more than semiconscious even now. There is a degree of fever, increasing restlessness, and irrationality. I could give her laudanum, but should not the fever be brought down first? I dislike this reliance on drugs; the effect is temporary, and there is no way to be sure the condition may not be worsened."

He eyed me sharply, picking up his bag. "Yes, quite so. If I may see the patient?"

Watching his gentle efficiency, I thanked Heaven that Dr. Robinson was sick—and I hoped he wasn't suffering, and wouldn't recover too quickly! Dr. Jermyn was much more competent. Even Nana was restored to a measure of calm as he closed his bag. Miss Amy's eyes were fixed blindly on space, but the powder was already taking effect. He left us three more. "One every two hours; expect some return of restlessness as you approach the next dose; don't be alarmed, it's quite normal. In between, see if she'll drink a small cup of clear broth—don't force it if she refuses. *No* laudanum or other medicines; give the powders a chance to work. I'll return this evening; then we'll see whether she needs a sedative."

For four days Miss Amy lay as if in a coma. Her eyes were sometimes closed, sometimes open and staring dully at nothing. Occasionally she accepted broth, or a few swallows of milk or orange juice. Dr. Jermyn came three times a day, and his cheerful satisfaction with progress bolstered the staff. "Doctor says the fever's gone! It's only to wait a bit, and she'll be right!"

Mr. Beltane put his arms about me ruefully for a light hug. "Poor Silence. Where was I in your hour of need? But your decision was correct; James will be proud of you. Jermyn's immensely capable. You couldn't be in better hands."

"So I think, sir." I grasped for courage. "In fact, would it be permissible for me to transfer Miss Amy permanently to his care?"

"Certainly. James placed you in full charge, Silence.

If you wish to change doctors, you may do so—but why?"

"Dr. Jermyn takes a . . . deeper professional interest." I chose my words carefully. "And I feel his training is modern."

But I did not tell the rector that Dr. Jermyn considered Amy Salford a fascinating case history! He was, amazingly, rather pleased by her continued inertia. "It is merely a temper tantrum," he informed me cheerfully. "I've never known one to last so long, but she'll come out of it when she is convinced it is useless."

"Temper? Not Miss Amy," I protested. "And she's gone four days without food."

Dr. Jermyn shrugged into his overcoat and grinned at me. *"Has* she? Every time I come, you tell me she's drunk a cup of soup or tea or something. You'd be surprised at how long the human body can live on that. She could go another week without harm," he said calmly. "Whenever she has a reason to revive, I promise you she'll be entirely lucid."

"I see."

Dr. Jermyn looked over his shoulder as he opened the front door. "Yes, I think you do," he remarked. "You're a very clever, sensible young woman, Miss Eddington, but think well before you wake Sleeping Beauty. It's a lot easier, and not dangerous, to keep the status quo."

I went upstairs and stroked Miss Amy's lifeless hand gently. "Dr. Jermyn says it may be a long siege, but he has no doubt of her safety," I told Mrs. Davenport softly. "What I wonder, Nana: Mr. Ormond was to come tomorrow. Do you think I should ask Mr. Beltane to wire a cancellation? It seems a waste for him to make the trip if she's unable even to sit up and play games or talk to him. And I dislike for him to see her in this condition. He is like Mr. Ffolliott: a man who finds female illness distasteful, however politely they bear with it. What shall I do?"

"I'd not know. But if there's to be no music, what will we do with the lad?" Mrs. Davenport pondered. "He can't see her this way, certainly."

"Let's wait until noon," I said finally. "Dr. Jermyn thinks she'll come to herself very quickly when it happens. It *could* be she'll astound us by demanding breakfast, and

Alfred could carry her into the morning room for a light dinner, or downstairs to listen to Mr. Ormond at the piano. What d'you think, Nana?"

Mrs. Davenport's eyes were shrewd. "A good idea, my dearie. We'll wait until noon."

But at eight o'clock on Saturday, Miss Amy's lovely blue eyes opened clearly and smiled at me. "Silence?"

"Yes, darling. Did you have a good sleep?"

"So good!" She stretched like a kitten, and suddenly looked at me squarely. "Have I been ill?"

"Yes, darling. For a while you worried us dreadfully, but Dr. Jermyn has made you well again. We had to have him because Dr. Robinson was sick, but I think you're going to like this doctor even better."

She vaguely brushed a wisp of hair from her forehead. "Where's Papa?"

"I expect he's partway across the ocean; he sailed Wednesday. He'll reach those lovely islands by the end of next week." I brought toothmug and washcloth, and stood waiting with the comb.

"He didn't come back," she whispered, burying her face in the damp cloth. "How could he go away when I was sick?"

"He had no choice, darling. He *had* to make this trip. You knew that." I combed her hair gently.

"Did he know I was ill?" She caught my hand and stared at me. "Didn't you tell him, Silence?"

"How could I? There was no way to reach him."

"No, I suppose not." Her shoulders drooped. "But he knew before he left; he could see for himself. . . ." Her jaw tightened. "How could you let him go, Silence? How could you not send for him?"

"What for?" I asked in surprise. "There was nothing wrong with you, darling. You swooned, and I thought it best to have a doctor. But you see? You are perfectly recovered this morning." I laid aside the comb as Sarah came in with a tray. "And now you must have some breakfast and be tidied up for visitors. There's the doctor, and Mr. Beltane; and Mr. Ormond will be here at teatime. Set the tray on the side table, Sarah. I'll wager Miss Amy has an appetite today!"

"Do you?" she murmured, eyeing the tray impassively.

"After four days of soup and milk and orange juice?" I

raised my eyebrows humorously. "You'd better have some solid food, darling!"

It seemed as though the fever had taken with it all Miss Amy's nervous uncertainties, and she emerged like a phoenix: more beautiful than ever with new life and interest. If (as I'd suspected) Mr. Ormond had tacitly accepted his cousin as a wise alliance, he was now sincerely head over heels in love—but amusingly enough, he no longer had a clear field. Dr. Jermyn's visits did not cease with recovery, and Miss Amy was well aware of him!

I felt a bit anxious about it as interfering with Mr. Ffolliott's plans, but on the face of it, Dr. Jermyn was as eligible as Mr. Ormond: a Cambridge man, of respectable family, with some private means and a growing practice, not particularly handsome but with a lively humorous face, and no more than thirty years old. Let Mr. Beltane deal with this, if he saw need. For my part, Dr. Jermyn added greatly to the life of Hazelhurst, and it was delightful to observe Miss Amy's enjoyment of two suitors.

Even better was Dr. Jermyn's guidance of Miss Amy's health: no more tonics or laudanum, fresh air at night, a walk before lunch and tea no matter what the weather, no necessity for naps. "You're far too young for such coddling! Backaches, nonsense! Don't lace her so tightly, Mrs. Davenport. Heaven knows, she's in no need of stays at all. She could take 'em off and be the despair of every woman in Chelmsford."

Miss Amy blushed and giggled, but she liked his mischievous forthrightness, and she did what he told her. Night after night she slept peacefully, awoke bright-eyed with anticipation for the day. Mrs. Potter provided sensible menus, and nobody fussed if Miss Amy didn't clean her plate, but in general she did. The staff could scarcely believe its eyes on the Saturday that Dr. Jermyn strode in briskly. "Put on your boots and cloaks. The snow's just right for a fight." All indoor work came to a stop; there was a face at every window watching Miss Amy and myself, teamed efficiently to defeat the doctor and Mr. Ormond, for he was regularly released on Friday these days "To take charge of you flighty girls."

I suspected a private word from Mr. Beltane to Mr. Hasworth for an arrangement that gave Mr. Ormond more chance to protect his interests, but there seemed no strain between the young men, and Hazelhurst rang with cheerful laughter at a dozen happy ploys and fresh schemes. Looking at Miss Amy's glowing cheeks and clear eyes, I was as incredulous as Mrs. Davenport! Could this be the same girl who wept and screamed hysterically four months ago? My heart was filled with joy, awaiting the master's return to a beautiful, healthy young lady, taking her place in society.

Mr. Ffolliott had cabled safe arrival to Mr. Beltane, and shortly there were letters. With the first, I worried a bit: might Miss Amy be distressed at the tangible evidence of distance? Her eyes certainly misted, but she was amazingly resigned to his absence. I noticed Alfred always delivered the envelopes when we were a group: "Dawson brought this from the last post, miss."

"Oh, it is from Papa!" She would open it eagerly, her eyes devouring the strong black script, while Mr. Ormond asked, "What does he say? Is he enjoying the trip? What a pity he's missing our fun here."

"Yes, but all goes better than expected." She would read aloud a sentence here or there, fold the letter back into its envelope with a tiny sigh. "It sounds very pleasant, doesn't it? How much I wish I were there."

"You will be the next time," Dr. Jermyn assured her. "Come, read it again later. It is your lead. . . ." He was teaching us to play cards, and as soon as we had mastered Euchre, we were to learn Whist as a surprise for Mr. Ffolliott. I was not very good at remembering the suits, and generally begged Mr. Beltane to take my place, but Miss Amy was persevering. Every so often she won a hand, until Mr. Ormond remarked ruefully, "You may be slow, Cousin Amy, but you always get there in the end. By Jove, this is fun!"

Everything was fun these days. There was an unusual amount of snow, and the old sleds stored in the coach house proved serviceable. The men made a long slide on the rear of the hillside beyond the lake, and we had coasting parties. We made a snowman in the center of the tennis court; we went for a sleigh ride with Dr. Jermyn, who had a patient to visit. "It's only to take his temperature and tell his wife *not* to give him hot buttered rum every time he asks for it." Mr. Beltane came nearly every evening to dinner, and we read cozily before the library fire until bedtime, choosing (at Miss Amy's request) books that were Mr. Ffolliott's favorites. I doubted that she would ever really care for literature, but as with the card games, she persevered staunchly.

Mr. Ormond brought opera scores. "Carmen is not written for your voice range, Cousin Amy; it is really meant for Silence, but she has not the strength. We will transpose; if Calvé can do so, why not you? And here is 'Cara Nome,' 'Sempera Libera,' 'Celeste Aida'—that is mine. 'Escamillo' must wait until Cousin James returns—he's the only one with a voice deep enough—but we can be ready and waiting for him to join us."

It was borne in on me that Miss Amy was *thinking*. She no longer prattled inconsequentially while we sewed, but seemed to be happily absorbed in working out something in her mind. Putting two and two together, I concluded that Miss Amy was occupied in becoming a *woman*. Where earlier she had played nursery games, they were now put aside. She was making every effort to learn the things enjoyed by *men*—more particularly, by Mr. Ormond! He read books, played cards, loved music and dancing, admired elegantly dressed females, and loudly praised her artistic ability.

"I say, you've caught me exactly, Cousin Amy! May I have this to send Mother?"

A blustery evening confirmed my suspicion. First, Mr. Ormond commented contentedly on the management of Hazelhurst. "After a week in lodgings, Cousin Amy, you can have no notion how good it is to be here! I hope you've ordered a good dinner, for I'm uncommonly hungry!" Second, Dr. Jermyn came in with Mr. Beltane's regrets. "He'd forgotten he must be present at the toffee pull in the parish house."

"By Jove, what a pity! It's the very night for a toffee pull. If we'd known, we might have made shift to join in."

"If Mrs. Potter has molasses to spare, we could have our own," I said involuntarily.

"I say, what a scrumptious idea!" Mr. Ormond exclaimed. "We can't practice satisfactorily without the rector. Do let's invade the kitchen, Cousin Amy."

"I've never heard of a toffee pull. . . ."

"Oh, it's the greatest fun!" he assured her. "You'll like it of all things, Cousin Amy."

"I'll speak to Mrs. Potter, shall I?" I smiled at her uncertain expression. "It's making candy, you know, and we have to have plenty of hot water afterward, or we'll stick to ourselves."

"Oh?" I could see Miss Amy was dubious that this could be classed as amusement, but she said, "By all means, Silence, ask Potter."

It was a sensationally successful pull! We took over the kitchen and I set everyone to work cracking nuts while I boiled up the syrup. And once she got the knack of it, Miss Amy's fingers were swifter and stronger than anyone else's at pulling the strands! We made enough to treat all the staff, and gave a package to Dr. Jermyn for a little girl who had the measles.

But the following day, Miss Amy was more thoughtful than ever. "Should I know how to cook, Silence?"

"You should know how properly to order a household, Miss Amy," I said slowly. "Perhaps not actually doing the cooking, but yes, I think you should know *how*. Otherwise, if you got a bad servant, you would not know what to do, and gentlemen expect their wives to manage everything for their comfort."

"Do you manage Hazelhurst, Silence?"

"No." I shook my head. "And now you mention it, Miss Amy, I don't know who does—perhaps Mrs. Davenport—but I think the servants have all been here for so long that they know exactly what Mr. Ffolliott likes."

"Do you know *how* to manage a household, Silence?" she asked presently.

"Oh, yes, in a simple way. I would know how to go on without servants," I explained. "I cooked Miss Carey's dinners, you know, and mended her clothes, darned the linens, polished her silver. It's unnecessary for you, Miss Amy; Hazelhurst runs itself."

"If you can do it, I must learn how. Will you teach me, Silence? I remember now," she murmured absently. "Mama used to make special dishes for Papa. She said Potter couldn't do them properly."

So we instituted a cookery session, and with Mrs. Potter's supervision, I learned as much as I taught. We spent one morning with Mrs. Davenport, inspecting the linen cupboards, and another morning teaching Miss Amy how to mend. "You'll not need to do it, my dearie, but Miss Silence is right: you should know how." We observed, while Sarah lectured on laundry and ironing, losing her shyness when I rolled up my sleeves and demonstrated a washboard. The tweeny went to pieces and broke a cup at the thought of Miss Amy *watching* the washing up, so I had to do that myself. The mysteries of polishing were thoroughly explored: copper pots, brass firedogs, silver tea service; the waxing of wood; and the use of beeswax for damask.

"What about blackening the boots?" Alfred asked cheekily.

"No *lady* is required to know how her husband likes his boots blacked," I returned snootily. "If *he* doesn't know, he doesn't deserve a good valet."

Hazelhurst was torn between pleasure at Miss Amy's intent interest in its operation and apprehension that she'd decide to change everything! In fact, although she persevered in learning *how,* she was primarily absorbed in cooking, determined to master the dishes Mrs. Ffolliott had prepared.

"I've your Mama's cookbook," Mrs. Potter admitted, and brought it forth: a compact book bound in crumbling leather with pages of faded ink. "Much of it was from her mother, and there's some goes even farther back. 'Tis hard to read, but here's the ones she used to make."

"Why should we not copy it for a book of your own?" I exclaimed. "And I'll make a second copy for Mrs. Potter."

"Dear Silence, make a third for yourself," Miss Amy returned tenderly. "And we must practice the special ones."

The results were . . . peculiar! Curries: "Your mama used to grind the spices. Mr. Ffolliott brought them from London, but I've no fenugreek or cardamom left."

"Mr. Ormond will get them for you, Miss Amy."

He not only brought them, but added a number of other recipes. "If you could make this, Cousin Amy— It's a dish Cousin James and I often order at our London club." Manfully, he ate what we placed before him, but he was immensely helpful in polite criticism. "You need a *touch* more cinnamon, and less salt, Cousin Amy. By Jove, what fun this is, experimenting!"

The days flew past; a tight freeze clothed the lake with ice. "Can you skate, Silence?"

"Yes, but I've no shoes, and I thought you said the lake wasn't safe?"

"In one section," she nodded. "Papa closed it to the townspeople, but Dawson will put a rope across to indicate where it's weak, and we can use the rest. It would be fun to skate again. I wonder if I can still wear my boots. Let us drive to Chelmsford, Silence! We'll buy skates, and take the designs to Madame Raimond."

It was the moment I'd been dreading! Silently, I got out the shattered remains. "I'm sorry, Miss Amy. The dresses are here, but the heads are broken."

For a moment her eyes clouded in the old way. "Yes, I remember," she murmured. "I broke them. Mama said I should have my own when I grew up, and then Langley took them. They never meant me to have these at all."

"I meant you to have them," I said after a moment. "The best I could do was to copy the fashion plates. I didn't expect you'd use them as they were, but I thought it would give you ideas for your own designs. Madame Raimond selected the colors; I wouldn't have known how."

"That's so." She fingered the rose silk. "They are for me, although this would suit you, Silence."

"It was chosen for you, Miss Amy." When she stood uncertain, I asked, "Shall we try to have new heads fixed on these, or throw them away and buy dolls for yourself?"

"Yes"—she threw up her chin—"I'll have my own, but you'll keep these, won't you, Silence?"

"What for? They're of no use, unless you'd like them for first fittings."

"But you could use them for yourself. Wouldn't you like Mama's dolls, Silence?"

"No," I said bluntly, stripping off the costumes and dropping the kidskin bodies into the wastebasket. "Which cloak will you like for the drive?"

"The sable cape. . . ."

All the way to Chelmsford, I apologized mentally to Macdonald. When we'd returned, the basket was empty. I said to Mrs. Davenport when Miss Amy had gone down to the piano, "You knew, didn't you, Nana?"

"I . . . suspicioned, Miss Silence," she admitted unhappily. "I'd forgotten until Sarah mentioned. I wasn't here, you see. That is, I'd been ill; the master sent me away to me sister in Kent. Mrs. Langley ordered the house, but it didn't answer. She'd her own ideas—fair put about Mrs. Potter was." The housekeeper shook her head. "The mistress newly dead, the master with all to do for the estate, Miss Amy naught but a grieving schoolgirl with no notion of how to go on—it was no time for innovations, Miss Silence!

"And no time for me to be sick," she said grimly. "I'd not know all that occurred, but finally Sarah sent for me. 'All's at sixes and sevens, getting worse every day: *she* says one thing, and Miss Amy says another, until we're distracted.' So I wrote to the master, and he sent Dawson all the way to bring me back to Hazelhurst in his own carriage."

"I'd better know the rest of it, Nana," I said presently. "Miss Amy broke the dolls because Madame Raimond reminded her Mrs. Langley had used them. She says the woman wanted to marry Mr. Ffolliott, and told him Miss Amy should be placed in an asylum."

"Aye, she may have done." The housekeeper sighed somberly. "Alfred thinks she'd the *hope* to catch the master, but 'twas too soon, and Miss Amy wouldn't have it. Like a wild thing, she was, jealous for her mother's memory, until at last Mr. Ffolliott sent Mrs. Langley away. Then we had the governesses and nurses until you came—but I should have remembered. I'm sorry, my dearie. Sarah said there'd be trouble when I told her I'd given you the dolls."

"It's no matter, we're rid of them, although it's a pity she destroyed them out of hatred for Mrs. Langley," I said regretfully. "They were so old and lovely, and her mother's, after all."

Mrs. Davenport flicked a glance at me. "As you say," she agreed. "You'll be skating on the lake, I hear—but not without one of the men! You wouldn't know, Miss Silence, but Mr. Ffolliott is firm on it: Alfred, Dawson, or Macdonald is to be there if there's skating."

"Dawson's to put up a barrier to mark the weak spots."

"Yes, but you'll not skate, even with the rector or the doctor or Mr. Ormond, without one of the men standing by. 'Tis a rule! Eh, I'm amazed she'll try it again," Nana murmured.

"Why not?"

" 'Tis how Mrs. Ffolliott met her death," Mrs. Davenport said, surprised. "She was skating with Miss Amy and went through to the water. Macdonald chanced to be observing and pulled her out, but in the dead of winter, the chill was too great. It turned to pneumonia, and in a week she was gone."

"How dreadful!"

"Yes," Mrs. Davenport agreed evenly. "So you'll take great care, Miss Silence, and obey the master's rules no matter how well you skate."

Two thick, sturdy ropes stretched from shore to shore midway of the lake. Dr. Jermyn was adequate; Mr. Ormond feathered his curves neatly; but Mr. Beltane was the star. "Whistle for us, Robert, while I teach Silence to waltz." Around and around we glided, the rector humming in tune with Mr. Ormond's lusty rendition of "Blue Danube," and Miss Amy adding a gay "Tra-*lah*-la-la-*lah*, pom-*pom*, pom-*pom*!"

Alfred and Dawson stood at either end of the ropes, suppressing shivers, until Dr. Jermyn said, "That's enough! Sun's going down. One last swoop! Come on, Miss Amy."

"Oh, I wanted Mr. Beltane to teach me," she mourned.

"Another day! One crack-the-whip before tea." We started at the ropes, with the men to swing up and Miss Amy's hand in mine; and it was a glorious swing—except that I lost her slender fingers on the turn. With incredible speed, I was hurtling directly for the guard ropes, to a chorus of horrified yells behind me. How strong was the barrier? Would it give beneath my weight coming at it full force? Could I even keep my balance, or perhaps fall and slide along the ice until I went *under* the rope?

Brrrr! The mere thought of that water stiffened my backbone, until I was digging in my skates, leaping sideways, and ending in a long lazy curve that brought me facing the others. *Then* I fell down, and skidded toward them, laughing at my ignominy. Alfred reached me first. "My God, Miss Silence! Are you all right?"

"Except for a cold unmentionable," I said cheerfully, hauling down my skirts. "Can you get me up?" The others clustered about, white-faced but relieved. "Not the first time I've fallen"—I hugged Miss Amy reassuringly—"and not your fault. Next time we'll put one of the men on the end."

"There will not be a 'next time,' " Mr. Beltane said, turning me toward the bank. "No more swings—understand me, lads?"

"Oh, you make too much of it, Mr. Beltane!" I ducked away from his protective arm with a laugh. "Come on, Miss Amy, one more go-around to warm us."

She blinked away the tears, and took my hands with a brilliant smile. "Dear Silence—forgive me?"

"For what? The strength of your wrists is for a piano, not holding onto a great lump like myself."

At evening's end, Mr. Beltane detained me while Miss Amy ascended the stairs with her cousin. "You will not skate again, Silence," he said quietly, "no matter who is present. That is an order, and you remember Mr. Ffolliott empowered me?"

"Yes, sir."

I understood easily enough. Miss Amy was marvelously recovered, but might there not be a relapse if she were reminded of her mother's death? And how terrible for Mr. Ffolliott if there should be a second disaster—not that I worried for myself. I was young and robust; a ducking would be uncomfortable, but with a hot bath I'd survive. However, Mr. Beltane felt himself responsible for my safety as well as Miss Amy's; it was not fair to object to an order when there was so much else for amusement.

The choice and measuring for spring clothes took three full mornings, because mine must also be ordered this time. We rarely sat in the morning room, the former free hours during Miss Amy's nap were ended, and I could not be dressmaking in the library or salon with men constantly present. She was more easily curbed, though, and was induced to agree that one suit for church would be sufficient, with two muslins and a challis afternoon costume to extend my existing wardrobe. The only point of disagreement was her insistence that *I* was to have the rose silk. "I've changed my mind, I don't really care for it; but Raimond's laid it by, and she's not to lose the sale, Silence. That would be unfair."

In vain, Madame said there'd be no loss; if Ma'amselle no longer wanted the silk, it could easily be sold to someone else. In vain I protested it was unsuitably fine for me, and reminded her Mr. Ffolliott had particularly liked the color for her. "He'll like it just as well for you, Silence." Miss Amy's mouth set stubbornly. "I *want* you to have it for Papa's homecoming dinner. It will please him."

"It would please him better on you, Miss Amy." But there was a tinge of the old imperious voice as she said, "Measure up for Miss Silence, please, and copy the design she chose."

"*I* didn't choose it, Miss Amy. It was for you, and it's completely wrong for me." I felt a bit mutinous. I'd spent so much time on making the dresses she had liked, had marked in her fashion books. I could accept the breakage of the dolls, but even at the risk of causing one of the old hysterical scenes, I would *not* have that silk pushed onto me in that style.

Miss Amy eyed me impersonally. "Well, choose whatever you think Papa will like better, then."

"He won't like anything better; he's expecting to see it on you. If you don't want rose, have it in blue or lavender —and I can't see why I have to have the rose when Madame says she can get rid of it. I don't much like it, either, now I see it again; I think I'd rather have yellow or green, if you insist on a new dress—which there's no need of, Miss Amy."

"Don't you want to please Papa, Silence?" she asked uncertainly.

"It won't please him to pay good money for a dress I don't need in a style and color I don't like," I said flatly. "So long as I'm clean and neat, it doesn't matter what I wear. I'm only a little girl, Miss Amy."

"You aren't really," she said after a moment. "You're nearly nineteen, Silence. Lot of girls are married and have babies at your age."

"Well, I'm not, nor likely to be, and there's no use in dressing me like a young society lady. What will I do with silk dresses when I go to my next position?"

In the end we compromised: I agreed to the rose silk, and she approved a simple style heartily recommended by Madame as *tout à fait comme il faut pour la jeune fille*.

Driving back from Chelmsford, Miss Amy asked, "What did you mean by a next position, Silence?"

"What I said," I returned in surprise. "I was only hired

SILENCE IS GOLDEN

to be with you while Mr. Ffolliott took this trip. When he returns, you'll have no need of me."

"You wouldn't really leave Hazelhurst?" she asked incredulously.

"I shall be sorry to go," I answered honestly. "I fancy no one ever had such a pleasant post for a first employment, but I must look for another."

"But what would you do?"

I shrugged. "Take charge of a small establishment—something in a modest way, you know—perhaps a widower with small children needing supervision until they reach an age for school, or I might be fortunate enough to travel with a young lady going from school to join her parents in one of the colonies. When Mr. Ffolliott returns, he may suggest something," I murmured absently. "One of his business associates might need me; and there are Mr. Beltane, Dr. Jermyn, Mr. Ormond, as well as Mr. Chisholm, who recommended me in the first place. I'm sure to find something," I finished cheerfully. "May I depend upon you for a good reference, Miss Amy?"

"*No!*" She stared at me. "I shall say you're a *terrible* person. I'll make it all up: you kicked and slapped and . . . and *bit* me; you can't carry a tune; you don't know spades from hearts." She looked innocently into space. "What else? You're a liar; you tried to drown me; you stole Mama's jewels; and all the plants in your room die because you're so evil; and . . . and you starve me at teatime—I'm not let to have any cake. . . ."

"Ooooh, what a whopper!" I chuckled. "You ate four slices yesterday."

She laughed lightly. "But you won't really leave, Silence. You don't mean to go away from Hazelhurst. If you married Papa, you could stay forever!" she said with the effect of brilliant inspiration, and I could not restrain my laughter.

"That is the silliest thing of all," I snorted. "You'll never get away with that one, Miss Amy! Of all the absurdities! You might as well say I've set my cap for the rector or Dr. Jermyn or your cousin."

"Why not? They're all in love with you, Silence." She smiled knowingly at my blank face. "Hadn't you realized? It's you they're after, and you can have any one you fancy, but *not* Papa."

"I never thought of such a thing," I protested. "Good heavens, Miss Amy, how can you be so silly! Mr. Ormond is madly in love with you, Dr. Jermyn is equally smitten, and Mr. Beltane is the age of Mr. Ffolliott."

We were turning into the driveway for Hazelhurst. "Dr. Jermyn observes me under a microscope," she said with detachment. "Robert Ormond is in love with my dowry, and Mr. Beltane is only about thirty-five—Papa is the older."

"He's still twice my age."

"What of it? Papa is twice mine," she returned. "And a rector ought to have a wife. It makes the parish feel better and protects him from the languishing old pussies who knit things that don't fit. It'd be the very thing for you, Silence. I don't know why I didn't think of it before."

"I wish you hadn't thought of it now," I said involuntarily. "Please, Miss Amy, I know you mean to be kind—"

"Do I?" she murmured, waiting for Dawson to open the door.

"—but it makes me uncomfortable to talk this way. Please never mention it again, not even in fun."

"I wasn't funning." She glanced at me, surprised. "I should think you couldn't do better, Silence. Then you'd be here, but not at Hazelhurst. We'd still go shopping together, visit back and forth every day. You'd let me be godmother for your babies, wouldn't you?"

"*Please*," I entreated, "it's absurd—almost shocking. And you won't be here yourself when you're married, Miss Amy."

"I thought you knew, Silence: I am to stay with Papa always. He promised; it was all settled years ago." She pulled herself forward to the carriage door. "So you see, I can't marry anyone."

She said nothing more of it, but the conversation stayed with me. I could quickly dismiss the three men who formed our court, although the first encounter with each was an uneasy moment. From never thinking of it, had I missed some significance in their behavior? With deep relief, I thought not. If anything, I'd become a sort of younger sister. I was "Silence" to everyone; my mistress was still Miss or Cousin Amy. The rector's expression was much that of a kennel master watching a basket of scrambling puppies; but if I was the inept runt of the litter, Miss Amy was marked for the blue ribbon and treated accordingly.

I didn't mind being joshed, the teasing and laughter at my helpless giggles. I knew the men sincerely liked me. Once Mr. Ormond said, "By Jove, Cousin Amy! What luck your companion isn't some stuffy old woman!"

"She'll never live to grow up if you don't stop washing her face in the snow, Robert," Mr. Beltane observed, helping me to my feet from Mr. Ormond's unexpected snowball. "Are you all right, child?"

Slowly my natural unselfconsciousness returned. There was kindly affection for me, but no hint of romance. If Miss Amy mistook a spade for a club, it was overlooked; if *I* did so, my partner unhesitatingly complained. When they undertook to teach me the polka, Dr. Jermyn rubbed his ankle with a grimace. "This damnable habit you have of *hopping*, Silence!"

But something remained of Miss Amy's words, not so much what she'd said as what they indicated. The glib outline of lies—how many times in the past had she said similar things? I did not really doubt I should have a good reference from Mr. Ffolliott—the staff, the rector, the doctor were well aware there was no physical abuse—but I disliked the possibility of any unpleasantness when I left. In the old days, Miss Amy would have wept and screamed, been subdued by laudanum; but that was then, and I began to think the undrugged, clear-headed Miss Amy was a creature no one had known before.

Sometimes I thought she was as much a creation as that of Count Frankenstein, for nothing in the past was a guide to now. I had taken her faint flashes of memory as exaggerated, and perhaps they still were—due to the years of clouded invalidism—but facing her clear eyes, hearing her calm, factual voice, it was difficult to be sure how much was real and how much was the residue of illness.

She said she was to stay with Mr. Ffolliott and couldn't marry anyone, but uneasily I felt he had very different plans. Everything said he intended her to marry her cousin and had privately arranged it before introducing Mr. Ormond to Hazelhurst. Of course, that was in the days of emotional crises. Now they were gone; a relative might not be the only solution—but a husband Miss Amy must have, I quite saw that. When the guardianship ended, Mr. Ffolliott would have no legal standing, but someone would have to handle her affairs. Who better than Mr. Ormond, already in the same field of business? In a way, Dr. Jermyn might not be so capable, although he would certainly keep her healthy.

"Have you been indoors all day?" he asked suspiciously. "No wonder your head feels heavy! Come along—into your boots and cloak. A little snow never hurt anyone. Sweet as you are, Miss Amy, you won't melt."

Neither did Macdonald. Breathing deeply and one clinging to each of the doctor's wiry arms, we went around the house and along the path to the greenhouse, laughing and shaking off snowflakes, while Macdonald surveyed us with disfavor. "Ye'll catch your death," he observed. "Did ye want the plants, ye should send me word. Forbye there's naught ready for the house this day."

"Och, we only came in fra' the rain for a wee crack, mon," Dr. Jermyn said cheerfully. "What hae' ye in the pots?"

Macdonald's face was a study at the sound of the doctor's broad Scottish burr. Miss Amy and I laughed helplessly until the gardener nodded austerely. "Ye'll be fra' Dumfries."

"Summers with my grandparents on Solway Firth, near Annan."

"'Tis pleasant country there." Amazingly, Macdonald relaxed and settled for a chat. I could hear the male voices back and forth behind us as I followed Miss Amy between the shelves of pots and soil, forcing frames in various stages of seedlings. She went across to the other aisle, while I lingered to examine the tiny shoots, trying to identify them and wishing I dared ask Macdonald for a frame of my own. Bending down, I could see Miss Amy wandering along the far side—until she suddenly stood still.

Unconsciously I bent lower, peering through the shelves. She was facing a plant covered with white flowers. The pot was large; the leaves were a glossy dark green; the blooms were (I thought) some variety of camellia. I couldn't remember ever to have seen that plant anywhere in the house, and as I was wondering why Macdonald said he'd nothing to give us, Miss Amy raised her arm and swept it to the floor!

For a split second I stood thunderstruck, while she disappeared from view as though kneeling over the fragments. I could hear her wailing sweetly, "Oh, my sleeve must have caught it! Oh, Macdonald, I'm so sorry! I'm afraid it's ruined! And I was just going to ask for it. It was so lovely, and now it's done for."

By the time I'd got around the end of the benches to come up behind her, Macdonald and Dr. Jermyn were striding toward us. She sensed my movement and turned sadly. "Oh, what a shame, Silence!" Her eyes were misted with tears; she stretched out her hand for me to help her to her feet. "Macdonald—forgive me!"

His eyes blazed at her, and were suddenly curiously cold as he picked the plant root gently from the shattered pot and inspected it. "Why, 'tis not harmed, mistress," he said deliberately. "Set back awhile, but you've not killed it. I'll have it ready again for the master's return. A pity the blooms are stripped; he's so fond of them. I mind it was your mother's favorite." Macdonald stumped away to the potting shelf. "I'd not know where she got it—she called it my 'Cape Jessamyn' and kept it in her bedroom— but 'tis a gardenia."

"You've cut your hand on the shards!" Dr. Jermyn whipped out a handkerchief and twisted it quickly about Miss Amy's hand. "Come back to the house and let me cleanse it."

For a moment I thought she hadn't heard him. She was staring after Macdonald, who was shaking off the free dirt and skillfully repotting. "Mama's plant," she muttered. "I thought it was dead, and all the time it's been alive. . . ."

"And will be again," said Dr. Jermyn. "It's nearly impossible to kill a healthy plant, Miss Amy. Come. . . ."

Firmly the doctor led her away without a glance for me—but that had been no accident. I had seen Miss Amy destroy that pot; and in the time it had taken for me to cross into the far aisle, she had deliberately crushed the flowers. They lay scattered amid the broken shards. Unconsciously I stooped to retrieve one; it was already discoloring at the edges but the scent was delicious.

Slowly I went toward the greenhouse door, and felt the

flower plucked from my hand. Wordlessly, I looked at Macdonald. "Now ye see, mistress," he said evenly, "and ye'll have a care for yourself. We canna be everywhere to watch. And a good day to *you*."

I stepped along the path to the house heedless of wind and snow in my face. All my shivers were inside and somehow a part of the shadow over Hazelhurst, yet was it? Why had she harmed the particular plant that Mr. Ffolliott kept in memory of his dead wife? Intuitively I knew that plant lived behind the door to which Alfred carried a key, and that was why I had never seen it before. I had thought that for all his apparent fondness, he secretly disliked Miss Amy, but did she perhaps dislike him equally? Then why should she not marry and leave Hazelhurst? What strange tie held them together? I could imagine nothing, but for the first time I felt afraid. . . .

CHAPTER EIGHT

It was a month, six weeks, then two months since Mr. Ffolliott had left. Miss Amy spoke of his return, but evinced no impatience for it. His letters were frequent and seemed full of description, although she never shared more than a few sentences. In time there were numerous small presents, ranging from pen-and-ink sketches of the localities to exquisite convent lace and delicate embroideries. By contrast, her replies were skimpy: a single sheet of her elegant monogrammed writing paper contained all she wished to say for an entire week! I wondered whether she meant her good health to be a surprise, but if so, I felt certain Mr. Beltane had given it away. From something said, both he and Mr. Ormond were reporting faithfully on the situation at Hazelhurst.

For myself, I heard nothing nor expected to. My second quarter's wages were duly paid over by Mr. Beltane, and again I was astonished. "Six whole months! I can't believe so much time has passed."

"It goes quickly when one is busy," he agreed with a smile. "There is one thing, Silence: have you a safe storage place? James raised the question. Thirty guineas is a tidy sum to have lying about, not that it would be lost or stolen at Hazelhurst, but you have no need for so much cash, after all. Would you like a small strongbox of your own, or shall I be your banker until he returns?"

"I'd rather you should take care of it, if it's not too much trouble, sir," I said gratefully, "for there's twenty guineas of the first quarter left as well." Running quickly up to my room, I found Miss Amy at the open drawer of the writing desk. "Oh! How you startled me! I thought you were practicing."

"I was," she said after a moment. "And I thought you were in the library."

Anxious not to delay the rector, I made directly for the chest and drew out the cloth bag in which I'd stored my money. At the hall door, I paused briefly. "Oh, did you want a stamp, Miss Amy? For I haven't any. We must ask Dawson to get some."

"No, I was looking for Papa's letters."

"Why? Don't you have them?" I asked, bewildered.

"My own," she nodded. "But where are yours?"

"If you mean the instructions he sent to Mr. Beltane, I'm not sure what became of it. I'll ask, shall I?"

Slowly she pushed in the drawer. "That's all you've had?"

"Yes, of course. Why would Mr. Ffolliott write to me?"

"I don't know," she murmured dully. "I just thought he had." She went into her own room, half closing the door behind her.

Puzzled, I ran back to the waiting rector. "You've had nothing from Mr. Ffolliott for me aside from the authorization to transfer to Dr. Jermyn, have you? Do you have it still?"

"It's in the top drawer. Why d'you want it?"

"Not I—Miss Amy. She seems to think I've had other letters."

Mr. Beltane's lips tightened momentarily. "No, there's been nothing. In fact"—he raised his voice slightly—"the only mention James has made of you was concerning your wages. I assumed he would include any messages in his letters to Amy." The rector looked over my shoulder. "Hasn't he, Amy?"

She came around the half-opened door and shook her head. "Once he said he hoped we were *both* well. I told you that, Silence," she said sweetly, wrinkling her forehead. "How strange of Papa! Why should he ignore you, Silence? He can't have forgotten you're here."

"Oh, he hasn't," I returned cheerfully. "He remembered my wages, Miss Amy, but he's too busy otherwise. Are you going to finish practicing before luncheon?"

"Yes. Come and sit with me, Silence."

It was a trivial episode, yet troublesome, for when I put away Miss Carey's next letter I realized all the others had been examined. They were not in the same order, and some had been crumpled when thrust back into the envelopes. It could only have been Miss Amy; the master had inspected my first letters, but never opened Miss Carey's replies. I found it disturbing as an evidence that some of the old cloudy suspicion still lingered in my mistress, although it was not surprising.

Poor Miss Amy! Some, at least, of her memories of bruises and slaps must be true, and after those years of opiates, nerve storms, and impatient nurses, it was not to be expected she could totally trust anyone all at once. In time it would come.

So did our trip to London, although the new Gilbert and Sullivan production had not yet opened. Instead we would attend an opera: *The Barber of Seville.* Upon learning this, Mr. Beltane firmly announced himself as our escort. "I shall enjoy it far more than poor Davenport! Robert, let us give the girls a full taste of life! A glimpse of Asprey's and Liberty, lunch at the Savoy, and Gunter's for tea and ices—what d'you say?"

"Couldn't be bettered!"

For me, it was fairyland! I consciously stored every impression to be written to Belliston Parva, and was nearly speechless with excitement. "Your eyes are as round as saucers, Silence." Miss Amy laughed, but I would not be teased. "Even our orphans who find posts in London do not see *these* places," I said, "and they will like to hear."

"Very true," Mr. Beltane remarked, "and I must say I should like to hear what you tell them, Silence."

"I'll let all of you read it, if you like, and if I forget anything, you can remind me."

Miss Amy was not equally happy. She held Mr. Ormond's arm very tightly when we were crossing pavements or walking past the shop windows. "I'd forgotten how big and noisy it is," she murmured nervously.

"It's getting more so every year," he said, "but there's no place like it, Cousin Amy! You'd soon grow accustomed. Even the fogs have a flavor all their own. Cousin James should take a house and give you a Season. How you'd enjoy it! Balls every night, the opera, ballet, theater! The court is not what it was, but there are still presentation days. How lovely you'd look with the Prince of Wales' feathers, making your curtsey, Cousin Amy. And nothing could be simpler for Cousin James, for he knows everyone of consequence, you know. I daresay there are a dozen peeresses who would vie for the privilege of introducing you, and as for a proper chaperone, we will coax my mother to leave Wales."

He smiled at me apologetically. "Silence, you do understand? You are the perfect companion at Hazelhurst, but in London, an older woman is necessary."

"I should think so," I told him severely. "Chaperones are not trained in orphanages, Mr. Ormond."

He laughed, but continued to entice Miss Amy with the delights of a London Season. "Don't you agree it's essential, Mr. Beltane? By Jove, what a famous time we'd have!"

I could see Miss Amy was intrigued by the idea, yet fluttered at the thought of grand society. "I shouldn't know how to go on, nor have the right clothes. Your mother would be in despair, Cousin Robert—the mere thought of meeting her frightens me to death."

"Oh, I say," he protested earnestly, "nobody could possibly be frightened of Mother. She's the dearest creature, Cousin Amy! She's much more apt to be nervous of you. She's not really a relative, you know—it was my father who was cousin to your mother—but the thing is that Mother will know best how to do, for she had her own Season and still has friends to put her in the way of it today."

From Mr. Ormond's insistence, I suspected it might be part of Mr. Ffolliott's plans. A London Season was certainly advisable, if possible, and in the present state of Miss Amy's health I thought it was. She would be the acknowledged Beauty of the Season. "And as for clothes, I wish you will study what you see about you, Miss Amy, for there is no one more elegantly attired than yourself. It is why Madame Raimond loves to make for you; you always have a distinctive touch of your own," I told her. "I shouldn't wonder if you were to have all London following your lead."

"Oh, Silence, you are prejudiced." She blushed, but I noticed her eyes moving from stall to stall with discreet glances, and she was increasingly thoughtful. "Would Papa like it, do you think?" she asked that night while we undressed for bed.

"How can I say?" I returned. "I think . . . perhaps. He was always used to gaiety, to friends and society with your mother, was he not? Why should he not enjoy that life again, unless," I added doubtfully, "he has grown too old. But even if he no longer cared for balls, there would be everything else, Miss Amy."

"Yes," she murmured, her fingers pausing, then moving slowly onward to unhook the stays. "Yes, I am old enough to make him happy again."

"His real happiness will be to find *you* healthy and happy." I caught her eyes directly. "That wave—has it gone, Miss Amy?"

She looked at me for a long moment, her face curiously blank. "No," she said finally, "but it is . . . different now. I'm no longer afraid; I know what I have to do."

The following week, Mr. Beltane came in with a cable: Mr. Ffolliott had sailed that very day and would reach Southampton in ten days or at most in a fortnight. "He'll telegraph when he lands, and depending on the time of day, he may be forced to stay the night in London, but you'll have ample time to prepare, Amy."

"Papa," she murmured mistily. "I can't believe it! He'll be *here!* We must go to Chelmsford; Madame Raimond must finish our dresses."

There was no doubt of Miss Amy's inner ferment, although she controlled it well. Still, the expectancy posed the greatest possible strain. Daily I feared a crisis after so many months of calm. For the first time since Christmas she was imperious and demanding—the menu, the flowers, the evening musicale, a dozen directions to Alfred and Dawson. The harness must sparkle. Were there enough cigars? What about brandy? She found minor faults: the fire brasses did not shine as they should; all the books in the library must be dusted. "You know how Papa loves his books!" She fussed until the staff was unnerved, walking on eggs, and agreeing to anything and everything.

Mr. Beltane came to dinner each evening; Dr. Jermyn seemed more often in evidence than usual. "I was driving by and turned in for a minute to see how you do, Miss Amy." Mr. Ormond arrived on Friday. "I say, the snow is perfect! Probably the last chance this year—we must have a sledding party and a toffee pull!"

Everyone was late.

Mr. Ormond drove into Chelmsford with a worried frown after a glance at the morning paper. "I must telephone or wire the office, Cousin Amy. This damnable Gladstone! But I'll be back in plenty of time."

Mr. Beltane's man brought a note saying the rector was detained by a parish matter; we should start without him and he'd join us as soon as he finished.

There was still Dr. Jermyn, but Mrs. Davenport said, "The rector's man passed the remark he'd seen the doctor going toward Calne Halt, and Mr. Fothergill's been took bad again."

Miss Amy and I ate lunch. We dressed for outdoors and fretted about until nearly three, when I said, "The light's going. Why don't we go along first? They can catch up to us, and at least we'll get in one go by ourselves."

"*Yes!*" She smiled brilliantly, "Do, let's! And when they arrive, we'll put our noses in the air and say 'you missed the fun.'"

Chuckling naughtily, we bundled into scarves, mittens, and close caps. It was already shadowy as we dragged the sleds up the hill beneath the snow-laden trees, and I had misgivings. "I think we waited too long. D'you think we can see the slope?"

"Of course we can!" She tucked herself onto the sled. "Push off! I'll do you next time, Silence."

I was tempted to belly-whop, which was strictly forbidden by Miss Carey, but it gives so much more speed when you're alone. Peering through the shadows to the last sunshine near the house, I thought I saw figures—some of our guests? Sedately I sat on my sled, dug in my heels at the top of the rise and skidded down until I reached my mistress. "I think they're coming."

"No, it was only Alfred closing the shutter on the terrace. Let's have one more!" In silence and panting a little, we dragged the sleds back up to the top, stood catching our breath and looking hopefully toward the house, but there was no sign of motion. "Your turn, Silence. Pull the sled a bit farther up. I can push better, and you'll have a faster ride." When I was settled, she said gaily, "*Bon voyage!*" and with a long breath, took several running steps, her hands firmly set to my shoulders until I was skimming forward like a bird—

—and suddenly realized I was not following the sled track.

Somehow from the higher starting point and in the dimness, I was veered to the right and hurtling straight down the bank to the lake—if I didn't run into one of the great trees first. . . . From side to side went the sled, for this was not snow but pure ice beneath the trees, where neither winter sun nor snowfalls reached. It was impossible to control the sled runners; as often as I tried to set my boots on the steering bar, we hit a bit of rock or buried shrubbery that jolted them off. For a space I slid sideways, and nearly capsized before we caught a tree root and were dashing downward again.

Ahead was the lake. At this speed I'd crash completely through the ice, and I knew there were submerged rocks somewhere at this end, rimming the underground springs where the lake wouldn't freeze. To the left were the great trees I'd so far avoided. To the right were mingled outcrops and shrubbery—but covered in snow, which was which?

I tensed my muscles, gathered my skirts together, and sprang for what I thought I remembered was a bush. I was only half right; it was mated with some rocks—but at least I was safe. Behind me was a muted splintering, the tinkling crash of thin ice: the sled had gone. I couldn't think of that now—I wasn't on it—but I was far too close to the brink for peace of mind. Painfully, I hauled myself up to the top of the rocks, bracing myself with my boots against a ridge and grasping a sturdy branch of the shrub. When I saw *how* close I'd been to the dark water, it took a number of deep breaths to steady me, but at last I was lying limply secure and wondering how I was ever to get back up that icy bank.

"*Silence? Silence, where are you?*" I could hear Miss Amy's distracted voice, but I couldn't summon the strength to call a response. Cuddled in the snowbank, I felt oddly lethargic; my eyelids drooped; I nearly went to sleep— except that I could see Miss Amy staggering frantically from the bottom of the sledding slope toward the house, screaming at the top of her lungs, "*Come,* come *quickly!* Help, *help!*"

Across the dark water, it seemed Hazelhurst erupted and blazed into life. The servants poured from the rear door, with Alfred stamping into his boots and wildly winding a scarf about his head. From the middle window of the salon, Mr. Ormond raced forward with Mr. Beltane behind him. Dr. Jermyn must have just arrived, for he came tearing around the front corner of the house. It was a pantomime. They were too far away for words to reach me, but Mr. Ormond reached Miss Amy first. He caught her in his arms, and held her tenderly, protectively. I knew what she must be saying: "When I got to the bottom of the slide, Silence wasn't there."

Drowsily I was pleased at the way Miss Amy clung to her cousin, burrowing against his shoulder, until he picked her up bodily and started back for the house. The others ran forward toward the slope, calling my name. At this distance my voice would never be heard. How could I reach them? I roused myself determinedly, stripped off one mitten and set two fingers to my mouth. Who would have ever dreamed naughty Tommy Six could teach anyone such a *useful* accomplishment?

"Silence? *Silence?*"

Again and again I whistled, feeling my breath warm on my fingers.

"Where are ye, lass?"

"I'm down here, Macdonald, but I don't know how to get up." I could hear trampings and cracklings. "Oh, do be careful! It's all ice."

"I've the right equipment," he said, towering over me with grim disfavor, "which is more than can be said for you, mistress." He put both hands to his mouth and shouted, "She's down the bank! Bring the ropes!" I was dimly aware of Alfred racing for the house, of Dawson appearing from the direction of the stable, and Sarah at the rear door with two lighted lanterns, but I was drowsy once more. Cautiously Macdonald settled beside me, pulling me against his chest and wrapping me within his heavy coat. "Dinna sleep now until we've hauled ye up. 'Twill not be long."

Macdonald smelled of clean green things, sweet soil, a tiny whiff of manure. "In the spring, if I'm a very good girl and don't bother you," I said dreamily, "could I have a forcing frame, Macdonald?"

"Mphhmph. What were ye wishful to grow?"

"Sweet peas," I said unhesitatingly. "At the orphanage it was always vegetables, because we needed them, you know, so I'd like flowers, to see what it feels like."

"Aye, but 'tis all one. Ye'll find a bean blossom is as beautiful."

"Perhaps, but this once I'd like something . . . something extravagantly useless."

"Beauty is *never* useless," he said so deeply that I was startled. " 'Tis an essential for all souls. Why else did the Lord make this fine earth for us? Wherever ye look, 'tis beautiful—a refreshment of the spirit. 'Tis only people are sometimes ugly." He shifted slightly and shouted to the calling voices above, "Come down fra' the back."

They strung a rope from a tree trunk at the top of the hill, and stiffly, hand over hand with Macdonald bracing me and Alfred digging in his feet to make steps for me, I hauled myself up to find Mr. Beltane and Dr. Jermyn. "Silence! My dear, *dear* child!" The rector put his arms around me thankfully. "In God's name, what happened?"

"Never mind now, Hugo. Silence, can you walk or shall we make a hand-carry for you?"

Now it was over, I felt light-headed. I raised my head from the rector's shoulder and said dramatically:

"Despite the bludgeonings of Chance,
My head is bloody but unbowed."

"Did you hit your head? Are you bleeding?" Dr. Jermyn asked sharply. "Where's the wound, Silence?"

I swayed against Mr. Beltane and laughed. "Nowhere. It's just something Miss Carey always says after a trustees' meeting."

"Hysterics!" the doctor said in an undertone. "Get her down hill as fast as possible, Hugo."

"Oh, nonsense." I straightened up and stepped back from the rector's support. "All I need is a hot bath, and a bit of ointment for various scrapes and bruises, and I'll be good as new." I took two steps forward, and turned. "Macdonald, thank you."

"I'll ready a frame," he said off-handedly, "and goodnight to ye, mistress."

In spite of myself I stumbled slightly in the snow, and Mr. Beltane swung me up into his arms firmly. "I'll carry her, Albert. Hold the lantern a bit lower. Alfred, go ahead and tell them to be ready for us."

"Get my bag from the carriage, and bring the brandy," Dr. Jermyn added.

"Yes, sir."

Slowly, steadily, we descended the slope. I closed my eyes, conscious of Mr. Beltane's strong arms, of soft whiskers brushing my cheek, the faint scent of lavender. "Is Hugo a family name?" I asked.

"Yes," his voice was amused. "It's not very suitable for a rector, but I'm the seventh, and my father never expected me to take holy orders."

"Actually, I shouldn't be surprised if you rose to be a bishop," I murmured when I'd thought it over. "Haven't you noticed how many are named Cyril, or Percival, or Cedric? I think Hugo fits beautifully."

Mr. Beltane stood still for a moment, shaking with laughter. "Oh, Silence!"

"For God's sake, Hugo, come *on*," Dr. Jermyn said urgently. "She said she'd struck her head—probably a mild concussion—her mind's wandering."

"No, it isn't—" I began indignantly, and the rector said, "Yes, it is, Albert, but Silence's wandering mind is one of her greatest charms."

"Whatever it is, I want her indoors where I can look at her."

We started forward once more. "What happened, Silence? How on earth did you end on the bank?"

"Oh, it was an accident because it was dark under the trees. We got tired of waiting for the rest of you and went by ourselves," I explained. "I pushed the first time. Then it was my turn, and Miss Amy thought she'd get a better start if we were a little higher, but I didn't steer properly. Somehow I missed the tracks, so I picked a likely looking snowbank and leaped for it. That's all."

"That's all!" he repeated under his breath, his arms tightening convulsively. "Thank God, James will be home next week! It's getting beyond us. . . ." Heedless of wet boots, he carried me from terrace to salon through the long window Dr. Jermyn had opened.

Miss Amy was sitting exhaustedly in the bergère, her face streaked with tears. Mr. Ormond held one hand, and Mrs. Davenport hovered, white-faced, with the smelling salts. At sight of me, Miss Amy leaped to her feet with a sob and ran forward. "Silence! Oh, thank God! I thought you were dead! I thought I'd never see you again."

SILENCE IS GOLDEN

I said to Mr. Beltane, "Put me down, please," and took her affectionately in my arms. "Silly! I'm perfectly all right. I simply missed the turn and went off to the side. There's nothing to cry about."

"How can I help it?" she hugged me closely. "Dear, dear Silence, what should I do without you?"

"You won't have to." Dr. Jermyn came back with his bag and took charge. "Let her go for the moment, please. Silence, get out of those damp things at once." Impersonally he detached Miss Amy and pushed her back to her chair, while the rector swiftly pulled off my cap and helped me unbutton my coat. When I was free, he commanded, "Sit down in front of the fire. Robert, get her boots *and* her shoes off. Put your feet on the hearth, Silence. Hugo, chafe her hands. Alfred, where's the brandy?"

"Here, sir."

He poured a small glass and handed it to me. "Drink it straight down, Silence—don't sip."

I choked miserably, and Mr. Ormond wiped my eyes with his handkerchief. "Cousin Amy, hand over the salts for a moment."

"Truly I don't need them."

"Yes, you do," Miss Amy said firmly. "Nana, is her bath ready?"

So many voices, so much confusion, so many hands patting and rubbing me . . . weariness swept over me and I drooped against the rector. "If I could just lie down for a while. . . ."

He picked me up like a baby. "Albert, bring your bag. No, Amy, stay here with Robert, please. Davenport, get them some tea. Sarah can take care of Silence."

"This isn't my room," I said when Mr. Beltane laid me on a bed and I'd opened my eyes.

"No, miss, but there's not the space for the bath L yours." Alfred's face was oddly grim as he emptied the copper cans. "I'll bring another while you're getting her undressed," he said to Sarah, "and mind, doctor says not to chatter!"

She nodded wordlessly. After that, time seemed to float until I was in and out of the hot water, into a nightdress and between fresh sheets. I think I slept instantly, with no idea of the hour when my eyes opened again. A lamp was turned low on a table in the far corner; the fire flickers danced on the ceiling. Scraps of conversation reached me dimly, but without significance.

". . . waiting in the salon, I thought . . . got past me somehow, sir . . . first I knew is Mr. . . ."

"Don't blame yourself . . . mistake to let her know. . . ."

"Gawd, those screams—s'help me, I *knew*—fair sickened me!"

"Shhh. . . ."

Involuntarily, I yawned, stretched, and was fully conscious. I did not even feel particularly bruised. A hand held my wrist. "How d'you feel, Silence?"

"Hungry!"

"Not surprising; it's nearly eight and you missed tea." Dr. Jermyn smiled professionally. "You'll have a tray as soon as Sarah's got you ready."

"A tray? I'm not an invalid." I sat up, tentatively exploring my limbs. "I hit my funny bone"—I winced—"and there's a sore spot on my left ankle. That's all. Why do I have to eat in bed?"

"Not all bruises are tangible, and you've had a shock."

"Not really—as a matter of fact, it would have been rather fun except for the water. The ice was much faster than snow. Besides, if you keep me in bed, Miss Amy will have the shock," I pointed out. "She'll be convinced I'm dying, go into a fantod, and upset the whole household, so if you don't mind, Dr. Jermyn, I'm not ill, but I don't want to *cope* with anything."

"I expect you're right, but I don't like it." He tugged at his earlobe thoughtfully. "The effort to dress will be more tiring than you realize."

"Would it be *very* shocking if I were to descend in my robe?" I asked. "There is only Mr. Ormond to consider. A doctor and a rector must be accustomed to such garments, even if not usually seen at a dinner table. But unless Miss Amy can see for herself that I'm not hurt, she'll insist on eating upstairs with me."

"Yes," he said slowly, "that's the best solution. Oh, Sarah! Help Miss Silence into her robe, please."

"Yes, sir." But within five minutes, Mrs. Davenport bustled in carrying Miss Amy's fur-collared velvet peignoir with a smile. "You're to wear this, my dearie, and Alfred's to carry you down," she announced. "Sarah, she'll need her

SILENCE IS GOLDEN

own slippers. Miss Amy's are too small. Eh, 'tis grand to see you're none the worse"—she hugged me heartily—"and Mrs. Potter's made the special custard you fancy!"

Held firmly in Alfred's arms, I was borne into the salon and set in a chair with a fauteuil thrust under my feet. Miss Amy knelt beside me. "Silence—darling, darling Silence—are you really all right?"

I kissed my mistress and laughed. "I'm a complete fraud," I stated. "There's *nothing* the matter with me, but if you wish to cosset me, you may! The rector may carry me in to dinner; the doctor may carry me out; Mr. Ormond is to play some waltzes; and you are to sing everything I like best. I intend to make the most of every fleeting moment, I warn you."

The men chorussed agreement. "You shall have anything and everything you wish! By Jove, there's nothing nicer than a pretty girl to be spoiled a bit, eh?" Miss Amy could not be so easily restored. She shook her head, misty-eyed. "Oh, Silence, how could I have done such a thing! What would I do without you?"

"Don't think about it. It was my own fault for not looking where I was going . . . *and there is no wave!*" I told her softly.

"No," she murmured after a moment. "I begin to think there isn't." She leaned her head against my shoulder, and whispered despairingly, "What *shall* I do?"

CHAPTER NINE

Mr. Ffolliott's return took me as much by surprise as his departure. His boat was expected at Southampton on Thursday, but from the circumstance of its having rained steadily from Sunday through Wednesday night, we had thought it unlikely he would reach Hazelhurst before Friday. It was the most difficult week of any since my arrival. The shadow had lain more heavily upon us than ever before, though I knew not why.

Despite my insistence that there were no ill-effects, my mishap contributed to the general tension. The staff hovered over me constantly. Sarah constituted herself my personal maid and bullied me unmercifully; Alfred firmly grasped my elbow the instant I stepped out for a walk. "Miss Amy's arm is not strong enough, miss." Mrs. Potter sent in glasses of egg and milk every morning, and Mrs. Davenport carried the smelling salts in her pocket. To all protests, they replied, "Doctor *says*. . . ." Mr. Beltane worked daily in the library, preparing parish reports and (I supposed) an accounting of his stewardship during the master's absence.

As for Dr. Jermyn, he came so often that I automatically opened my mouth as soon as he entered; he always put a thermometer in it! I continued to sleep in the guest chamber. "The exposure is better, Silence. At this season, the weather is changeable; night winds veer suddenly; or the temperature drops inside an hour," he said.

So much supervision inevitably made Miss Amy uneasy. "What is wrong, Silence? There is something you haven't told me!"

"No, no, truly. . . ."

Her great blue eyes searched mine intensely, grasping my arm convulsively, until at last she relaxed with a sigh. "If anything happened to you, Silence, I couldn't bear it.

SILENCE IS GOLDEN

I can't think how I came to do it," she shivered.

"Will you stop teasing yourself! In the dimness, I didn't steer properly and missed the tracks. You didn't 'do' anything, silly."

"Didn't I?" She sank onto the floor beside me, laying her cheek against my hand. "Are you sure, Silence? I thought I had . . . but perhaps I only imagined it. It's always so hard to remember, and afterward they said I did . . . things. . . ."

"That was long ago, and anyway, Davenport says you didn't," I scoffed gently. "Today is all different, and tomorrow we must go to Chelmsford for the last fitting. I hope the rain stops."

It didn't, and both Mrs. Davenport and Alfred went with us. "You'll not mind, Miss Amy? Mrs. Potter has a commission, and Alfred's to pick up a parcel."

The finished gowns were brought out by Dawson next day, and Miss Amy insisted on trying them on. Almost at once we were in difficulties. She found nothing wrong with the deep violet moiré of her own dress; she had taken out the jewelry, and was debating the advisability of an amethyst set versus her mother's emerald parure when I came to exhibit the rose silk.

By comparison with Miss Amy's gown, it was extremely simple, but I was the more pleased with it. It suited my notion of propriety. Miss Amy, however, took one look and grew stormy. "How *could* Madame have made such a stupid dress! I knew I should have gone into the fitting room yesterday, but Davenport distracted me." She stamped her foot angrily. "There'd have been time to add some ruching or braid or something. As it is, you look like a . . . a nursery child. What will Papa think?"

"Nothing," I said pacifically. "He won't be looking at *me*, after all. Would you rather I wore the amber taffeta?"

"With Mama's diamonds!" She turned eagerly to the jewel boxes and drew out the necklet.

"No! Remember, you agreed I was too young for diamonds?"

Her eyes filled with tears, her chin quivered, and Mrs. Davenport was twisting her hands together in anguish. I went forward and laid one finger gently on my mistress's hands hovering over the caskets. She recoiled violently, staring at me, and I thought of a small wild animal, startled and wary. "Dear Miss Amy"—I smiled—*"There is no wave!* Mr. Ffolliott comes tomorrow. Let him see you as you are?"

Her glance wavered and slid away. "Yes," she whispered, "yes, you're right, Silence, but I wanted him to see you as *you* are, so I would know. . . ." She dropped the diamonds with a long breath. "And if you insist on wearing this horrid dress, you must have something to finish it off, or I shall lose my appetite," she stated flatly. There was a tap on the door. "Come in."

"Beg pardon, miss"—Alfred was breathing hard, as if he'd been running—"but the rector says Mr. Ormond's here unexpected-like, and it's near teatime. They're in the salon, waiting for you."

"Thank you, Alfred. We'll be down shortly. Wait!" She whirled impetuously, pointing to the jewel boxes. "Take these with you, Alfred. Come along, Silence. We'll see what the men have to say. Are you willing to abide by their decision?"

"Yes."

"Even if they want you to wear jewels?" she insisted. "Go on, Alfred, we're coming."

"Yes," I agreed valiantly. Mr. Beltane would extricate me somehow—and eventually he did, but not before Miss Amy had tried the effect of every neck ornament she owned. Mr. Ormond provided innocent assistance. "Either her neck's too short, or the dress is too high, or the color's wrong. Nothing seems to go with it, or her. I'm sorry, Silence."

"*I* think she needs something simpler, Amy," Mr. Beltane observed mildly. "Haven't you some pearls?"

"Yes," she said after a moment. "I never wear them. Pearls are for tears." Slowly she drew them out: a double strand, pink-tinged.

Mr. Ormond loudly approved. "The very thing! All young girls begin with pearls, Cousin Amy. I say, Mr. Beltane, you've more of an eye for feminine fripperies than is quite respectable for a rector, sir!"

"How could I guide my flock if I were not versed in its pitfalls?" Mr. Beltane returned blandly. "Yes, Robert is right, Silence: the pearls it must be."

"If you say so, sir."

Miss Amy was inclined to crossness. "So insignificant!

Why not the garnets? I'm sure we could contrive to shorten the extra links somehow."

"You made me promise to wear what the men chose," I reminded her merrily, "and you have to accept it, too! No fair fussing!"

Reluctantly she smiled. "But I did so want you to appear at your best, Silence."

"Why, so she does," Mr. Ormond said heartily. "Put the doodads away, Cousin Amy, and let's have tea."

I took the caskets upstairs first, and was returning when I heard a carriage. It was probably Dr. Jermyn—he'd only stopped twice thus far today—but Alfred came dashing along the lower hall and threw open the door with a most undignified cry of welcome. Surging through the kitchen passage were Mrs. Davenport and Sarah, Mrs. Potter hastily tying on a fresh apron, with the tweeny bringing up the rear.

And stepping down from the carriage was a tall, smiling figure, shaking hands heartily with Alfred: the master had come home.

Mr. Ormond, the rector, and Miss Amy passed me from the salon door, and still I stood on the lower steps of the staircase, looking at Mr. Ffolliott. He was so much *more* —handsome, assured, vital—more everything than I'd remembered. How could I have forgotten? The mere sight of him inspired confidence. Mr. Beltane and Dr. Jermyn had the same quality, but in Mr. Ffolliott there was a touch of extra warmth, laughter, something debonair, almost reckless and imperious. He was a man among men, a born leader. "Robert, how are you?" He slapped Mr. Ormond's shoulder, then turned to the rector. "Hugo!" Silently, the two friends clasped hands for a long moment.

Miss Amy had advanced no farther than the top of the steps. "Papa," she said softly, and stood waiting. I couldn't see her face, but by the proud set of her figure, she was entirely calm and controlled.

Mr. Ffolliott looked up at her, and for a second he stood transfixed, his expression unfathomable. Then he released Mr. Beltane's hands and walked up slowly, his lips curving in an odd smile. "Amy! You've grown very dignified while my back was turned."

She laughed delightedly. "I am learning to mind my manners so you can present me at Court," she confided;

but when he was standing beside her, she threw herself against him with a deep sob. "Oh, Papa, Papa, it's really you! You have come back to me." She clung to Mr. Ffolliott, kissing him wildly and pressing her cheek to his. "They said you would, but it was so *long,* Papa . . . sometimes I thought. . . . Oh, Papa, *please* never leave me again!"

"Now that is the old Amy, after all." He hugged her closely. "And they told me you were so grown-up I wouldn't recognize you."

"*Who* told you?" She leaned back, smiling brilliantly at him.

"Hugo and Robert," he chuckled. "They wrote me faithfully twice a week with all the news of gay dinner parties, whist evenings, and I don't know what all. You are a very poor correspondent, darling!"

"I left it to Silence; she doesn't mind writing letters," Miss Amy said sweetly. "Didn't she tell you everything?"

"No, she was worse than you; she never wrote at all." He laughed. "Where is the naughty thing?"

"Here, sir."

Something else I'd forgotten was that kingfisher flash of blue in his eyes. With Miss Amy folded against him, Mr. Ffolliott stared at me impassively while I came from the hall. "Welcome home, sir."

"Thank you, Silence. It is . . . good to see you again. Come! We mustn't stand here or I shall be the one to take a cold! After two months of sunshine, England is terribly damp." With a pat on my shoulder, he went into the hall with Miss Amy. There ensued a great bustle of greetings, boxes and trunk being unstrapped from the carriage, Mr. Ffolliott stripping off his greatcoat and directing matters: "The trunk upstairs, that box to the library, this to my room, the others to the salon. . . . Hugo, will you keep me company while I change? Robert, amuse the minxes. No, I don't want any tea, thank you, Potter."

"Oh, I say, Cousin James, could we have an Allahabad Aperitif?" Mr. Ormond inquired eagerly. "I've been practicing it, but there's something escapes me. Mine don't taste the same."

From the stairs, Mr. Ffolliott raised an eyebrow superciliously. "It's the nutmeg does it, Robert," he said, and went away laughing.

"Nutmeg! By Jove, I never thought of that," Mr. Ormond was muttering as we went back to the salon.

It was true that Hazelhurst came alive when the master was within. I had never realized it so clearly as in the next days. While all had functioned smoothly during his absence, and my only exercise of authority had been the transfer of Miss Amy to Dr. Jermyn, the staff was infinitely happier to have Mr. Ffolliott at the helm. So was I, although Miss Amy did not—as I'd half feared—break down from joy. The new calm continued, and I saw that he observed it narrowly.

I could not be sure he was entirely happy about it; he seemed at times almost disconcerted. Occasionally there was an ironic twist to his lips when her fluting voice produced an incisive remark, but in general his expression was as fond as ever. There was a difference in Miss Amy's fondness, though. She still kissed him frequently, but not in quite the old artless, childlike manner, and she rarely sat beside him holding his hand. Instead, she sat opposite, smiling over the tea tray or the length of the dinner table, for she had decided, "I am grown enough to play hostess, am I not, Papa?"

Now, for the first time, I felt myself to be outside the family circle. On two different mornings, Mr. Ffolliott sent for Miss Amy alone. "It's to do with business," Mrs. Davenport said confidentially, "though how much she'll understand of it—" He spent several hours with Dr. Jermyn, and nodded to me approvingly at teatime. "That was a wise decision, Silence. You like him, Amy?"

"Very much!" She smiled mischievously. "He has taught me to play whist. Will you be my partner, Papa?"

More and more I left them alone together, making an excuse to go upstairs after the coffee tray and not returning at once; or if the card table were set in the salon, I slipped away to the library with a book. I saw that my employment was drawing to a close; it did not disturb me beyond a terrible pang at the thought of never seeing Mr. Ffolliott again, but I had always known it to be inevitable. Would I ever again have so handsome and kind a master?

Daily I expected a summons to the library for my dismissal. Miss Carey had written that she had a superb position for me: "Lady Lester's daughter's sister-in-law will need a companion for her girl coming out to India in September! If nothing transpires sooner, the trustees agree you may come 'home' (if I can call it that), but it will be refreshing to see you, child."

Meanwhile I made myself useful with household mending while Miss Amy practiced; I was at hand or not at hand according to circumstances, and as spring came toward us, I went down to the greenhouse and said daringly, "Good day to you, Mr. Macdonald. Have you my frame?"

"Aye, 'tis there." He jerked his head toward the side shelf. "Have ye the seeds, or will ye try your hand at what the master's brought fra' the Islands?"

I looked at the packet of sweet peas Dawson had gotten for me in Chelmsford, and the seductive envelope beside the frame. "I'll try my hand, thank you, Macdonald," I told him arrogantly. Side by side we stood, while I read the handwritten directions and set the seeds into the frame. I knew he was observing me—and I was engulfed with curiosity for the other envelopes he was setting into pots and frames—but we said nothing. When I'd finished, there was still some space at the edges. Defiantly, I made a small trench and scattered in the sweet pea seeds. I wiped my hands on the cloth beside Macdonald, and without a word I sauntered down the aisles, looking for a suitable spot.

It was so bare and so obvious, I knew it was meant for me. Carefully, I transferred my frame, and went on, inspecting the seedlings and occasionally snipping out a dead leaf from one of the pot plants. When I'd completed the circuit, Macdonald looked at me austerely. "And where had ye this training, mistress?"

"From Angus Maclachlan, who cares for the orphanage land," I said limpidly. "He's from Kirkcudbright, but I think you'd find him very sound. And a good day to you, Macdonald."

I could hear a deep chuckle as I carefully closed the greenhouse door, and looking back through the glass, I could see Macdonald's head thrown back, guffawing!

After that, whenever Miss Amy was busy with Mr. Ffolliott or practicing with her cousin, I ran down to the greenhouse fearlessly. I can't say we became cronies, Macdonald and I, but gradually we were comfortable together. "This Angus Maclachlan ye mentioned—would he be fra' Dalbeattie or Carsphairn?"

"I've no idea, but it's near Lake Doon."

"Mphhmph." He nodded—but when Macdonald permitted me to assist him with an intricate layering of camellias, I knew I'd been trained by the right Angus.

"Silence, where have you been?" Miss Amy demanded at teatime.

"In the greenhouse with Macdonald. Oh, dear, I expect I lost track of time," I apologized, "but I thought you were busy with Mr. Ormond."

"In the greenhouse?" She stared at me. "What are you doing *there?*"

"Growing some of the seeds Mr. Ffolliott brought home," I said cheerfully. "I don't know what they are, but some of them are starting to come up." I grinned at Mr. Ffolliott. "Oh, don't worry, sir. Macdonald's right behind me; I won't be let to make a mistake."

"That you won't," he agreed with a smile. "It will be interesting to see what survives. By the way, Hugo, Macdonald has been successful with the lilies; you'll have them for Easter, which reminds me. . . ." He plunged into parish business.

Miss Amy did not forget my seedlings, however. These days she forgot nothing—in particular, the subject of a London Season. The very next day she demanded gaily to be shown my labors in the greenhouse, "for nothing would be better than that the ball flowers should come from Hazelhurst, Silence! Only think how impressive to have something rare in London."

"Yes, but I'm not sure whether these are flowers or simply house plants," I said dubiously. "You may have to settle for my plain old garden variety sweet peas, Miss Amy."

She would not allow them to be despised. "I love them! Such tender colors and the delicate scent—they suit any gown. Best of all to have a corsage you grew for us." She hung over the frame, exclaiming at the infinitesimal specks of green, while I stood amazed at those words "for us." Macdonald towered beside her, and for Macdonald he was positively garrulous! He led her about, explaining the contents of various frames, which would be potted and which bedded out. He pointed out the Easter lilies, gave her a carnation for the master, and finished by rapidly creating a tiny corsage of valley lilies and the one opened lilac spray. "For your dinner gown, Miss Amy." He bowed gallantly.

I suppressed amusement. Poor Macdonald! How he disliked "weemen" in his bailiwick! He'd tried the tack of a personal tour, a floral tribute—but he couldn't make himself smile, and now he'd got us back to the door; he had it open in two-twos with the effect of sweeping us out. I could hear him saying to himself, "And a good riddance to *you*, mistress!"

He did not succeed so easily. Miss Amy sniffed her flowers with delight. "But there must be one for Silence, too."

"I doubt he has anything more, Miss Amy," I put in swiftly; the gardener was exasperated enough. "It's a wee bit between seasons, you know, and I don't need flowers tonight—it's only family."

"What of it? Macdonald, *find* her something!" Miss Amy's color rose slightly. "This can't be all you have."

"No, mistress," he said after a moment, and silently went into a side forcing room, to return shortly with a delicate white flower. He twisted a bit of silver paper about the stem, and extended it to me, while Miss Amy bent forward eagerly.

"How beautiful . . . but it has no scent," she exclaimed, disappointed. "What is it, Macdonald?"

"An orchid," he told us deliberately. " 'Tis one of the plants the master brought, a sort of vine that drapes itself among the trees. Verra difficult to grow in this climate, but he was wishful to give me the chance to experiment." He looked at me grimly. "Ye'll tell him this is the first blossom, mistress."

I gulped. "Oh, *why* did you cut it? Wasn't there a camellia or—or some daphne?"

"Aye, but he'll like to see this; forbye, it'll die by evening's end," he returned casually, pulling open the door again. " 'Tis a parasite, ye ken? It has no life of its own. . . . And a good day to you, mistress."

Stumbling along the path with Miss Amy, my eyes were blurred with tears; I could scarcely attend to her fluting voice commenting on buds and trees, the loveliness of spring emerging. I felt distracted, almost physically wounded by Macdonald's words. Was that all I was: a parasite? Something like mistletoe and honeysuckle, clinging to a sturdy tree and creeping ever closer until at last the tree strangled? Surely I'd earned my wages as much as Macdonald earned his. Hadn't I produced by helping Miss Amy to be herself? Would I not produce equally by accompanying Lady Lester's relative to India next fall?"

Someone had to do these odd jobs, with the added uncertainty of short tenure. I knew I was going to have to earn my living; there'd be scant chance of marriage for a penniless orphan, despite Miss Amy's fond suggestions. At Hazelhurst I'd been supremely fortunate in meeting only gentlemen who treated me with dignity, but it might not always be so. The one thing any orphan knows is the result of easy virtue! Between farm animals, my companions, and Miss Carey's succinct explanations ("I do not wish to bring up your children!"), any graduate of Belliston Parva unquestionably knew more of the proclivities of high-spirited young men than Miss Amy.

It would still never be a life of my own. At best I'd be respected by household males or surreptitiously bussed behind the baize. At worst, I'd have difficulties with men servants and need to lock my bedroom door at all times. If I were ever offered a wedding ring, it would be in the expectation of eternal gratitude, and perhaps in time I should be able to feel it for some man who would pay for my keep. Right now, with spring in the air, I couldn't bear to contemplate such an ending . . . yet what else could there be?

At the top of the path, Miss Amy turned impulsively. "It's not too late! Let's go down to the lake and see if the wild ducks are here. They come back every year, and sometimes there are babies."

Automatically I consulted my Christmas watch. "All right, but only down and back, or we'll have no time to dress."

She laughed. "How you love that timepiece!"

"Of course! You gave it to me."

"No, it was from Papa. I gave you the furs, and Cousin Robert gave you the gloves. I told him your size. Mr. Beltane gave the books, but the watch was from Papa."

"Was it? There was so much, I'm afraid I forgot which

was whose." With an effort, I put aside the dismal thoughts and followed her, waving my hand to Sarah at the scullery door.

The ducks had arrived. They eyed us warily and scudded away to the opposite side while we sat on the iron bench. "Silence, what's wrong? You're not listening to a word I say," Miss Amy complained.

"I'm sorry."

"What is distressing you?" she persisted tenderly. "You're twisting Papa's flower until it'll be dead before you have a chance to pin it in place to show him."

"Am I?" I stared vaguely at my hands, and laid the orchid aside. "Macdonald said it was a parasite, but what he really meant is that I'm a parasite, too. That's why he gave it to me—so Mr. Ffolliott would see—" I couldn't go any farther, my voice was trembling too badly. She wouldn't let it rest there; I had to explain the meaning of parasite, and I was so distracted that I poured out my thoughts.

"Oh, Silence." Miss Amy's arms went about me. "Dearest sister, stop, please! It is every way absurd. Hateful, hateful old man—how could he say such things?"

"Because they're true," I said, valiantly mopping my eyes. "Kind as you are at Hazelhurst, dearly as I love all of you, it is *not* a life of my own, Miss Amy. And he is right that I shall never have one. I suppose I always knew that, but now he's made me realize that the most I'll ever achieve is a share of other people's lives."

"Don't you like sharing my life, Silence?"

I smiled weakly. "Yes, of course, but it is nearly over. You will be going to London for your Season, and I shall go to another household."

"Never!" she said fiercely, springing to her feet and dragging me up with her. "You're to be with me always; I've told Papa and he agrees. But perhaps we'll find you a husband in London, Silence. Should you object to being married?"

"Not in the least," I said frankly, and chuckled. "How absurd you are, Miss Amy! Who would marry me, a portionless orphan!"

"Anyone, when you've had a Season," she crowed triumphantly, tugging me to walk along the bank path with her. "Yes! It's all arranged, Silence: you will make your bow with me. Cousin Robert's mother will be our chaperone; Papa means to take a house in Eaton Square; and Lady Desborough will present us. What d'you think of that?"

"I think you are raving mad, Miss Amy"—I laughed heartily, leaning to kiss her cheek—"and I love you for it, but it is still absurd."

"Why?"

"Because London high society would never forgive you or Mr. Ffolliott for introducing your hired companion out of an orphanage," I told her affectionately. "My dear pretend-sister, only think of the embarrassment if Mr. Ffolliott were to receive an offer for my hand and be forced to say we *think* I am legitimate but are uncertain who I am, and that my dowry consists of fifty guineas!" I chuckled again. "You'd never live it down! Come! We must go up to dress for tea."

I went past her to pick up the strange flower for Mr. Ffolliott. She'd left her own corsage on the bench, but the boutonnière had slipped to the ground. I bent to pick it up, and something went over my head into the shrubbery beyond. "What was that?" When I straightened up, turning in bewilderment, Alfred was holding Miss Amy's arm firmly, and with a gasp she sagged against him. He fended me off as I ran forward. "She's only frighted by the robins, Miss Silence. They swoop-like at this time of year."

"Has she fainted?"

"No, no. You'll be able to walk, Miss Amy. Or shall I carry you?"

"I can walk," she said after a moment. "What happened? What are you doing here, Alfred?"

"The master sent me to say tea's ready, and when I come around the bush I saw you nearly tumbling backward into the lake from the flight of robins," he said glibly. "Eh, a rare scare you gave me, miss!" Slowly, she went up the path leaning on Alfred's arm, while I retrieved the flowers and a mitten she'd somehow lost. As I followed, I glanced about the lawns and shrubs. There were only two robins, pecking avidly in the distance; the others must have been frightened away by our voices.

The summons came that night with a tap on the door leading to the next room. "Miss? You're awake?"

"Yes, but I've put off my dress."

"No matter," Alfred said. "The master wants you, and there's Davenport and myself for propriety. Put on your robe and come with me." We went from one shadowed room to another, through a softly lamplit bedroom with a huge canopied bed and a leaping fire in the grate. Mrs. Davenport stood, white-faced and twisting her hands together, summoning a tiny smile as I passed. "Miss Eddington, sir." Alfred ushered me into the corner room above the library and stepped back.

"Leave the door ajar, Alfred," Mr. Ffolliott said evenly, "and Davenport is to wait, you understand?"

"Yes, sir."

I had time to glance about the chamber, to see it was a sitting room hung in red and gold with its own fireplace large enough to hold logs instead of a coal grate. The master sat in a low-backed fireside chair, holding a small balloon glass of brandy. "Come in, Silence."

"Yes, sir."

"Sit down." He nodded to the chair opposite his. Silently I sank into it, while he sipped and gazed at the fire flames. Finally he said, "The time has come for you to leave me, my golden girl."

"Yes, sir. I knew it must be so. When shall I go?" I managed to hold my voice steady, but my eyes were filled with tears.

"As soon as may be," he said harshly. "Tomorrow, if it were possible, but at most by week's end."

"Very good, sir." I could not trust my voice further.

"You are very resigned, very calm," he remarked. "Does it mean nothing to you to leave Hazelhurst? Where will you go, with those fifty guineas Hugo is holding for you?"

"It means a great deal to me to leave Hazelhurst, sir"—I suppressed a sob—"but I had always known it must come. I was hired only for your absence, and you have already retained me far longer than necessary."

"Far longer than wise," he muttered, tossing off the brandy and refilling, "and where will you go, my golden girl?"

"Back to Belliston Parva," I said simply. "Miss Carey says the trustees will allow her to take me back temporarily, and in September I shall accompany a schoolgirl to India."

Mr. Ffolliott sighed deeply. "The excellent Miss Carey—I should have known!" He hauled himself erect from his chair. "India in September, eh? How fortuitous!" He laughed deeply, leaning to pick up the brandy glass. "Suppose instead that you fill in those weeks with the job I have found for you. Hugo's mother, Mrs. Beltane, requires someone to assist in a general way: light gardening, flower arranging, reading aloud, writing letters." He shrugged. "I've no idea of the exact duties, but it will be a household like this, Silence, where you'll not be a servant. Would that please you?"

"*Very* much, sir!" Indeed, my heart did leap at the thought of being still in some sense connected with Hazelhurst. "Where does she live, sir?"

"In a London suburb called Wimbledon, but it's nothing like your visit to the matinée," he warned, "and I fear she's elderly. It will be a quiet life."

"Yes, sir. That's what you said about Hazelhurst, but I've not found it so," I murmured involuntarily.

"Ah? How have you found us?"

"It was a sort of challenge, sir," I said after a moment. "I think I met it fairly well, although I've no idea how." I looked up at him earnestly. "You'll give me a good recommendation, sir?"

"Yes, my golden girl." Mr. Ffolliott set the brandy glass on the mantel shelf and suddenly extended his arms to me. Instinctively, I rose and went to him, nestling against his chest and savoring the strong arms about me. "All right, Nana, take her back to her bed," he said over my head. "I've had a minute at least. . . ."

"Yes, sir. Come along, my dearie. . . ."

"You'll say naught of leaving," Mrs. Davenport said when we were back to my room. "Sarah'll pack against the moment, for there's no knowing how Miss Amy'll take it." She drew a deep breath. "But there's Dr. Jermyn now, and the master's home, and 'tis best you should be safely away, Miss Silence, although what's to happen then, I'd not know. . . ."

Neither did I, and it caused me some anxiety. I disliked the possibility of any reversal. Miss Amy was incredibly changed, but it was too recent to be sure of permanency. Even now there were occasional moments when all hung in the balance. Thus far the old hysteria had been averted, and with each successful control, Miss Amy grew stronger within herself; but lacking the strategic word from me, could she do it alone? I felt that if she once broke fully into the tears and screams, she might go completely, irrevocably, to pieces through discouragement. I could not question Mr. Ffolliott's decision; it must surely be based on consultation with Dr. Jermyn. If they felt Miss Amy capable of standing alone, no doubt she was, and my apprehension was really fallen pride, humiliation to learn I was not indispensable.

I scolded myself severely for my dejection; I was really a most fortunate girl: my very first position had been extraordinary; I'd been highly paid for learning all sorts of social niceties among well-bred people, and I would go directly to a similar household without a moment's anxiety for the future, for in September I was promised further employment.

Yet, no matter how firmly I reminded myself of all I had gained, all I had to anticipate, with each succeeding day it was harder to think of leaving. I thought of Mrs. Beltane only in the likelihood that she received letters or an occasional visit from her son, who would give me the news of Hazelhurst. Would I be allowed to write to Miss Amy? Perhaps, but in the expansion of her life she'd have scant time to reply. Mrs. Davenport might keep in touch, but it would not be the same as being here, seeing with my own eyes, sharing Miss Amy's social triumphs.

Would I ever see Hazelhurst or any of these kindly people again? I scarcely saw Miss Amy even now, except at mealtimes. She was much occupied with Mr. Ffolliott, for there appeared to be a great deal involved in ending her trust.

"Papa is explaining everything to me, and I have to understand it because he cannot care for it after the first of June when I am twenty-one," she said. "Isn't that peculiar, Silence? But however, that is the law, and I must appoint an agent, and know how to instruct him. Only fancy"—she widened her eyes—"those sugar plantations belong to me, as well as all the Salford godowns and the firm that employs Cousin Robert. Even Hazelhurst is mine! Papa says there must be a new arrangement when I am of age, and it will not be proper for him to live here." She laughed merrily. "Did you ever hear anything so absurd! Where else should he live?"

I was at a loss to answer; I suddenly realized it was true. As Miss Amy's guardian, Mr. Ffolliott could reside in the same house without question; there were always companions and Mrs. Davenport. Once she was of age, he became a man who was in no way related by blood, and continued residence without a mature chaperone would be unthinkable—nor did I think he meant to live here when his duty was ended! In a flash, I knew—*that* was why he'd laughed, said "India in September? How fortuitous!" He thought to return to the Orient himself.

With a pounding heart, I felt half faint with relief, for wherever I was and whether or not it was possible to encounter him, the master would certainly say a word on my behalf in his business circles that would give me protection.

Miss Amy was unaware of my abstraction, prattling on of her day while Mrs. Davenport dressed her for dinner. "Cousin Robert is to administer for me. Isn't that a good idea, Silence, since Papa can't do it? I still think it's silly, but at least we'll keep it in the family, and Papa has absolute confidence in Mr. Hasworth."

She whirled away from the mirror and hugged my shoulders with a mischievous smile. "But the best of all, Silence: Papa believes he has the house in London! Mrs. Ormond agrees to chaperone; our names are approved for presentation at the final Drawing Room in June; and Papa gives our ball on the night of my birthday! Ah," she laughed, "I *thought* that would amaze you, darling Silence."

"Indeed it does, Miss Amy," I said with an effort. "I can hardly believe—my head is in a whirl, I assure you."

"We must commission Madame Raimond at once." She was planning. "I think you are right, Silence: we saw nothing more modish the day we went to London, and she knows best how to cut for us, after all. Let us go tomorrow, so she can put it in hand at once. I have in mind the colors and fabrics that will go well together—it is so fortunate you are brunette, Silence!—and if they cannot be found in Chelmsford, we must go to a London warehouse." She sighed rapturously. "Won't it be fun?"

"Exciting beyond words," I agreed, avoiding Mrs. Davenport's anxious eyes.

She smiled dreamily. "Papa will open the ball with me; you will follow with Mr. Beltane, if he can be persuaded. We'll select a waltz. And you must *practice*, Silence, for you are naturally graceful; it is only a matter of learning the steps. Our gowns will be white, of course. I shall wear the emerald parure, and I mean to give you the string of pearls for your very own, Silence!" She hummed softly and did a few swaying steps from one side to the other, her eyes half closed. "We go once around the floor, and then everyone can dance—but we are *out*, Silence. We are introduced; we can go anywhere in society; and once we are presented at Court we will be invited everywhere.

"Think of it, Silence! With Papa to escort me, and Cousin Robert for you—"

"Not unless I can learn how to *bounce*, Miss Amy!" I chuckled. "I only hope Mr. Beltane can be persuaded, or my first appearance is likely to be my last."

She opened her eyes and stared at me blankly, before laughing. "Oh, poor Cousin Robert! I expect I had better learn to bounce, too!"

Chelmsford tomorrow put me in a quandary. Miss Amy could not be ordering gowns I would never wear. I glanced meaningly at Mrs. Davenport and received a tiny nod of comprehension. Quietly I followed my mistress downstairs to the salon. At her command, I placed my hands on the piano, and obediently slid my feet back and forth, back and forth, back and forth in time to the waltz music. "That's better. Now, go forward down the room, Silence. Keep in time, hum to yourself if necessary. Go *on!* don't think about yourself; just think about the music."

Slowly, concentrating, making my feet fit to her strong rhythm, I proceeded over the rug—and halfway down the room I realized I'd got it. My feet moved almost of themselves; I could raise my arms and sway as Miss Amy when she was thinking of the debut. And when I'd reached the far end, there was suddenly a strong masculine arm about my waist, a hand grasping mine. "Go on, Amy. She has to learn how to reverse," said Mr. Ffolliott. "Don't lose your step, Silence. You simply do it backward as well as forward, and my hand tells you which way to go."

I gritted my teeth; I *would not* stumble! But oddly, it was much easier with a partner. My eyes were fixed on Mr. Ffolliott's middle waistcoat button, but finally I was following him in circles down the floor and I could look up from my feet, let them move automatically whichever way he indicated by the light pressure on my back or a faint tightening on my hand. Mr. Beltane had been a smooth guide, but dimly I knew he was not to be compared with Mr. Ffolliott. So this was waltzing! It was exhilarating. Birds must feel like this when flying!

We were back to the piano. "Thank you, Miss Eddington." The master bowed formally, with a twinkle in his eye, and escorted me grandly to my chair with a second bow before throwing himself into his own chair with a laugh. "Amy, she's not your equal, but very adequate, very adequate."

"I knew it! It's only to practice a little until she gains confidence, for she's naturally graceful, don't you think so, Papa? I expect her card will be filled in five minutes for every ball, with terrible heartburnings over the encores." Miss Amy slid behind the tea tray with a happy laugh. "Shall you need Dawson tomorrow, Papa? We must start the consultations with Madame Raimond."

"I do not so much need Dawson as yourself, darling," he returned smoothly. "I'm afraid there are more of those beastly papers to be signed. And if Silence does not object"—he cocked an eyebrow at me hopefully—"there are some letters that should have been written long since, but I have not been to London for a clerk. Silence, do you mind to stay at home tomorrow, and make a fair copy of my fly-tracks?"

"Of course not, sir."

"Then you and I will go to Chelmsford in the morning, Amy, and when the business is finished, I expect there'll be time for a preliminary discussion with Madame Raimond."

She pouted slightly. "How can anything be decided if Silence isn't there?"

"I should think you could do a lot, Miss Amy. You'll see whether she has what you want and select what's suitable, which will reduce the list for London. And I shouldn't wonder if she mightn't do better at getting it than yourself, once you've explained to her."

"Of course she will," Mr. Ffolliott stated with faint impatience. "She knows far more of London warehouses than you, Amy. In any case, *I* need you tomorrow, and I need Silence to write some letters for me. And if you cannot settle anything without her, you must come in to Madame Raimond the following day."

She widened her eyes at his curt tone of voice, but she said only, "Very well, Papa."

I waved good-bye to Miss Amy the next morning and went back to the library, where Mr. Ffolliott had left his letters. There were only two. They seemed very insignificant formal notes to people who had entertained him in the Islands, but I wrote them out as neatly as possible. It was only eleven o'clock; I went upstairs feeling peculiarly aimless, and in the chamber next to mine was a neat traveling trunk. Brass nailheads on the top said S.E.

"Aye, you'll leave tomorrow morning, my dearie," Mrs. Davenport said behind me. "Sarah's packed all but a traveling suit, and a dress for this evening that can go in last." She put her arms about me, holding me close. "Eh, 'tis hard to part with you, child"—she sighed—"but 'tis best. He thought we might be able to keep you to the end, but it can't be. You'll like Mrs. Beltane," she went on cheerfully, releasing me to inspect Sarah's packing. "I remember her—it'd be ten years or more that she came to stay with the rector when his father died. A sweet lady she was, looks like him—the same white skin and masses of black hair. It's probably gray by now, but you'll be happy there, Miss Silence."

"I'm sure I shall, but— Oh, Nana"—with a sob I burrowed against her shoulder—"you will write to me, let me know how all goes on?"

"Indeed I will, child." She stroked my hair gently. "Shhh, my dearie, remember 'tis always darkest before the dawn, and there's naught but two months before all's settled."

I drew a long breath. "Yes, and I've really nothing to cry about, Nana. Actually, I'm a very lucky girl with a good job to go to at once, and India in September—one of the trustees is arranging it—but I can't help but worry." I looked absently from the window at the outbuildings, the grounds of Hazelhurst. "I expect it must be so beautiful in spring and summer," I murmured. "I wish I could have seen how Macdonald will bed out, and what my seeds will be. And I always hoped I'd have a chance to see the sea. I'm from inland, you know."

"The sea? Why, 'tis only a mile or so over the rise," she said, briskly refolding a dress in my trunk to suit herself. "Miss Amy'll not go near it; she'll not even allow Dawson to drive her along the cliff road."

"It's because she was badly frightened when she was a child," I said. "I didn't realize it was so close. Listen, Nana, this might be a help . . . later." I told her Miss Amy's description of the wave. "You see? I'm not certain she's outgrown it, but she says it is different now and she knows what to do."

"Bless my soul! Does she still remember that?" Mrs. Davenport exclaimed, astonished. "Why, she was quite a big girl; it was just before she went to school. I mind they took their lunch—they often did so—and the master did say Miss Amy must be taught to swim, and a wave had bowled her over, but she seemed none the worse. She was in and out of her mama's room until Mrs. Ffolliott was dressed. The master was taking her to London for a birthday treat, and Miss Amy had her supper as usual and went to bed with never a mention of being frightened."

"I expect it came later, when she remembered it."

It was a lonely, melancholy day. I didn't know what to do with myself. Everything saddened, from the volume of *Nicholas Nickelby* I'd be unable to finish unless Mrs. Beltane possessed a copy, to the sight of Mr. Ffolliott's hookah when I returned the book to its place. I fingered the Rubaiyat, and couldn't face rereading; the memory of that night dimmed my eyes. Mrs. Potter's luncheon was composed of my favorite dishes, but while kindly meant, it only brought more suppressed tears. The silent affection of the staff was unnerving—even Macdonald. He was in the upper hall after lunch when I was wandering toward the morning room with a vague notion of working one of the puzzles.

"And a good day to ye, mistress," he said impassively. In his hands was Mr. Ffolliott's plant, restored and blooming once more.

"I'm leaving tomorrow morning, Macdonald."

"Aye, they tell't me," he nodded, "and a good thing, mistress. Ye shouldna hae been endangered so long, but he's willful, is Master Jaimie. He would have it he could keep ye safe, but ye see 'tis impossible."

I stared at him, perplexed. "I don't understand you."

"Mhphmph, ye've an innocent heart." He gestured to the plant. "Ye'll mind the day it was broken? But 'tis grown again." He broke off one white flower and handed it to me. "That's to console ye meanwhiles, lass. Tuck it out of sight in your trunk."

"Oh, thank you, Macdonald. What a delicious fragrance!"

"Aye, but put it out of sight," he repeated warningly, and stumped away to Mr. Ffolliott's room, where he took out a key and unlocked.

I took my nose from the gardenia. "Macdonald, you'll finish growing my frame?"

"I will." He paused and looked at me over his shoulder, and amazingly, *he smiled!* "Och, aye, ye're a sonsy lass," he murmured half to himself. "And a good day to ye, mistress, until we meet again." He disappeared, and I heard the bolt thrown behind him.

I went on to my room, but the connecting door was locked; I couldn't get at the trunk, and suddenly I could stand no more of Hazelhurst with its shadows and locked doors. If it was only a mile or so to the sea, why not walk over to look? Swiftly I donned cloak and walking shoes, tied a kerchief over my hair and stuffed the flower in my pocket. The kitchen was deserted; I could hear cheerful voices at lunch in the servants' hall, and suddenly Alfred emerged. "Bound for the greenhouse, miss?" he asked jovially. "Macdonald's upstairs with the plants."

"I know; I just saw him. I thought I'd walk to the sea, unless it's too far. D'you think I could get back by teatime?"

"Easily!" he assured me. "Keep to the right-hand path over the hill—the walking's better—but once you reach the cliff road, bear to the left and you'll find a track down to the shore."

Some of the melancholy left me as I went around the lake, past the spot that had been our coasting slide, and ventured onto unfamiliar ground. The path was clearly evident, though not part of the formal plantings, and in no more than twenty minutes I was standing among the windbreak trees, with a carriage road running past me and beyond it: the sea!

I stood breathless, open-mouthed, transfixed! The limitless expanse of water, the tiny curling waves foaming white, the thought of what lay beyond my sight: all the countries of the world! How much I should see on a boat bound for India! Seasick or not, it would be worth any discomfort to pass through the Mediterranean and the Suez Canal, with Europe, Africa, Asia on either hand. I ran down the path to the road, and halted at sight of a trap: Dr. Jermyn.

"Hello! Where are you off to?"

"I'm going to see the sea!"

"Come with me. I'm driving a good five miles along the cliff. The views are superb, and once I've finished a call, I'll take you back to Hazelhurst for tea."

"No, thank you." I looked at the breaking waves. "This will be good enough. I think I'd rather like to be . . . alone this time."

" 'Silent upon a peak in Darien'?" He smiled. "The sea does have that effect on people. I'll see you later, then."

When he'd gone, I went down to the sand for a while, but there was a tempting rocky bluff to the right. It was thrust out into the sea with baby rocks around its feet, causing the water to swirl and break restlessly. There seemed no way to scale it from the shore, and I finally went back to the road, until I found the other side of the bluff. It took care to get to the top; it wasn't a single piece of rock but cleft here and there with fissures as wide as two or three feet in some places, and extending down to the sand with water washing at the bottom. Eventually, I was up and thought it worth the effort. I was literally monarch of all I surveyed. Before me was the water, and behind me, far across the rise and beyond the trees, I could see the top of Hazelhurst.

I sat down cross-legged for a while, drawing out the gardenia blossom. It was already discolored, but the fragrance was strong, mingling with the sea smell. I thought of the sea stories in Mr. Ffolliott's library, and could understand the fascination of writers for the subject. No two waves were exactly alike, nor was the rhythm constant: it lulled and hypnotized, yet crashed into excitement when least expected. Of all the experiences of Hazelhurst, this was the best.

I was not disappointed in the sea.

"Silence?" Miss Amy was picking her way toward me.

"Yes, darling! Oh, *ought* you to have walked so far?" I asked anxiously. "Sit down to rest before we go back for tea. I didn't expect you so early."

"Nor I"—she shrugged—"but Chelmsford was stupid without you. Raimond had nothing I wanted, and I couldn't see Dawson anywhere. I thought he'd brought Papa home and was to come back for me, but I didn't feel like waiting, so I got a livery hack and came home alone."

"What a shame!" I exclaimed as she sat down beside me. "I quite thought Madame Raimond would have something. Did you look in at the warehouse?"

"No, I was so out of patience with Raimond . . . and I thought Papa was *here*. . . ."

"He hadn't arrived when I left"—I consulted my watch—"but that's nearly two hours ago."

"But he's been here, hasn't he? You have one of his flowers."

"This?" I was suddenly wary. "It's only a broken blossom that Macdonald gave me in the hall." Casually I tossed it into the water, watching her unobtrusively. Mrs. Davenport had said Miss Amy couldn't bear the sea, the sand—not even the carriage cliff road—yet here my mistress was. Had she come to exorcise her "wave"?

She sat staring at the water for a long time. Finally she said, "You're going away, aren't you, Silence?"

It was useless to lie. "Yes, darling. Mrs. Beltane needs someone for a while, so Mr. Ffolliott is lending me to her."

"Are you ever coming back?"

"I don't think so," I said steadily. "I'm going to India in September as companion to a schoolgirl, and if there's any hiatus between that and Mrs. Beltane, I'm to visit Miss Carey. Besides, you no longer need me, Miss Amy. I was only to be with you while Mr. Ffolliott went to the West Indies. Now that he's back, you'll be busy with your Season."

"I shan't enjoy it without you, Silence."

I took her hand gently. "Dear Miss Amy, it was never possible. It's like you to wish to include me in your come-out, but Mr. Ffolliott knows better—and so do I. I shall be quite happy in Wimbledon with the rector's mother. Perhaps one day I might be able to visit you and hear all your conquests at first hand."

"Wimbledon," she murmured. "That is London . . . now I understand."

"Understand what, darling?" I tried to release my hand, but her grasp tightened convulsively. "It's a suburb, I think, nowhere near the section in which you'll live, but I'm sure there'll be some sort of bus or train by which to reach you."

"Or for Papa to reach you." She sighed deeply. "Oh, Silence, why *did* you! I told you and told you—you could have anyone you fancied, but not Papa! Why can't you understand that he belongs to me? I know he's better than the others, *but you can't have him!* Why couldn't you be content with Dr. Jermyn or Mr. Beltane?"

I stared at her uneasily, but I couldn't pull my hand from her grip. "Please, Miss Amy, I've told *you* before that I don't want any of them, and that includes Mr. Ffolliott. I wish you will believe me; this sort of talk makes me uncomfortable. It is merely kindness for Mr. Ffolliott to transfer me to a good job that will keep me employed until I go to India."

"And keeps you nearby." She nodded indulgently. "He'd not like you to be so far away as your orphanage, but in Wimbledon, it's no distance at all. He's known to Mrs. Beltane—that was a clever idea! How men stick together! He'll be welcome at any time . . . and if she's in need of a companion, it's the first I've heard of it." Miss Amy laughed lightly. "Wait until you see the rector's mother, Silence! She's a militant feminist—doesn't believe in stays, wants votes for women; we should all go to college and be able to earn our livings."

"Well . . . well, that sounds stimulating," I said blankly. "I expect she needs someone to write letters and accompany her to the meetings."

"Not she!" Miss Amy shook her head and laughed again. "No, no, she'll leave you at home to receive Papa for tea. You must be sure to have what he likes—but you know his tastes, don't you? If her cook doesn't equal Potter, you'll make the sponge slices and madeleines, won't you?"

By now I was beginning to be thoroughly frightened. Her tone of voice was completely reasonable, almost conversational, but the words were absurd. Was Miss Amy developing some new and different sort of nerve storm? We were alone together on the outcrop; I doubted a passing carriage on the cliff road would even see us; and the tide was evidently coming in, for the spray from the waves at the base of the bluff was dashing upward and turning the front edges of the rock into a slippery carpet tilting down into the fissures.

"Don't you know you can't leave Hazelhurst, Silence?" she asked wonderingly. "You have to stay with me, so I can see what you do. You sent Papa away, and never told him I was ill. But you see, he came back to *me*. And now you think he'll follow if *you* go away, but he won't." She patted my hand sympathetically—but the grip on my wrist never slackened, and I realized those piano-playing hands were phenomenally strong.

"Darling, you're being absurd!" I protested gently. "It's quite the other way 'round: Mr. Ffolliott is *dismissing* me, because you no longer need anyone. And if you're right that Mrs. Beltane doesn't need a companion, then it's simply kindness on the rector's part to give me a breathing spell before the next job."

She sat beside me for a long time, staring out over the rolling waves, oblivious of the spume dashing up the front of the bluff—but her hand never relaxed, and when I said, "Miss Amy, your dress will be ruined by the sea water," she merely shook her head. "It doesn't matter."

"It matters to me," I said. "I don't like water in my face. Shan't we move back a bit, Miss Amy?"

"No." Her hand constrained me, forcing me nearly prone on the rock, wincing under the increasing spray bursting up and over us. "Oh, Silence, why did you?" She sighed despairingly. "I'd have taken you to London, given you every chance for a respectable establishment, given you a dowry—I can afford it! Why must you insist on enticing Papa? Is it only because he belongs to me? Do you hate me so much—like Langley?"

I lay quiet beneath her hand, gathering my strength for what was to come, because now I knew what everyone else had suspected was true: *Miss Amy was quite definitely insane*, and this I had not encountered before in all the years at Belliston Parva. I had no guide at all, except my own will to survive.

"I don't hate you at all," I said steadily. "I've loved you like the sisters you pretended we were—but it was only a pretense, wasn't it, Miss Amy? You're the one who lies, and spies, and cannot believe truth when you hear it, aren't you?" Cautiously I'd twisted until I found a firm rock ridge to brace my feet. "How many times do I have to tell you *I don't want Mr. Ffolliott?*" I cried, glaring at her. "You *told* me I could have Mr. Beltane—I've just got everything arranged—why must you ruin it for me?"

Briefly, she hesitated, her eyes clouding with the old uncertainty, and I seized the chance. With all my strength, I dug in my feet and pulled her with both hands until she flipped over to my other side, releasing her grip with a gasp as she hit the rock. I struggled to my feet, and turned frantically to the rear of the outcrop, but between the spume and my own terror I couldn't find the safe crossing of the fissures—and Miss Amy sprang onto my back like a tigress. She nearly choked me, screaming indistinguishably and dragging me back full force toward the outer edge of the bluff. I was no match for her, but with a strategic foot between her legs I tripped her and made good my escape as far as the other side of the wet rocks. She was between me and the safety of the road, if I ever accomplished it. . . . We were dodging back and forth, slipping in the sea slick to the front.

Oh, *please* let me forget those minutes!

They'd said she was a wild thing—it was too true. She tore at me, her fingers curved like cat's claws catching to rip my coat. She spat and leaped at me, screaming violently when I eluded her. The long golden hair came free of its pins and lashed about her face in the sea wind; so, too, did my brown mane, and both of us tossed our hair aside to continue the fray. I wasted no breath on protests or expostulations. I knew she was beyond reason. I merely fought for my life, but try as I would I could not get her away from the retreat to the road. Slowly, slowly, she was forcing me back to the sea edge, until I felt it might be best to let myself slip into the farthermost cleft. If I could do it—the water was not deep—at most I'd be bruised and scraped on the side rocks, but once down to the sand I'd have at least a chance to get away.

From side to side I went, feinting to avoid her grasp. If she once got her hands on me, I knew I was finished. My only advantage was that my arms were longer than hers. I could push her away before she could grapple—but I dared not spare a glance to identify the widest part of the fissure.

"*Amy? Silence?*" Male voices, figures scrambling indistinguishably up from the road. "*Amy,* stop, stop!"

She heard. It increased her fury; she had me cornered and would be balked of her prey. Oh, *God,* the maniacal glitter in her eyes as she sprang toward me full force! Sobbing with exhaustion, I felt myself slipping on the wet stone . . . and as I went down sideways, was not *there* to block her; the violence of her movement carried her beyond me to plunge over the edge with a last terrible scream. Simultaneously, in the spume showering the bluff, I rolled uncontrollably backward . . . briefly plummeted into the fissure. Then my head struck something, and I knew no more.

CHAPTER TEN

I opened my eyes.

I was in a bed, in a sort of cocoon of pillows, with bright sunlight filtering through the jalousies at the windows. My head felt . . . peculiar. Tentatively I raised a hand, and encountered a soft padding above the right ear.

I closed my eyes again and lay inert. Very slowly memory returned, at first only tiny scraps: I'd fallen on some rocks somewhere . . . yes, that accounted for the bandage. Vaguely I recalled screams and confusion . . . arms around me . . . lips pressed to mine, wet cheeks, a frantic voice imploring, "Beloved, sweetheart, speak to me! *God,* Hugo, I think the hellcat's killed her . . . my little love, open your eyes, speak to me, Silence, Silence. . . ."

Silence? Yes, that was my name . . . and this was Hazelhurst. Now it was coming back. Hugo was Mr. Beltane, the rector, and tomorrow morning I was going to companion his mother in . . . in Wimbledon, that was it. It was a suburb of London, but very, very quiet. Sarah had packed my trunk; it was in the next room. But how could I go with a bandage on my head?

What *had* I done to myself? I'd been alone for luncheon; it was lemon sole, cold roast beef with potato salad, a plum tartlet . . . I'd gone upstairs and spoken with Macdonald . . . then what? *Yes!* I'd walked to see the sea, and gone up on a rocky headland for a better view. . . .

Miss Amy. . . .

"*No!*" I struggled to sit up, and Mrs. Davenport's strained face bent over me.

"Hush, child! 'Tis all over." She gently pushed me back among the pillows.

"Nana?" I stared at her fearfully, and her eyes widened.

"Eh, you're back to yourself, my dearie! Thank the good Lord. . . ." Swiftly, she tugged the bell and hastened to mix a powder in water. "Let Nana brace you to drink it. Doctor *says* . . . but it's been *so* many days." She was weeping gently, setting aside the glass as Sarah burst through the door with Alfred behind her. "She's conscious—she knows me!"

"Oh, thank God!" Sarah broke into tears. "Oh, Miss Silence, you'll never know—"

"Stop chattering!" Alfred reminded her. "Doctor said *quiet* at first."

Sarah nodded, sniffling into the corner of her apron, and finally smiling at me weakly. "Tea and a boiled egg, you're to have. I'll see to it."

"Wait!" I looked from one to another. "Miss Amy?" I knew by Sarah's averted head, Mrs. Davenport's lowered eyes. "Alfred?"

He swallowed hard and met my eyes with an effort. "She's buried beside her mother, miss . . . six days past. You've been sick near ten days."

"I see. Thank you, Alfred."

He looked at me steadily. "Doctor says you're not to think on it till he comes, Miss Silence, which'll be no more than an hour. He's regular in his visits."

I said again, "Thank you, Alfred."

I was a good patient; I lay still until Nana propped me against the fat pillows and gently bathed my face and gave me toothmug and basin. I drank the tea and ate the egg with a strip of toast when Sarah brought the tray. I sat forward, conscious of aches and twinges, seeing scraped arms and sore hands, while Nana combed my hair into a plait and set a bed jacket about my shoulders. We said nothing but, "Sit up, my dearie," and "Thank you, Nana."

At last I was alone, staring dully into empty space, and the tears ran silently down my cheeks. How could I *not* think?

"And a good day to ye, mistress," said Macdonald austerely. "Ye'll permit me to change the plants?" He stumped forward, substituted a pot of ivy for the verbena on the windowsill, a shallow dish of flowering narcissus for the pansies on the table, and set a small duplicate of Mr. Ffolliott's gardenia plant beside my bed. He stood at the foot of the bed, holding his plant tray. "For what do ye weep, mistress?"

"I'm a murderess, Macdonald," I said simply.

"Nae, that you're not," he returned strongly. "Ye'd not believe me when I called her daft, but she killed her mother, mistress, and broke her neck trying to kill you." Staring into his pale gray eyes, at last I saw Truth.

"But . . . *why*, Macdonald? I meant her no harm. All I ever wanted was to make it possible for her to live normally, to be a pride to Mr. Ffolliott when she had her Season."

"Aye," he nodded. "I said ye'd an innocent heart, but ye made a trifling mistake: ye forgot to consider what *other* people wanted. Yon cousin wanted control of her money; she wanted Master Jaimie." Macdonald's lips twisted sardonically. "Och, there was a spiel when she'd killed to no purpose—'tis forbidden for a man to marry his wife's daughter."

I drew in my breath, aghast, and he nodded again. "Master Jaimie only wanted his freedom; he'd had enough with his career ruined by the mother without being trapped by the girl into the bargain." Macdonald eyed me somberly. "And then you came, mistress. You set all straight, and verra cleverly you did it, but she was the more clever. She knew; so did we all! She knew he'd leave her the day he'd finished his duty—and take you with him if he could."

"He's going back to the Orient, isn't he?" At Macdonald's nod, I said, "I'm still . . . sort of a murderess, am I not? If I'd left well enough alone"—my tears flowed again silently—"he'd have been able to carry out his plans, wouldn't he? She'd have had a London Season, married her cousin, and Mr. Ffolliott could have left with no responsibility."

"Aye, but she'd not have married. She'd be placed where she always should have been: in an asylum," Macdonald returned stonily. "Ye dinna ken the ways of the law, mistress . . . nor I, for that matter . . . but 'twas so placed that before she was twenty-one, he'd inherit all, and after twenty-one, it'd go to the cousin. And Master Jaimie'd no wish for it."

I covered my eyes with my hands, weeping uncontrollably, and after a moment he said, "I tell't ye on the hillside, when she tried to kill ye the second time, mistress: 'tis only people are sometimes ugly. Six years o' hell he's had. Inadvertent, ye've released him, lass, and that's good. But can ye give him the reward he wants?"

Before I could answer, the door swung open again, and Dr. Jermyn came in with a broad smile. "Good day, Macdonald. Silence, how are you, child?"

Silently, the gardener ducked his head and went away with his tray of plants.

Hazelhurst revolved about me. The shadow was gone. I saw now that it had been Miss Amy herself; and despite the tragedy and the occasional sighs, regretful tears, and shaking of heads, the staff was bearing up well. When I was permitted out of bed, to sit at the window and look at the burgeoning of spring flung across the trees and shrubs, I watched for a solitary moment and went across the hall.

My room had long been empty since I was transferred to my present bed. Now Miss Amy's was equally silent and deserted. There were no plants, the grate was swept clean, the closets were bare. "Come away, my dearie," Mrs. Davenport said behind me.

"Yes, Nana. But all her lovely clothes and scent bottles—"

"Shhh. The master had us pack them up and sent to charity."

"May I look at the morning room, Nana?"

"If you like, child, but all's cleared away."

Silently I looked at the impersonal room. The shutters were open again, the shelves of games were bare, the fashion books were gone. So, too, was the great Winterhalter portrait of Helen Ormond Salford Ffolliott. I stared at the faint discoloration of the wallpaper and wondered where it hung now. Had it gone back to the library, where Mr. Ffolliott could look at his beautiful dead wife?

Mrs. Davenport caught the direction of my gaze. "He's presented it to a great London museum," she said briefly. "Come away, Miss Silence. It's time for your nog."

A week, two weeks . . . the painful scrapes and scratches healed gradually; I could walk without limping; the head bandage was removed . . . but I was still peculiar! "We had to shave a path through your hair, Silence, but it's already growing in nicely."

"I hope you're right! At the moment I look like a scrubbing brush."

Everybody loved me, took care of me, sneaked in on some excuse to make *sure* I was recovering. Mrs. Potter brought a caramel custard; the tweeny peeked timidly around the door jamb with my Christmas hair ribbon ineptly tied: "I never had one before, miss."

"Come here, then, and let me show you how."

Dawson carried in a parcel and said, "Eh, 'tis good to see you're progressing, little miss! And Madame Raimond's sent this. . . ."

It was a peignoir of softest gold velvet, bordered at throat, wrists, and hem in sable. *"Chère Mlle. Eddington—avec mes souhaits les plus amicales. . . ."* She'd put it on Mr. Ffolliott's bill, but I wrote a polite note of thanks in my best French, anyway.

Mr. Ormond sent me two books: *Bab Ballads* and *The Owl and the Pussy Cat,* with a formal visiting card saying, "to cheer your convalescence." I was a bit unstrung by that. If I'd understood Macdonald correctly, Mr. Ormond had missed a fortune by a scant six weeks because of me.

I asked Dr. Jermyn, "Was she always deranged?"

"No. I fancy it was caused by puberty," he said absently.

"By what, sir?"

"Oh, the devil," he muttered, embarrassed. "It's a medical term, Silence. I'm sorry."

When he tugged at his earlobe and regarded the toes of his boots, I said, "It would be easier if I understood, Dr. Jermyn, because I truly loved her."

"I know you did—and the devil's in it that she truly loved you, too." He sighed, rubbing his chin thoughtfully. "Oh . . . you're not miss-ish, Silence. You're innocent, but not ignorant. . . . You'll not faint, will you?"

"No. I already know some of it, I think."

He nodded. "Well, then—puberty is the point when a little girl starts to be a . . . big girl. Her body changes and develops, but there are changes inside—in her mind. She begins to be conscious of men, as different from women. It's part of getting ready to marry and bear children. . . . Do you understand?"

"Yes."

"At that point, Amy Salford fell in love with her stepfather. As best I can reconstruct, this was not realized at first," he went on impersonally. "The nerves and hysteria were ascribed to shock at her mother's death, and by the time Ffolliott recognized the truth, he was entangled by his guardianship. She belonged in an asylum, but if he committed her, he'd appear a wicked stepfather trying to misappropriate her fortune—and that, in turn, would cast doubt on his business probity. So he kept her at Hazelhurst and under sedation much of the time, arranging that Robert Ormond would assume control on the day she was twenty-one.

"Robert's a good lad. For a space, he thought perhaps you'd brought her back to normalcy and he could marry her, but when she began trying to kill you, it was obviously hopeless. She pushed you free of her on the ice, Silence, and deliberately steered the sled down the ice bank, and Alfred was only just in time to deflect her aim when she threw a rock at you after a visit to the greenhouse. I don't know what occurred to set her off...."

"Macdonald gave *me* the first orchid on a plant Mr. Ffolliott had brought from the West Indies."

"Ah? Well, the point is that she was perfectly sane until he was concerned; then she reacted violently. She was furiously jealous of any other woman, no matter how old or ugly—except you. Ffolliott says she looked on you as a younger sister for months; it was the first peaceful interlude he'd had in years." Dr. Jermyn shook his head with an intent smile. "And I wish I knew how you got her to abandon that hysteria! You don't realize it, Silence, but what you accomplished with Amy Salford is at this moment the subject of some highly controversial medical experiments in Vienna!"

"They must not be valid, sir—or I didn't do the right thing—for she's dead," I said presently. "I can't help but feel I killed her, because I was ignorant."

"On the contrary, you came within Ames' Ace of succeeding," he said authoritatively. "The blame lies with us: we should have got you away that very night, Silence. But where to send you? The rectory's a bachelor establishment, so is mine; Hugo suggested Davenport could come with you for chaperonage, but Ffolliott wouldn't have it. Ormond offered to come from London next day to drive you back ... and I fear it's my responsibility." The doctor sighed. "Amy's attacks were always impulsive, Silence. An opportunity presented itself, she seized it—and was devastated afterward by what she'd done. She didn't *want* to kill you when she was sane.

"Each incident was connected in some way with Mr. Ffolliott. The ice skating reminded her of the way she'd gotten rid of her mother . . . and I'm not sure she intended the woman's death," he interposed. "I think it was her first impulsive action, out of desire for—" He stopped abruptly. "I shouldn't be saying such things before you, child."

I smiled faintly. "You cannot live in an orphanage without learning the . . . the technical facts of the human body, Dr. Jermyn. The results of . . . sensual desire are all too tangible, and I think you are right that Miss Amy never anticipated the actual end," I murmured. "She was angry. Mrs. Ffolliott had sent her away to school in order to accompany her husband on business trips; Miss Amy was to be returned for the next term while they went to South America. I expect she wanted to . . . to punish her mother with an unpleasant cold bath. When it resulted in death, she was sincerely shocked—and when Mr. Ffolliott simply continued the original plans, she went out of her mind.

"Yes"—I nodded thoughtfully—"that must have been the way it was. Inadvertently, she'd cleared the way, but she was only fourteen; there'd be at least two to four years to wait before she could marry. I suppose—he was young and handsome—she was frantic that he'd remarry before she was old enough. She didn't dare take her eye off him, so she made herself sick and the school sent her home. *Then* she found out he could never marry her in any case; it'd be forbidden by the Church of England. I remember now, she said once that it was all for nothing."

"Go on, Silence." Dr. Jermyn had got out a big pad and pencil, and was busily making notes. "Please, this is invaluable," he said quietly. "Can you bear to help? Is it too painful? But don't you see how it could assist in other cases?"

"That's all she ever was to you, wasn't it? A medical case," I remarked sadly. "She said Robert only wanted the money, and you put her under a microscope, but to me she was a beautiful, loving, tender woman. I wanted her to be able to enjoy life, and I wanted Mr. Ffolliott to be proud of her—but as Macdonald said, it was only what *I* wanted because this was my first position, you know, and I wanted to justify Miss Carey's retaining me two years longer than the other orphans.

"I expect I was very stupid not to realize, but there was always another explanation for everything. I thought she destroyed the design dolls because they'd been misappropriated by a companion she hated, and I thought she'd abandoned her music because she didn't like to sit alone in the salon. Now I see that everything was meant to erase the memory of her mother. She deliberately smashed the gardenia plant that day we were in the greenhouse—I saw her. I suppose it was always in Mr. Ffolliott's locked suite, and she didn't realize it was still there, reminding him."

"He had to keep his rooms locked," Dr. Jermyn muttered. "She got in once, in the middle of the night. . . ." He cleared his throat. "And a day or so later she got in again, when he'd gone to breakfast. The place was a shambles; all her mother's belongings were broken or cut to ribbons. After that, only Macdonald, who was from his family home in Scotland, and Alfred, who'd been his batman in the Crimea, had keys."

"And barred the door behind them," I nodded. "Yes, I understand now; I can see a dozen small clues. But you see, Dr. Jermyn, it isn't the thing you *think* of. She pleaded for the Winterhalter portrait, and never looked at it, but I thought perhaps she did when I wasn't there. She was determined I should wear her mother's jewels, in the hope he might think I'd misappropriated them. She taught me 'Lady Greensleeves' because in some way it would make him unhappy to hear it sung badly.

"I can even tell you when she fell in love with him," I said steadily. "It was a picnic at the shore: a wave knocked her down and he pulled her out. But she wasn't a baby, Dr. Jermyn. She was fourteen—and if I understood you correctly. . . ." I looked away with a sudden shyness.

"By heavens, this is incredible!" he muttered, scribbling quickly. "You can't know! My dear child," he added anxiously, "I don't mean to distress you in my wish for facts while they're fresh in your mind."

My cheeks were wet with tears, but I shook my head. "I think perhaps it's good for me to put everything into words. I can't help but cry, we had such pleasant times together." Slowly I began from the beginning, recalling everything I could, and as I talked it did come clear in my mind. The tears flooded down, dropping onto my lap in uncontrollable sorrow.

"If only I'd known more, not been so ignorant, realized . . ." I said despairingly. "It was the gardenia Macdonald gave me; I had it in my hand when she came up to the headland—and it was like the letters: she never believed Mr. Ffolliott and I weren't corresponding when he was away—and when she saw the flower, she was certain he'd left her in Chelmsford and come back to see me."

"He left her at the dressmaker; Dawson had an errand at the harness shop, but he'd plenty of time to come back for her. But as he turned into the street, he saw her in a livery hack. By the time he got Ffolliott and they were back to Hazelhurst, Amy had disappeared. No one even knew she'd come home; madness makes people incredibly sly." He shook his head sadly. "Presumably she hunted for you, and from the attic windows she'd have seen you at the shore.

"Alfred said you were bound for the sea; I came along while they were searching the house for Amy, and said I'd met you on the cliff road. My trap was better suited than the carriage—we drove directly across the grounds and over the rise. Don't think about the rest of it." He grasped my hand firmly. "Silence, she's better off dead! Would you condemn that beauty to a Bedlam?" At my muffled sob of protest he continued, "There was no other future for her. You came close to saving her, but when she'd attained her majority and discovered Mr. Ffolliott had left her forever"— Dr. Jermyn shrugged— "Robert would have had no choice but to commit her, Silence. He'd have given her every chance to pull around, but he was prepared for the inevitable, much as he hated it. He's a very good, responsible lad, and Ffolliott's trained him well."

Releasing my hand, Dr. Jermyn stood up briskly. "You're discharged as a patient, Silence. I'll stop in as a friend, if I may? How long shall you be at Hazelhurst?"

"I don't know, sir—a day or two, perhaps," I said helplessly. "If I'm well again, I must not trespass longer on Mr. Ffolliott's kindness."

The doctor frowned at me faintly, tugging his earlobe as always when thinking. "Have you understood anything at all of what we've been discussing?" he demanded. "Do you really not know that Amy Salford tried to kill you because James Ffolliott fell in love with you, Silence?"

I found my voice. "That was only her imagination, Dr. Jermyn. You said she thought everyone wanted to take him from her."

"For once she was right," he remarked. "Poor devil, he was in as much of a state over you as she was over him. He couldn't bear to send you away; he kept hoping he could keep her occupied with the plans for a Season until her birthday; and for a while it appeared to be progressing safely. Macdonald and Alfred were told off to guard you; the servants were always alert; and the rest of us—Robert, Hugo, and myself—were at hand as often as possible. But when she attacked you at the lakeside, Alfred flatly said he'd not take the responsibility any longer."

Dr. Jermyn eyed me with suppressed amusement. "Poor Ffolliott! He could easily discount Robert and myself, but Hugo Beltane is no mean adversary in the romantic stakes, Silence! Oh, they were two dogs with a choice bone that night; it'd have been hilarious if it hadn't been so serious." He laughed reminiscently. "Ffolliott was for sending you to Belliston Parva, while Beltane's urging you should go to his mother, and James only agreed to Wimbledon because you'd be close enough for him to see you occasionally." Dr. Jermyn chuckled teasingly at my incredulous eyes and patted my shoulder. "Pick either one, please, or I'll have to offer for you myself; and frankly, much as I enjoy your company, Silence, I'm not a marrying man!"

He went away, still chuckling—but to me it was no laughing matter.

In my mind I still heard that passionate deep voice calling my name . . . or had I imagined it? Was I, in my way, as bemused by my master as poor Miss Amy? Once he'd kissed me, when he was leaving for the West Indies. I'd not refined upon it—I'd been far too busy and anxious in those first days of her illness—but when I saw him again, I'd envied her the right to kiss him. As best we knew, I should be nineteen in July, but as Miss Amy had said, many girls were married and had babies by that age.

And after Dr. Jermyn's impersonal explanation, I could no longer hide my head in the sand like the ostrich. I knew I loved Mr. Ffolliott as a woman should love a man. I trembled at the memory of his hand on my hair when I had read the poem to him, at the memory of his arms the night he told me I must leave Hazelhurst. I longed to feel him, smell him, touch him; to be held, protected, loved; to go anywhere that he went; to be with him always. I knew it could never be so. Now that he was free to go back to his own life, there would be no place in it for an uneducated orphan twenty years his junior. The last thing he would want was another adoring child, particularly one who had stupidly complicated matters.

Dr. Jermyn might praise me for what I'd done with Miss Amy, but that was merely his medical mind for a case history. Mr. Ffolliott would infinitely have preferred a semidrugged girl to a healthy young lady demanding presentation at Court. In a few months he could have turned everything over to Mr. Ormond, washed his hands of her estate, and if Miss Amy had to be placed in an institution, she would at least be alive—nor was I so certain she might not have been cured of her unhealthy infatuation, given time and understanding. For nearly six years he'd endured it, and within sight of the goal, I had ruined it all.

I knew that I loved him, but if he ever could have loved me, it was finished. He had no wish even to see me; in these past days he was the one I'd not seen. There was no constraint in the staff; they spoke casually of the master: he'd been at home, given this or that order, gone to London and would not return for two nights, and so on. Alfred was in high fettle, hauling out great trunks to be polished and packed. "Going back, we are!"

"Oh, *where,* Alfred?"

"Singapore, Madras, Kandahar"—he shrugged—"somewhere out there, miss. It'll be good to see it again!"

"I'm so glad, Alfred. I didn't realize you'd been to the Orient, too."

"O'course I have, miss," he said in surprise. "I was always with the master from the war time. I knew old Mr.

Salford—a *great* gentleman he was—Mr. Ffolliott's godfather. They lived in Bombay. Miss Amy was a baby, and there were older children, but they died."

"How sad! No wonder Mrs. Ffolliott was so choice of Miss Amy."

Alfred's sharp face was cynical. "She was choice of herself, Miss Silence, and finely she diddled him!"

I could go up and down the stairs alone, with Sarah or Mrs. Davenport at hand, but I knew I was perfectly recovered physically. Nothing was said of my departure; the staff appeared to think I would be here forever and often consulted me on small household decisions, as though I were still in charge as during Mr. Ffolliott's absence. I knew that *I* must make the move. Mr. Ffolliott must find the presence of an unemployed employee distasteful while preparing for a long voyage, but in view of the circumstances he would feel unable to *ask* me to leave.

Mr. Beltane was my most faithful visitor; he came every day, usually at teatime, and he was as kind as always. But after Dr. Jermyn's words, I felt oddly shy. No look or word said that he was more than a family friend, but I was unable to speak freely as in the past. "Albert says you are no longer a patient," he remarked cheerfully. "That is very good news, Silence."

"Yes. Now I needn't drink that horrid nog every morning!"

He laughed. "What shall you do, Silence? My mother would like you to be with her, if you feel able," he said quietly, "but if you feel . . . shaky, Miss Carey writes she wants you to return to her."

"Thank you, sir."

"D'you think you could bring yourself to call me Hugo?"

I looked at the intent black eyes regarding me, the warm hand holding mine. "Perhaps in time," I said steadily, "but not just yet."

He sighed deeply, and released my hand with a slight pressure. "I was afraid of that. Well, I shall lick my wounds in solitude and continue to hope a little. . . . And meanwhile, will you go back to Belliston Parva?"

"I think that would be best," I murmured tremulously. "I'm . . . sorry."

Mr. Beltane shook his head. "The heart goes where it must, Silence, and the best is always yet to come." He stood up with a faint smile. "But I doubt that I shall ever be a bishop without you, my dear." He suddenly tilted up my chin and kissed me gently. "James will never miss that one," he murmured, "and perhaps, perhaps. . . ." While I stared at him mutely, he drew a long breath. "Shall I arrange your trip? Dawson can wire Miss Carey, and look up the trains and coach connections. Will you like to have your money in coins, or shall I give you a bank draft for part of it, for greater safety? Shall we say . . . the day after tomorrow, if it proves possible?"

"Yes, please, Mr. Beltane."

"You're quite certain you cannot like to be with my mother?" he asked after a moment. "You must guess that she has no need for a dog's-body, Silence, but it is a pleasant home in which to restore yourself. Nothing arduous would be expected of you."

"I know. But actually, I think it would be better for me to be very, very *busy*," I said. "It will not be arduous at Belliston Parva, but Miss Carey will have a dozen things to occupy me." I smiled reminiscently. "There will be mending, or Elizabeth Two will need help with her sums, and Angus Maclachlan will have planted more peas than beans . . . or something."

"You look better already, just thinking of it," he remarked with a sigh. "But yes, you're right. It will be best for you to renew yourself in familiar surroundings." He reached for my hand and held it against his cheek for a second. "I shall miss you, Silence," he said quietly. "No matter what happens in the future, never go completely away from me, please?"

"I shan't," I said clearly. "You are my first dear friend, and I think one cannot have love without friendship first."

"Yes, you are very wise," he agreed. "I'll instruct Dawson. . . ."

I shed a few tears when Mr. Beltane had gone. If all I wanted was a respectable establishment—as Miss Amy had said, I couldn't do better than the rector—but *he* deserved more than cupboard love. If I went back to Belliston Parva and talked to Miss Carey, if Mr. Ffolliott closed Hazelhurst and went away from the neighborhood, perhaps in time I could give Hugo Beltane real devotion.

Dawson had arranged everything; it would be tomorrow, or I must wait another two days. "I'll go tomorrow. Sarah, can you help me to pack?" The staff was faintly tearful, but resigned. "Eh, I'll not know what we'll do with ourselves come June when the master leaves us, too." Mrs. Davenport sighed. "We're to keep the house open for Mr. Ormond, but it'll not be the same."

After dinner I went into the library and finished *Nicholas Nickelby*. The master was in London and not expected for the rest of the week. The tall case clock chimed eleven, and I thought I would take a last look at the grand salon in which Miss Amy and I had spent so many happy hours. I stood in the doorway, but it only brought tears to my eyes: the Christmas tree, the birthday concert, the New Year's waltz, and the night before Miss Amy's death when she'd played for me to practice my steps, and Mr. Ffolliott had said, "She must learn to reverse."

The music was stacked neatly on the closed piano. Who would ever play it now? In my ear I heard the voices blending together, Mr. Ormond's dashing rendition of "A Policeman's Life Is Not A Happy One," Mr. Beltane singing *"Adeste Fideles, laeti triumphantes. . . ."* Sadly I turned away and went back to the library, but there were memories here, too: the books we'd read—the rector's voice was superb, but Mr. Ffolliott added a touch of expression that had us convulsed with laughter. There was the night of my arrival, the night of my first wages, the night of Miss Amy's nightmare—except that I knew now it had not been an upset stomach.

My eye went to the fourth from the left on the third shelf. Defiantly I pulled out the tooled leather-bound book and settled under the reading lamp. I didn't *have* to tell Miss Carey, after all. . . . Now I considered the meaning of the words. There were still stanzas that were lovely but without significance to me, but others meant even more.

Vaguely I heard footsteps; the salon lamps went out; a door was opened and closed—Alfred, shutting for the night. And suddenly the library door swung back, and a deep voice said, "Silence!"

"Yes, sir?" I knew I'd no business to be caught reading that book at that hour, but *oh!* it was so good to see him once more.

Slowly Mr. Ffolliott stripped off his coat into Alfred's

waiting hands, and came forward to his chair while I scrambled to my feet. His face was impassive; his deep blue eyes never left mine, nor could I look away from him. "I'm sorry, sir," I apologized breathlessly. "I understood you'd not be returning tonight."

"You meant to leave without even a handshake?" Mr. Ffolliott raised his eyebrows.

"I . . . thought you'd prefer that, sir."

"Why?"

"I've trespassed on your kindness too long, sir. And with all that's to be done before you leave, it must be easier to have the undivided attention of the household."

He nodded indifferently, sitting down to exchange boots for the slippers Alfred had brought and rising to exchange business coat for house robe—and still his eyes never left me, until I was trembling uncontrollably. When Alfred had poured the brandy and departed, Mr. Ffolliott said, "Why are you going back to the excellent Miss Carey instead of to the position I found for you?"

"I don't feel able to undertake an unfamiliar household, sir."

"Jermyn says you're entirely fit," he remarked impersonally. "Isn't it a bit reckless to squander your savings on a summer holiday? Mrs. Beltane understands the situation; she'll not expect anything physically exhausting."

"I'm sure she'd be very kind, but there are many sorts of expectations, sir, and I should prefer to abide by my decision."

"Why?" he asked again.

I threw discretion to the winds. "Because I cannot bring myself to call Mr. Beltane 'Hugo,'" I said simply.

Mr. Ffolliott's eyes were like blue fire, and I was suddenly suffused with confidence. "Must I really leave you—*James?*"

EPILOGUE

Can it really be five years?

We reached Hazelhurst last night at teatime, and it was the same, yet not the same. Dawson fetched us at Windsor, where Her Majesty made us Sir James (and Lady) Ffolliott. She was a dumpy little woman in Stygian black lace, but she *smiled* when James looked at her before bending to kiss her hand! His black hair is more powdered than before, but the kingfisher flash is still in his eyes—and more devastating than ever. I had a dreadful time extricating him from the wife of a French chargé d'affaires in Lucknow.

Robert Ormond and his wife live at Hazelhurst. I do not know who owns the estate, but somehow James and Robert amicably split things between them, and our rooms will always be ready. Alice is a darling: a tiny bird of a girl, with a voice like a lark. Robert has placed a second piano in the salon, and they play together every evening.

The shadow is truly gone forever. The morning room is now the day nursery for Master Robert Swithin Ormond IV; Miss Amy's bedroom is the night nursery; and my former room is occupied by a nannie so starched you can hear her from one floor to another. Master Charles Hugo Ffolliott demanded, "Why does she *crackle*, Mummy?" Miss Emily Ffolliott merely widened her blue eyes and screamed until Lallit swept forward to murmur consolation in incomprehensible Hindi.

I can see there may be a problem with the Ormond's nannie. . . .

Mrs. Davenport is looking forward to retirement; Sarah is married to a local farmer, but "obliges" whenever Alice is between parlormaids; and the tweeny is "walking out"! Mrs. Potter is still making everything the way Mr. Ffolliott liked it, no matter *what* Alice says. Alfred thinks poorly of George, who is Mr. Robert's valet, and Robert has (understandably, I think) packed away some of James's beloved books, to which James takes exception.

It bids fair to be a . . . stimulating sojourn, although nothing could be kinder than our welcome. Nevertheless, I am slightly unnerved by Nana's heartfelt and tearful embrace. "Eh, now you're here, my dearie, all will be put right in a trice!"

Dr. Robinson is dead; Madame Raimond sold the business to her head cutter and returned to France. Dr. Jermyn has succumbed to the blandishments of a lady called Jennifer, and is to be married in two weeks; we are asked to the wedding, but Hugo Beltane will not officiate. Three years past he went to a very superior London living, a fine step toward his bishopate, and he is understood to be interested in the charming widowed daughter of the Diocesan Head. James says it will be a very good thing.

This morning I stepped along to the greenhouse. "And a good day to you, Macdonald. What have you to show me?"

He eyed me carefully. "There's orchids, and gardenias, and roses, and camellias." Slowly his craggy face broadened into a smile. "Ye can have what ye fancy, lass. Naught's too good to pay you for the look on Master Jaimie's face this day."

"Thank you, Macdonald. Is it too late for a frame? I've brought some seeds."

I went down to the lake and looked at the quietly lapping water, the far bank where I'd hung on a shrub, the glossy privet and foaming syringa bushes. Such a lovely place to be the setting for tragedy! But Macdonald had been right that it was only people who were sometimes ugly, and the ugliest had been Helen Ormond Salford Ffolliott.

In the Royal Museum I'd seen the Winterhalter portrait again, and silently cursed her for the unhappiness she'd caused; yet she'd paid with her life, and James had escaped her to become a knight, to be loved and fulfilled in contentment. I knew that he was; it required no words, although he told me constantly. It was as though a floodgate had opened, and he delighted in freedom of expression. Sometimes I suspected he was wickedly *trying* to shock me. There was a certain *gleam* in his eye when he casually imparted a sensational titbit of gossip, and quite often I *was* shocked; but no matter what language he used nor how startling the tale, I would *not* give an inch.

I had determined on the night he told me of his marriage that he was always to feel free, to be a man and fully comfortable with his home and wife, to say or do what came naturally to him, without apology for an oath or racy story. Some of them were very racy indeed, but I would *not* blush. Instead, I asked him innocently to *explain;* and when he said, "I shouldn't have mentioned it to you, darling. Ladies don't know such things," *I* said, "But if you know them, how can you talk to me if I don't?"

I must say a number of things sounded rather disgusting, but I put them in a mental pigeonhole—they did not concern me—and James had a complete companion rather than a delicate female with smelling salts in her hand . . . like his first wife.

"I'm too old for you—old enough to be your father. Half my life is gone," he'd muttered hoarsely.

"There's lots of years left—and I have *never* thought of you as my father," I said breathlessly. "Oh, *please!* It's not kind to kiss me if you don't want me."

"Want you?" he groaned. "But wanting isn't the answer, my darling. I wanted Nellie—and paid with twelve years of my life."

"I expect you'd better tell me about her. Not that I care, but you'll feel better," I said presently.

"She was the living proof that beauty is only skin deep," James said grimly. "James Salford was my godfather; we were extremely fond of each other. She was his third wife; it amused him to marry a callous little beauty. He denied her nothing—he'd the money—but if he'd ever dreamed I'd lose my head, he would have told me explicitly what she was, or forbidden me the house.

"As it was, she came back to England when he died—rich, beautiful, widowed—but found she was no longer a queen of society. When I came home, I was exactly what she needed. By then she'd realized someone must take charge of all the business interests, and to enter society she must have a permanent escort." His lips curled sardonically. "She . . . bowled me over, Silence. I didn't want for money—my godfather provided for me generously when I came of age—but Nellie was accustomed to the

Orient, knew what was required of a diplomat's wife, and she could still bear children despite the age difference.

"So I married her, and within a year I found out: she never intended to go anywhere; she meant to stay snugly in England with a presentable husband who would manage her affairs for her." James buried his head in his hands. "She was very careful for a long while; she did everything she could to increase my ardor. I had a magnificent establishment, a beautiful, fond wife, acceptance in the best social circles, the suggestion of Parliament held before my nose; but in time she felt secure, and the mask began to slip. *Then* I opened my eyes—and instead of the career for which I was expensively trained and to which I was suited, I discovered I was only a businessman irrevocably married to a beautiful bitch.

"As much as I thought I'd loved her, I came to despise her, not that she cared. So long as she could wear fine clothes and jewels, give parties and go to balls, nothing mattered. She didn't give a tinker's curse for Amy, aside from a useful weapon to prevent my accepting a foreign assignment—and actually it did, Silence. Amy was only five or six years old. She was a most endearing little girl"—James sighed—"and because she was Uncle James's daughter, I tried to take care of her." He snorted violently. "I remember when I refused to leave her: she had some childhood disease, but she'd taken it badly and Robinson wasn't happy. . . .

"Nellie was all dressed for the ball, and if you think Amy created storms, you should have heard her mother!" James laughed mirthlessly. "I could always have left; I was always in touch with the Foreign Service; the door was always open—but I couldn't bring myself to desert the child until she was old enough for school. So I waited it out."

James stood up abruptly and turned away from me. "This isn't pretty, Silence," he muttered, "but I think you have to know it all. When Amy was thirteen, I told Nellie I meant to finish her business affairs, place responsible men in charge, and return to my career. I would take her with me, if she cared to come, or leave her at home . . . and she was no longer quite so beautiful. She'd put on a bit of weight with the good living, and there were some gray hairs. It didn't suit her at all to be left without her permanent escort, to be forced to make explanations of why she wasn't with me.

"Not that I wanted her," he remarked. "I'd done without her for several years. I'd have been entirely happy to leave her here, but for once she was frightened: what would people think?" He chuckled deeply. "When I let her know *what* people would think, she made haste to pack Amy off to school and came with me, rather than—" He stopped short.

"If you mean that Mrs. Langley became your mistress," I said calmly, "I have long supposed it, James, but I cannot see that it affects me." He whirled, his eyes incredulous, until I smiled faintly. "Men are men, James, but," I added warningly, "you will never have another, you understand?"

"Ah, you are jealous! You would fight like a tigress to keep me?" he asked hopefully, pulling over the ottoman to sit down and clasp my hands. "You would tear your hair and scratch out my eyes?"

"Well, not precisely that," I said apologetically. "It's to be expected that gentlemen will enjoy looking at pretty ladies, and I shouldn't wish to do anything that would interfere with your pleasure, James."

He laughed heartily, holding my hands to his lips. "Oh, my dearest darling, where had you such wisdom about 'gentlemen'?"

I laughed with him. "From the excellent Miss Carey, of course. But"—I was serious—"if you were ever tempted to do more than look, would it not be my fault?"

"Why?"

"Well, it might be partly your own fault," I conceded after a moment, "because it is up to you to make me into a wife to your taste, isn't it? I won't know anything but what you teach me, so you must correct me at once if I am not learning properly. I do not know what the masculine of 'miss-ish' may be, but you cannot be *that* with me, James."

His eyes were deep blue pools of light. "I promise I shall not. What I felt for Nellie was infatuation, the normal . . . physical desire of a healthy young man for a beautiful woman," he said steadily. "It was no more, and I paid dearly for it, but now I understand love, my golden girl. . . ."

I wandered back along the path to the house, and every step was a memory—yet, amazingly, not wholly tragic. My heart still wept for Miss Amy: so beautiful and so doomed. It was the one subject we never explored, James and I. "You said it was a nightmare, that night in the library. It was all of that and more, until you came," he said under his breath, "but it's already nearly erased in my mind. I can remember, but it seems another time, another life. Let us not talk of it, Silence. Let me live normally, in sanity. . . ."

So I said nothing beyond impersonalities. Her beloved jewels were parcelled out to Robert's mother and wife—with the exception of the pink pearls. "These were my mother's," said James. "Could you bear to wear them, beloved?"

"Yes. . . ."

I would wear them tonight, because it was supposedly my birthday and Mrs. Davenport had whispered that Potter was preparing a special menu. "Oh, dear! Don't tell her, Nana, but my real birthday is December 28th! We only thought it was in June because that's when I came to the orphanage," I said, aghast.

The report from Pinkerton reached us in Rangoon. James brought it when he came in for luncheon. "Your genealogy, dear heart."

I'd been amazingly close! My mother was Louise (not Lucy) Victoria Myrrdhin, born in Wales, but raised in Belliston Magna by her aunts who ran the Misses' Watkins Seminary. That was why the trustees couldn't find a family with the initial M that had died out. My father was of French extraction, Charles D'Aubigny Eddington. He was the overseer of a vast plantation to which Miss Myrrdhin came as governess—on the *Alison Castle* in 1854. There were some D'Aubignys in New Orleans and Eddingtons in Atlanta, but in the war Charles was killed, the plantation devastated. Apparently my mother took what money she had and went to Atlanta, where she found the Eddingtons were dead. In 1864 she'd no hope of reaching New Orleans for the D'Aubignys. She went on toward the coast, and found an English Blockade runner in a seaport called Savannah.

I shivered at the thought of my young mother, alone

with a small child and scant money, in an unfamiliar country. Due to the war it must have been several years since she'd had word of her aunts, and by the time she reached Belliston Magna, they were both dead. Evidently, too, in the ten years of her absence, such acquaintances as she'd had had also removed from the locality.

All the terror and suspense of
ROSEMARY'S BABY . . .

THE SURVIVORS

A spellbinding novel
by Anne Edwards

A beautiful and lost girl . . . a man obsessed with learning the undiscovered truth about the shocking slaughter of an entire family . . . a high-speed journey along the razor edge of madness into the jaws of unimaginable horror . . .

A novel that grips the imagination like a vise until the final shattering turn of the screw . . .

"You'll be reading THE SURVIVORS right to the breathless end."
—*Dallas Times Herald*

A DELL BOOK 95c

If you cannot obtain copies of this title from your local bookseller, just send the price (plus 15c per copy for handling and postage) to Dell Books, Post Office Box 1000, Pinebrook, N. J. 07058. No postage or handling charge is required on any order of five or more books.

How many of these Dell bestsellers have you read?

Mile High by Richard Condon $1.25
The American Heritage Dictionary of the English Language 75¢
Soul on Ice by Eldridge Cleaver 95¢
The Andromeda Strain by Michael Crichton $1.25
The Doctor's Quick Inches-Off Diet by Irwin M. Stillman, M. D., and Samm Sinclair Baker 95¢
Catch-22 by Joseph Heller 95¢
Commander Amanda by George Revelli $1.25
Naked Came The Stranger by Penelope Ashe 95¢
The Doctor's Quick Weight Loss Diet by Irwin M. Stillman, M. D., and Samm Sinclair Baker 95¢
The Midas Compulsion by Ivan Shaffer $1.25
Your Heritage of Words: How to Increase Your Vocabulary Instantly by William Morris 60¢
How Children Learn by John Holt 95¢
The Richest Man in the World by J. P. $1.25
Whipple's Castle by Thomas Williams $1.25
Once An Eagle by Anton Myrer $1.25
The Victims by Bernard Lefkowitz and Kenneth G. Gross $1.25
Judas, My Brother by Frank Yerby $1.25

If you cannot obtain copies of these titles from your local bookseller, just send the price (plus 15c per copy for handling and postage) to Dell Books, Post Office Box 1000, Pinebrook, N. J. 07058. No postage or handling charge is required on any order of five or more books.